Toxic Shock Syndrome

Volume 5 of the continuing adventures of Glen Wilson...

What people are saying about Ken Coffman...

Ken, I love your work.
- Robert Ferrigno, New York Times bestselling author of *Sins of the Assassin* and other novels.

Ken, you are a marvelous writer.
- Seymour Garte, Author of *Where We Stand, A Surprising Look at the Real State of our Planet* and *Molecular Environmental Biology*.

Other books by Ken Coffman

Fiction

Steel Waters
Alligator Alley, by Ken Coffman and Mark Bothum
Twisted Shadow, by Ken Coffman with Mark Bothum
Glen Wilson's Bad Medicine
Hartz String Theory
Endangered Species
Fairhaven

Nonfiction

Real World FPGA Design with Verilog

The Armchair Adventurer
www.ArmchairAdventurer.net

Books can be ordered from:

www.bytechservices.com
1500A East College Way #554
Mount Vernon, WA 98273

About the author:

Ken Coffman is a Field Applications Engineer and Member of the
Technical Staff at Fairchild Semiconductor.

He is the coauthor of six patents, a member of the standards association
of the Institute of Electrical and Electronics Engineers, part-time concert
promoter and a guitar player. He plays golf exactly the way his boss
wants him to: very poorly.

For the latest news, see www.kencoffman.com

This book is a work of fiction. Names, characters, places and incidents
are the products of the author's fevered imagination or are used
fictitiously. Any resemblance to actual, real life events, locales or
persons (living or dead) is entirely coincidental.

ISBN 0-975-4314-4-7

Published by:
The Armchair Adventurer
1500A East College Way #554
Mount Vernon, WA 98273

Dedication

For the rockers who inspire while I wrestle with words in my basement. They include Steve Vai, Mike Keneally, Francis Dunnery, Steve Morse, Ritchie Blackmore, Josh Zee, Marc Bonilla, Joe Satriani, Ty Tabor, and Glenn Hughes.

Also, for my Strange New Toys bandmate and friend, Douglas Paasch, taken too soon at the age of 49 in 2008. RIP, my brother.

Where's the Puppeteer?

For literary inspiration, I thank Dan Simmons. He's creating a highly interesting, remarkable, varied and prolific body of commercial literary fiction. I don't think there is anyone writing better in our generation.

I want to thank my "editorial board" for encouragement, guidance, proofreading and commentary.

Judy Coffman
Stacey Benson
Ken Lomax
Dock Brown
Gary Croft
Mark Bothum
Dale Edwards
Mick Wilson

Barry Otterholt
Maureen Blando
Mark Collins
Tommy Lee Bolser
Mike Irvine
Craig Ranta
Karen Wespi

Author's Notes

This book is a long love letter to music and the musicians who channel notes from heaven. I've loved music from the first songs I heard on the radio in the 60's. As a country bumpkin, I didn't know anything about recorded music and I thought The Association and The Electric Prunes were singing live into microphones at the radio station. Oh my.

For those who know me, I have guitars and I play them in my low-budget Pirate's Cove studio. I remain a mediocre, though enthusiastic, musician, song-writer and patron of the arts.

About the cover...

In 2002 I lost a fair amount of money bringing the Flower Kings to Seattle for a show. It was a great night and I remain a big fan. I don't regret doing it one bit. My old friend Dwight Freeman took the photograph of the unrecognizable Hans Fröberg and Guy Corp turned it into the distinctive pixelated cover. Judy Coffman, the futile voice of reason, took the rear cover photograph. As always, I am fortunate to have talented artists who serve my artistic ambitions.

Contact:

E-mail me if you have questions, complaints or comments:
kcoffman@sos.net

My Writing Process

My writing skill continues to evolve. I can't take full credit for this; I am assisted immensely by the great people in my Gather.com writing group, the Writin' Wombats. For this book, I got helpful comments from my "editorial board", but it was Lisa Fredsti, Beth Hill and Pat Shaw that dug in deep and helped me correct the worst of my quirks and deficiencies. If there is anything good about the writing craft in this book, they deserve much of the credit.

The Writin' Wombats include Pat Shaw, Lisa Fredsti, John Philipp, Pat Bertram, James Rafferty, Judi Fennell, Jill Lynn Anderson, Rand Phares, Jamie Chapman, Sia McKye, JK Sather, Vivian Archer, Ann Barks, Sherrie Super, Beth Hill, JC Alexander, Steve Prosapio, Dale Cozort, Gina Robinson, Dave Saari, Wendy Christy, Sy Garte, Dana Fredsti, Brenda Vander Linden, Adina Pelle and Mike Stromer.

As always, these folks are great fun to hang with. I'll see you all at The Hicken and Spleen.

- Ken Coffman February, 2009

Little Alligator

I could read your mind and all its freakish desire
A full on femme fatale with an elegant face of fire
Through the haze of your senses and your defenses
God only knows how long it is till you hit the bottom
But that's all right, I'll get you through paradise

Don't need your wings for the queen
Little alligator

From the fangs the poison is so sweetly injected
The words that fall from your tongue are so filthy
Your mouth must be infected
Not a man but not quite a lady
Hopelessly androgynous
Hell only knows how it goes down south of the border
But that's all right, your secret is safe tonight

There is no shame, glory and fame
For little alligators

In the jungle it's coming down for those who live in the lost and
found
Can't mistake your attitude, you're so heavy
Now get over here
You can hang your image in a brand new dimension
'Cause I don't even think your mirror understands your reflection
But that's all right, as long as you're not uptight

And in your brain, it's all the same
Little alligator

- Little Alligator, Steve Vai, from *Fire Garden*

The True Story of how Paco Menendez became David Allen Smith

The ruthless sun assaulted the earth in Mazatlán. Inland, there was no breeze and thus, no respite. A hundred children lived at the city dump. Their homes, patched together from rubble, were decorated with roving chickens and scraggly patches of tomato vines. Scavenging, the kids followed colossal trucks hauling garbage from the hotels that lined the Mazatlán shoreline. There was a pecking order—the bigger kids chased the smaller away from the richest garbage collected from exclusive resorts such as Pueblo Bonito and the cruise ships.

Fred, Pastor of La Viña del Pacifico Christian Fellowship Church, wiped his forehead with a bandana. The sandwiches were gone, as were the little plastic bottles of shampoo donated by Zona Dorada hotel dwellers. After final goodbyes and hugs, his missionary team piled into their fellowship van and headed back to the city. As they navigated massive potholes in the unpaved Colonia road, they passed a dusty Jeep Cherokee hidden between ramshackle buildings.

After the church van was out of sight, the Jeep driver, Hector, eased the Jeep from its sheltered nook and weaved around potholes toward the dump. Puffing the stub of a noxious cigar, he shaded his eyes and gestured.

"I think I see her," he said to his companion, Martin.

Martin took a pull from a long-warm bottle of Pacifico beer.

"I didn't think the bible-thumpers would ever leave. It must be a hundred and fifty degrees out here. Let's get this done and get back to the beach."

Maria was dressed in a dirty smock and wore a huge, ragged straw hat to shield her sad eyes from the unrelenting sun. Her brown face was etched with deep lines. Standing by a rusty barrel overflowing with beer bottles, she held tightly to the hand of a dirty, squirming boy.

The men exited their vehicle. The dump was a hellish cacophony of seagulls and rumbling diesel trucks. Martin fanned currency and handed it over. As agreed, 1,000 pesos. She took the money, stuffed it in her ragged apron and pushed the boy forward. He'd been crying. Tears made muddy tracks down his filthy face. Hector took the kid's arm and gently tugged him toward the Cherokee.

"Adios, amiga," Martin said.

Hector opened the Jeep door and lifted the kid in.

With the air conditioner leaking tepid air, they sat for a moment and watched the activity at the dump. On their haunches, kids sorted through trash and pulled out scrap metal and other treasures. Bundles of cardboard were piled on a horse cart made from a pickup bed.

"How can they stand the stench?" Martin said. "I'll smell this in my dreams."

"I told you to light a stogie. It helps."

"I'd rather stuff a turd in my mouth."

Hector backed up and they drove through deserted Colonia streets. After passing through the village, they slowed for an extra-large pothole. The kid, working his skinny arm vigorously, rolled down the window and jumped out. With puffs of dust flying from each footfall, he ran back to the dump. Hector stopped the Jeep. They got out and watched the kid sprint.

"As if the devil's on his heels."

"And it's too damn hot to chase the little fucker," Hector complained.

Martin laughed. "Look at this," he said.

Toxic Shock Syndrome

A slight figure, covered in dust and wearing only a pair of cut-off jeans, clutched the spare tire on the back of the Jeep. Martin lifted the kid by the shorts for examination. His hands and feet were black with grime and a crusty wound on his arm seeped fluid.

"It's a twenty-pound rat."

"Is it a boy or a girl? The doctor said he prefers a boy."

"I can't tell under the dirt. Fuck it, who cares? If he bitches, we'll come out and get another one."

Martin tossed the kid in the back seat and handed over a partial bag of fried pork rinds and a warm orange soda. The silent kid ate as if he'd never seen food before.

Back in the city, they arrived at their rented apartment near Plazuela Machado in the historic center of Mazatlán. In a claw-footed bathtub, Martin scrubbed the child, and then rinsed and scrubbed again. A four year old boy emerged from the filth. Except for stubborn stains on his feet and hands, his brown skin came clean. Martin put peroxide on the wound and taped it up. He led the naked boy into the living room.

"What do you think?" he asked Hector.

"I think there ain't much to him. There's leftover Dorado on the table. See if he'll eat it."

The kid pulled at the fish with his hands.

Martin sighed and put a fork in the kid's hand. He made motions to demonstrate its use. Gracelessly, the kid did his best.

"This is going to take time," he said.

Sucking a Tootsie Pop, the kid was dressed in a tiny three-piece suit and Panama hat. He looked like a prince. At SeaTac International Airport, a U.S. customs official knelt.

"What's your name, son?"

3

The kid, with lips stained pink, pulled the sloppy sucker from his mouth.

"David Allen Smith," he said with only a trace of accent.

He stuffed the sucker back in his mouth.

"Cute kid," the agent said as he stamped the paperwork.

"We know," Martin replied.

Doctor and Mrs. Smith waited in the concourse by a gift shop. The doctor wore a suit and tie, and Mrs. Smith wore a taffeta dress and white high heels. Her brown hair, rolled into a beehive, was topped with a wide lavender ribbon. Kneeling, she held the boy at arm's length and inspected him. She pulled the sucker from his mouth.

"My sweet little boy," she said, "don't you know candy is bad for your teeth?"

"David Allen Smith," the boy said.

"There is the matter of the donation to the church..." Martin said.

"Yes, of course," said Dr. Smith. He handed over an envelope. "Five-thousand, cash. It's all there. Let me know how the orphanage construction project comes along."

"I certainly will," Martin replied while pocketing the cash.

INTRODUCTION

Glen Wilson

It was a game he had not played for many years.

Where the hell am I?

A slice of blinding light slipped through heavy curtains and stabbed directly into his brain. In the domain of his skull, pain reigned. Only one of his eyes seemed to work.

I hope this is the residue of a colossal hangover and not a massive stroke or tumor or another of God's cruel pranks.

It was a cosmic puzzle.

Where the hell am I?

On a high floor, he deduced from muffled traffic noises drifting from below. A plump breast was six inches from his face. It was unfamiliar; deflated and dusted with flecks of gleaming glitter. The woman attached to this breast lay on her side. She had jet-black hair, dyed. The roots had grown out, but not much. An eighth-inch of sedimentary gray. She was not a hideous woman, but older than he typically liked; her pale skin was decorated with pastel blue veins that made him feel all too mortal and human. He hated to be reminded of the plumbing.

Another body pressed against his flank; it was a soft rump, warm and firm.

The previous evening was a jumble of strobelit images with everything lurid and bright. From the remembered cacophony of slot machines and drunken Asians smoking and throwing their money away at a backroom poker table, he surmised he was in Las Vegas. He had a vague memory of staring down a beefy man with a sweaty, red face. Red like raw salmon. If his memory could be trusted, there was a side bet of two show girls and a cowboy hat.

Did I beat an angry Oklahoma oil man with three threes?

Something tugged at his mind, but he could not capture the thought.

What am I doing in Vegas?

He felt as if he was missing something important.

Slowly, he raised his abused body and looked around the room. The thick carpets were adorned with a pair of silver Patrón tequila bottles. A chubby, phallic Dominican cigar butt was stubbed out in a plate of congealed pasta. A matchbox implied the room was at the Bellagio.

Twisting, he could see the ladies were similar, like twins. It had been a long time since he felt cocksure enough to tackle two women at once. He was too old for the novelty to be worth the effort. If you paid them well, he guessed it would be okay; professional women would hide their harsh judgment of an inadequate man. It must have been a late night. The ladies slept hard.

He slipped out of bed and threw the bedspread over them. They slid together and spooned. An unconscious hand with perfect pink nails sought a familiar breast and gently massaged.

Cozy.

He couldn't find his underwear, so he slipped wrinkled trousers over his nakedness. He spent a few minutes looking for his wallet and watch before thinking of the Coach handbags hanging on the bedposts.

The girls apparently shared everything—he found his wallet and credit cards in one handbag and his money clip and cheap Casio watch in the other. Between them, they had a few thousand dollars which he guiltlessly liberated.

To ease a head filled with sharp, rusty edges and swirling tidepools of pain, he washed down three Tylenol with a cup of bitterly cold water dipped from an ice bucket. With head hanging, he waited for the dope to kick in and his brain to start working. Something important nibbled. In the inside pocket of his jacket, he found a plane ticket. Bush Intercontinental Airport.

What could possibly be waiting in Houston?

His name was on the ticket. First Class. The plane left McCarran in a couple of hours if the hotel clock could be trusted. He could make it if he gathered his wits and left right away.

Standing with his hand on the door, he took a last look around. It hit him. His left hand was mutilated, so the wedding ring rested on his right hand. He raised this hand. Heavy gold glittered in the dim light. He had a vague recollection of standing with a stunning blond in an Olde England-themed chapel. Was it delusion or was the minister dressed like a low-budget middle-earth wizard?

Whose stupid idea was that?

And who did he marry? One of these dancers? No, no—both had black hair.

An image popped in his mind like a champagne bubble. The image included a grinning blond, sloppy drunk, wearing a tiny, expensive-looking white cocktail dress. Her name was Gerusha.

His superior, first-class, top-notch intellect refused to engage. If he was married to the oddly-named Gerusha, then why did he wake up in bed with two exotic dancers and a massive hangover? It was a brain teaser. He needed to get moving or he'd miss his flight.

To where?

He remembered.

Houston.

Raz

Dave couldn't quite get the timing of his drum fill right. What Raz wanted was a double-bass lead-in to a triplet on the snare finished with an accent on the high hat. Over and over they worked at it, but Dave's timing did not improve.

Two union cameramen, filming for VH1, wandered with high-def digital cameras, futilely seeking interesting POVs. They were tailed by a sound and light crew bearing furry boom microphones and bright portable lights. After a while the film crew blended in the background and became part of the scenery, like wallpaper. No one noticed them. Raz's bodyguard, Murphy, sat in a corner reading her newspaper and listening with half an ear.

Raz stood and stretched his back. He sipped from a cup of iced rice milk and stared at the wall. He was tall and very thin. Lanky dark hair flopped around his face like wings.

"Where's my girl?" he shouted.

There were lots of these girls; often he didn't bother with their names. He pointed when necessary to identify a specific one. This particular girl was young, perhaps 18, with a wide, innocent face sprinkled with light-brown freckles and bearing a baby bump under her shirt.

David Allen Smith went by the stage name Rusty Razor Blade, or Raz for short. He was smart, but no one knew how smart because he didn't use big words or talk about deep subjects.

As the motive force behind the post-grunge-metal phenomenon called Toxic Shock Syndrome, he'd recently signed a one-release CD/DVD deal with EMI for ten percent of gross.

Generally, a desperate new rock band would sign any one-sided deal put in front of them. They'd get a multi-record contract and a cash advance on royalties. Buried in the fine print, they'd find recording, marketing and tour support expenses were loans repaid from future royalties. Basically, the band would pay themselves with their own money, minus record company expenses and fees, of course.

Typically, the bills piled so high that under pressure from company lawyers, they'd sign over publishing rights. Then, the record company would reap long-term rewards by licensing the music to sell car insurance, toilet paper and soft drinks. The band, stuck with debt impossible to repay, would be dumped. Then, it's back to the convenience store gig, hope you socked away some of that upfront cash, because that's all she wrote, the end, fini, so long, farewell, goodbye.

Raz didn't play that game. He had enough money from touring and merchandise sales to fund the recording sessions himself and avoid the accounting scam. His lawyer wrote a simple contract. If the record company got a dollar, then Raz got a dime, period. The audit trail was clean and the paycheck, like clockwork, was cut at the end of the quarter or EMI could find themselves a new rock god to reinvent music.

Leaning back, he stretched and whispered in Girl's ear. She knew how he wanted his Starbucks order: Tazo Chai with a splash of soy milk, half a teaspoon of honey and topped with a dash of Tahitian vanilla. He whispered because he was not under contract with Starbucks and did not want to give them free publicity.

After she left, Raz dropped his pencil on the music notation pad he scribbled on and leaned back in his chair.

"Okay, Dave, that's it," Raz said.

"We'll pick it up tomorrow?"

"No, that will be all. I want to march to the tune of a different drummer."

The camera crew, sensing momentous events unfolding, maneuvered into position to capture the scene. Murphy put down her newspaper and leaned forward.

Dave paled. "You know I'll get it. I always get it sooner or later. You're tired. We'll talk about this tomorrow."

Raz sighed.

"Yes, I'm tired. Tired of inefficiency. You get it, but it takes too long. I want someone who rocks me. Don't worry. If I need your special talents, I'll seek you out. In the meantime, Seymour will cut a check and I'll authorize a month's severance pay. That's my best offer unless you want your lawyer to talk to my lawyer."

"I'm a drummer, not an sellout, asshole businessman. I don't have a fucking lawyer."

"Don't make this ugly. We had good times, but it's time to move on."

"When you fired Erik, I knew this day would come. The only thing you care about is the paycheck, you soul-less creep."

Raz smiled. "Now you're showing passion. If you had the same passion for practicing paradiddles, things might be different. I'm going to close my eyes and count to twenty. When I open them, you will be gone."

Murphy sighed and walked over. In her head, she counted.

"Don't touch me, bitch. I'm going," Dave said, shrugging off her hand.

He slammed the studio door as he left.

Nineteen, twenty, Murphy thought.

Raz opened his eyes and looked around. "Yes, that's an improvement," he said. "Thank you, Murphy."

Toxic Shock Syndrome

The girl came back carrying a hot cup. The Starbucks logo had been carefully eradicated with an indelible black pen.

Raz's eyes lit up. "Perfect timing, girl," he said while gently patting her protruding tummy. In a loud voice, he said, "Someone call Chad Wackerman and see if he's available. That man knows how to syncopate."

He waved for a cameraman to approach, then took a sip of his drink.

"Damn that tastes good," he said. "Howard, if you're watching, we can CGI the logo back in if you'll sign my damn contract."

He walked to an array of guitars hanging on the wall. Running his fingers over the strings, he considered a Vox 12-string and a Gibson SG before selecting a weathered 1957 Stratocaster. He handed it to a technician to be tuned.

"We'll work on overdubs until we find a new drummer," he said while gazing intimately into the camera lens.

Gerusha Andersen-Wilson

Pain. Her backbone was twisted like a pretzel. The taste of something foul like bad cheese filled her mouth. Sitting up was hard, but she pushed herself erect and peered through tinted windows into blinding sunlight. She was wearing a dress; white and luminescent except for a large stain where something orange had dribbled down one side. Her temples throbbed.

Where am I? What day is it? What happened?

With gummy eyes that would not open completely, she saw a photograph laying face down on her lap.

This is going to be bad.

She flipped it and gasped. In a low-budget wedding chapel, a man dressed in a cheesy wizard costume stood on a pulpit. She was drunk, laughing while hanging off Glen's arm. The picture captured him lecherously leering down the front of her dress.

She fumbled with the window control and barely got her head out the window before a flood of hot vomit erupted. It wasn't the first episode; the side of the limousine was caked with dried chunks. After spitting, she looked for something to rinse out her mouth. Her stomach churned at the sight of a nearly-empty bottle of Mescal.

No.

She pushed it aside and fumbled at the door of a tiny refrigerator. Inside, among cans of soft drinks, were several pint bottles of Arrowhead spring water.

Oh God, yes, thank you.

She pressed icy bottles to her temples and wept.

The limousine idled, but the driver was missing. They were parked in a corner of a parking lot next to a chain link fence topped with razor wire. The nearest vehicles were RVs, radiating heat waves. Fifty feet away, an old woman under an awning, pulled from the side of her Winnebago, knitted and watched. Gerusha pressed the control and the window slid up. The driver, walking slowly, approached, sipping from a paper cup. He was dressed neatly in a uniform and hat. After he got in the car, Gerusha slid open the privacy screen.

"Is that coffee?" she asked. "Hand it over."

"Oh, you're up. I fixed this one just the way I like it. We can find a drive-thru and you can get your own."

"Don't mess with me, hand it over. And aspirin."

The driver sighed and held up the cup. She reached through the window and grabbed it. It was a latté, sweet with vanilla syrup. After digging through the glove box, he offered a bottle of Excedrin.

"I can't open it, just hand me some."

He poured three pills onto her palm and she took them, one at a time, washing them down with the sweet coffee. She did an inventory. Her bra was unhooked, but otherwise, she seemed unviolated.

"Do I have luggage in the back?"

"Yes, ma'am," the driver replied.

"Good. Find me a place where I can change my clothes."

In a CITGO restroom, she stuffed the wedding dress in a trash can and put on clean underwear, jeans, and a blouse. Her shoes were missing. Discovering a toothbrush, she brushed her teeth for a solid five minutes, rinsing and spitting until the rancid, cheesy taste faded.

Even after a strenuous brushing, her hair was matted from hairspray. She desperately needed a shower. There was a tap on the door. She opened it a crack. The driver offered her handbag. She grabbed it and shut the door again. Inside, she found money, credit cards, and a marriage license. Mrs. Gerusha Wilson.

What had she done? Where was her husband?

After splashing cold water on her face and drying off with a paper towel, she stood up, and turned her head back and forth.

Not good, but better.

She smoothed the wrinkles on her blouse and was ready—or as ready as she would be—to face the day.

"Where to now?" the driver asked.

"First, anyplace that sells shoes, and then the airport," she replied.

13

CHAPTER ONE

Glen

On the plane, Glen had time to think, but his brain would not cooperate. His headache bounced around his skull like a pinball, but the drugs did their job and some of the pain was transferred to a Glen of an alternate universe.

Who cares, screw that Glen, I never liked him.

He slipped off the wedding band and looked it over. No clues were engraved on it.

The previous days were a blur of random images that included hours of tedium while watching Gerusha feed dollars into a slot machine, an altercation of some sort with a pit boss at Caesar's Palace and drinking mescal in a hired limousine. He remembered groping someone in the limousine, probably Gerusha, but he had no memory of sexual release, just an endless build-up. Somehow that build-up concluded with two ladies-of-experience in a king-size bed at the Bellagio. How that came to be, he could not grasp.

Gerusha worked at a company started by Glen's friends in Seattle and he'd been trying to get into her panties for a long time. He wasn't sure they'd done the deed and he considered that a bad omen for a happy marriage. The flight attendant brought two bottles of beer which improved his mood, but did not help him make sense of the weekend's events. He'd gather his nerve and call Gerusha to see if she'd shed light on things.

Slowly, it came to him that he was flying to Houston to meet Murphy. Murphy was an ex-cop, stocky and plain, but tough. She'd taken a chief-of-security gig for a whacked-out rock musician. She'd asked for his help.

What could he do?

He was compelled to offer expertise, skill and genius.

When the going gets weird, you call me, Glen Wilson.

He hated airports and the George Bush Airport was one of the worst. Jostled by a mob, he looked for Murphy, but she was not at baggage claim or parked outside. Hot and humid, Houston smelled like an over-ripe armpit.

He did the only reasonable thing he could think of. Found a bar, bought a mug of beer and nibbled from a basket of free pretzels while watching the crowd flow and swirl like debris in a gutter. He saw her walk by. Her gait was unmistakable; she marched like a constipated bulldog wearing a pinched, sour expression. He let her walk. If she was any kind of a cop, she'd find him. It didn't take long. Two minutes. She bruised the meat of his arm with a knuckle.

"Dammit, Murphy, that hurt," he complained while rubbing the sore spot.

"Be where you're supposed to be and I won't slug you. How long were you going to let me run up and down the terminal?"

"Here I am, innocently having a well-earned beer at McDonoughughs like you told me."

Murphy laughed, but without humor.

"We were supposed to meet on the curb by the skycap station where the traffic is lighter and you know it." It sounded familiar now that she mentioned it. "That way I wouldn't have to find a parking place and tromp up and down looking for your sorry ass."

"It's great to see you, Murphy, did I mention that already?"

She took the beer mug out of his hand and set it on the bar.

"Let's go, Wilson."

"Hey, I wasn't finished. Sit down and relax for a minute."

"You'll have plenty of time to relax after I kill you," she said, before turning on her heel and walking away briskly.

Glen tossed a random assortment of bills on the table and kept her in sight as she marched up the corridor.

Sourpuss, he thought.

Murphy drove a brown Taurus with Florida plates. The Taurus was the most boring car ever built and brown was its most boring color. It was clearly her personal vehicle, so Glen kept these well-known facts to himself.

"Why didn't we ever get married?"

She tried to hold it back, but laughter escaped.

"Well, for one reason, you're an asshole and I don't like you. Ha, that's two reasons, but I can think of a lot more. You won't keep asking now that you're married, will you? By the way, how was your honeymoon? I liked the picture you emailed. Gerusha is a pretty bride. How you talked her into getting hitched, I do not know. Was it hinky Glen Wilson hoodoo bullshit? Did Walter hypnotize her?"

This was a lot of words for Murphy to string together and he learned a lot. He and Gerusha had flown to Las Vegas to get married... He felt better knowing for sure.

"Don't underestimate the power of true love, Murphy." Without thinking, he added, "I'd like to see that photograph—"

He didn't say it very loud, but Murphy was onto him. Putting his life in danger, she studied his face instead of watching traffic. Glen turned his head to look out the side window, but it was too late. Laughter erupted from her chest like hiccups.

"You don't remember a thing about it, do you?"

"Goddam it, Murphy, watch the road."

She pounded on the steering wheel.

"That's a propane truck!"

"I see it," she said. "The almighty Glen Wilson blacked out on his honeymoon. That's too rich."

"I don't know what you're talking about. I officially withdraw any and all marriage invitations. You can rot in your grave as a dried-out lonely spinster, for all I care."

"Is she good in the sack, Glen? How does she like it? Slow and sensuous or fast and rough? Is she satiable? Oh, I'm sorry, that was cruel since you have no clue."

Convulsing, she clapped her hands.

"Go ahead, Murphy, have your fun."

"Elke will love this when I tell her."

It was going to be an endless fucking day.

After a few miles of stopping-and-going in bumper-to-bumper traffic, Murphy wiped her eyes with a tissue and calmed down.

"If you're done having fun at my expense, could we talk about the job?"

"Sure, Glen."

After exiting the freeway, she weaved through a rundown industrial area—block after block of railroad tracks, loading docks, graffiti and broken windows. She parked in a gravel parking lot and waved at a sign. Lawnmower and Garden Supply.

"What's this?"

"A sign Raz bought somewhere. It doesn't mean anything." She scooted around on the Taurus's cloth seat and faced him. "I need you to be the bag man. Raz's contract stipulates cash up front, or the band doesn't go on stage. It can be a lot of money."

"How much?"

"Just over three-hundred-thousand is the most I've seen so far, but the band is building buzz, and the next leg of the tour will be more profitable."

"Why me? You could contract this out to Brinks."

She looked out the windshield and rubbed her face.

"Cogs in cogs."

This was the Murphy Glen knew. Bleak and humorless. Serious. She knew when she was in over her head. She knew, when things got complex and out of balance, she'd need professional help. Glen's help.

Glen Wilson, the master of mayhem, the king of chaos, the fearless survivor riding a silver horse to the rescue.

"Let's not make this complex; you owe me and I want you onboard for the tour. If things are cool, then I'll use armed money carriers for the next leg and you can go annoy your blushing and unviolated bride instead of me. Can you deal with it?"

Deal with it? I was made for it. When large sums of cash are at hand, Glen is the man you want at your side. When the sun rises in the west and tornadoes appear on the horizon, you want Glen Wilson riding shotgun. When the stars spin like cartwheels in the sky—

"It's not a complex question, Glen. Are you in or not?"

She stood at his window, staring through the passenger-side glass with the question etched in her eyes.

"Why are we wasting time, Murphy?" Glen motioned for her to get out of the way so he could open the door. "Do you expect me to sit around and gather dust? Let's move out."

That earned him a small smile. By hurrying, he kept up as she marched toward the brick building and metal door under the Lawnmower sign. At the door, she stopped and put her hand on Glen's arm.

"Raz…"

"Yes," he said, motioning for her to continue.

"He's smart. Scary smart."

"Come on, Murphy. He's a guitar-plucker, not a nuclear physicist. Don't get overwrought."

She tapped on the metal door with the car key.

"You'll see," she said.

A huge glass window provided the view between the recording room and a 128-channel mixing desk. While two sound engineers chatted, pushed faders and adjusted knobs, lights flashed and flickered on rack-after-rack of sound equipment.

On the far side of the window, Raz stood with eyes closed. Black hair fell around his face as he riffed on a Fender Stratocaster. Music pulsated as he played sweeping lines across the neck. His fingers were long and he could reach almost an octave across the middle of the fretboard. The Fender sounded like a violin; notes cascaded in a mad flurry. If mad scientist Nicolai Tesla played electric guitar, this is what it would sound like, all angular and electric. It was too soon for Glen to measure Raz's intelligence, but he had to give credit—the kid could play the guitar.

Murphy dismissed the security guard. Glen was unimpressed; the guard's belly pushed at the buttons on his uniform tunic and brown stains ran down the front of his shirt. After the recording session, Raz huddled with the sound engineers for an intense conversation. After that, Raz stood and stretched his back. Murphy touched his shoulder.

"Raz, I'd like you to say hello to—"

"Walk with me, I need to talk to a drummer."

In the narrow hallway, a young black girl waited. Raz kissed her and nuzzled her neck. She was about six months pregnant. A narrow silver ring bearing the TSS logo rested on her finger. After a few moments of whispering, Raz patted her on the rear and continued walking. The corridor weaved and twisted, and then opened up into a large room. A skeletal, dark-skinned man adjusted the hardware of an elaborate drum set.

"McCloud?" Raz said.

The drummer stood; he was very tall. They exchanged an elaborate sequence of hand gestures.

"I enjoyed your work with The Toy Symphony."

"Thanks, man," McCloud said. "That was a cool gig while it lasted."

"Are you up to speed on my Soundtrack for Revolution project?"

"Yes."

"Could you show me what you would have done with Frank's Last Supper?"

"The middle section? Do you want me to vamp on it?"

Raz smiled. "I want you to play it your way. A busy version."

"Okay, I have some ideas."

He gathered Remo sticks and settled on the drum throne. After three clicks, he played military rolls which evolved into a raucous thunder.

Raz waved his hands.

"Stop. I don't like the cymbals; they wash out the midrange. Start again."

"Still a busy version?"

"Yes," Raz nodded.

McCloud started again with military rolls and built the wild pattern with less ride cymbal. Raz nodded and stopped him again.

"Okay, I get it, you can play a complex pattern. Let me hear something sparse."

McCloud nodded and thought about it for a second.

"Okay," he said. "I'm ready."

He started with the same snare roll, but stayed in the beat's pocket.

Raz waved his hands again.

"Are you okay with my guidance to get what I want?"

McCloud shrugged. "If you pay the bills, you're the boss."

A dreamy look drifted across Raz's face. "Yes, the boss." He snapped back into focus and talked quickly. "Here are the terms: I pay travel expenses, five-thousand a week and five percent of concert net. It's an at-will employment contract with no royalties or residuals. Between noon and midnight, carry a pager and get your ass into the studio within a half-hour if I call. For all band publicity, you go by the name Stix McClot. That name is trademarked and I own the trademark. It's my intellectual property, get it? Are you in?"

"Yes," McCloud said.

"Good," Raz said, "welcome aboard."

Clever, Glen thought. *He can change drummers and the album credits stay the same. Modular, plug-and-play musicians.*

Glen got five grand a week too, but without the profit sharing. His bank account balance was nearly two million dollars, so he wasn't hurting for cash, but still…

Raz walked to Glen and studied him. Face-to-face, Glen was measured, evaluated, and analyzed. Glen did the same.

"You'll carry my money? How can I trust you?"

"Trust as a refuge when you have no other choice."

"Maybe," he said. "You knew Moshi?"

Did I know Moshi? Mush? Hearing her name caused an icy finger to run up my spine. She took a bullet for me in Alaska and died in my arms. Raz knew her too?

"Yeah, what about her?"

21

"I liked her. I heard the story. What did she whisper before she died?"

"That's none of your damn business."

Raz hesitated and then laughed.

"As you wish," he said. He gestured at Glen's mutilated left hand. "Bummer."

"I can still play a blues lick that makes a girl's nipples perky."

Raz leaned over with his hands on his knees, laughing.

"Okay, Szabo, you got the job," he said.

The first and only time Raz asked Glen to make a coffeeshop run, they were listening to a playback in the control booth. Raz expertly equalized the sound and arranged each instrument with certain placement in the sonic spectrum. Raspy guitar here, a wash of chorus there, and individual drums placed at specific stereo locations. Fascinating, but tedious. He'd spend ten minutes diddling a reverb control before it met his approval. Glen napped and daydreamed about past adventures.

"You'd like a Tazo chai tea with a splash of soy milk, half a teaspoon of honey and a sprinkle of Tahitian vanilla? I'd like your girlie to suck my dick, so life overflows with sad, unfulfilled expectations."

Generally, Glen could peer into a man's soul and know him better than he knew himself, but Raz was complex. He defied easy categorization. Eventually, Glen would factor him like a polynomial, but it would take time.

Raz flicked his eyes to his girl.

"Hey, babe, will you see to my tea?"

She stared daggers into Glen, but nodded slowly in response.

"I'll take a double espresso," Glen said.

She didn't reply, but her expression suggested that Glen should die. Soon.

"Leave her alone, Glen," Murphy said, warning him with her eyes.

Glen was surprised when the girl brought the espresso. He inspected it carefully, but did not find anything wrong.

She was remarkable. Never saying much, her large brown eyes were always on Raz. It would be easy to presume she was a mindless groupie. A warm and disposable place for Raz to seek relief. But the babies added a twist to things. Several of the girls were noticeably pregnant. Raz was gentle with her. Were they married? She wore a ring, but Raz didn't. It was a mystery.

Raz resumed his work. The song they mixed was called *Empire of Love*.

> When the Emperor calls
> And the army gathers at the gate
> We'll raise our flags and banners
> And topple the state

The chorus was dense, like a Viking choir. It was a scary wall of sound.

Did it mean anything or was it just a stupid song?

Glen could not decide.

He watched for the rock and roll clichés. How did Raz take his dope? Snort? Inject? Smoke? Ingest? But, there were no signs of extreme bad habits. He was a vegetarian, though he ate cheese and eggs. He meditated and did something like Yoga with chanting and stretching. Otherwise, beyond an occasional cigarette, there seemed to be no destructive behavior.

The recording was nearly finished. Raz played the bass lines on the recording by thumbing patterns on an old Jazz bass or plucking notes on an Alembic. He loved counterpoint and could work out lines quickly, but wanted a bass player for the live shows. The first guy he interviewed had a great pedigree, but Raz didn't like his attitude. The next guy was better.

"I suppose I should tell you up front that I'm a Scientologist," the bassist said.

The young man, Tom LaRoe, had a huge bushy head of red hair: a white-guy Afro.

Scientologist? That was different.

Glen scooted his chair closer to hear them talk. Raz glanced up, but did not comment.

"Will that be an issue?"

Raz turned his attention back to the bassist. "No proselytizing."

"I wouldn't dream of it."

"Then it's not a problem," Raz said. "I want to hear you play. Can you do Bach?"

"Note for note or a classical jam?"

"Surprise me."

Tom walked to an SWR practice amp and plugged in his Kubicki five-string. He quickly checked the tuning and then played slowly. By tapping his fingers on the fretboard, he could play simultaneous ascending and descending lines. Glen had never heard anything like it. When he was done, Glen jumped up and applauded. Raz looked at him coldly until he sat back down.

"Thumb?" Raz asked.

Tom responded by playing a funky riff.

"Fretless?"

"I'm not Jaco. I can play quarter notes in tune, that's about it."

Raz handed him headphones. "Listen to this and see what you can come up with. Capture the feel, not the notes."

He gestured to the sound engineer who played the track. When it stopped, Tom rotated his finger in the air and the engineer restarted it so he could hear it again.

"Your bass line is busy. Not bad, but this is the way I hear it," Tom said.

He played a simple melodic pattern with muted notes and lots of space. The amp rumbled with low notes. "Shall we try it with the music?" he suggested.

With eyes closed, Raz concentrated while listening.

"Okay, it's good," he said. "What's with this Scientology thing? Chick Corea is a Scientologist… Stanley Clarke used to be one."

"Was that a question?"

"No, I'm thinking out loud. No preaching?"

"No preaching or recruiting. You do your thing and I'll do mine."

"Okay, you're in. Your band name is Jazz Berlin. Anytime you're on my payroll, you go by Jazz. You can be Tom when someone else pays you. Clear?"

Jazz laughed. "Yes, that's clear," he said.

Glen found Murphy deep in conversation with a husky, young Hispanic wearing a tank top. Tattooed from neck to wrist, his arms were densely covered with disturbing, writhing shapes. He looked like a former football player.

A running back?

He walked with an emphasis to his right side as if he'd had a knee blown out. If Glen ever had trouble with this guy, he'd start the festivities with a hard boot to the right knee and go from there.

"Give us a minute, amigo?" Glen asked politely.

He tugged Murphy's arm and they moved a few feet away.

"Play nice. Jesus is a good guy," Murphy said.

"Jesus?"

"Yes, 'Hey-Zeus'," she said with exasperation. "He's a friend."

Jesus is her friend.

"Of course, Murphy. Nice is my middle name. Don't get unhinged."

She looked at him with naked curiosity. "Is it my imagination or has your vocabulary improved?"

"I didn't have much else to do in captivity so I read some books. No big deal. Look Murphy, for this job, I'll need a piece. Firepower."

She sucked on her teeth and frowned. "I'm not sure that's a good idea."

"Don't make me taxi downtown and buy heat from a crack dealer. You can spare one, I know you can. Don't get all sour-faced about it."

"All right." She opened her briefcase, pulled out a bundle of bubble wrap and unwrapped a 1911 Colt .45 with a spare clip. It was old, but in good condition. Well-oiled and rust-free. "I'll loan you this one until you get your own."

Making sure Jesus got an eyeful, Glen weighed the weapon in both hands. His left hand was mutilated, but he could still shoot with it.

"Hey Wilson, what happened to your hand?" Jesus asked.

"Nothing," Glen replied. "What happened to your knee?"

"Stop this macho posturing right now," Murphy insisted. "Shake hands and be friends."

Glen held out his left hand. Jesus hesitated, and then shook it awkwardly as if he did not want to touch Glen's mutilated fingers.

"I'm pleased to make your acquaintance," Glen said.

"The pleasure is all mine," Jesus replied.

Murphy latched the clasps on her briefcase.

"Damned dickhead machismo," she muttered before walking away.

"Better follow mama," Glen suggested while slipping the pistol into his belt and arranging his shirt to cover it.

The tattoos on Jesus' neck twitched.

"Buenos tardes," Glen called after him before walking away.

Jesus didn't respond.

Gerusha

By arriving at Immortality, LLC early and using the back stairs, she got to her office unseen.

What would she tell her friends?

They'd want juicy details and she had none. She couldn't tell them she'd blacked out in a limo and had no idea where her husband was. That would not do. Her mood alternated between anger and fear.

What kind of man abandons his wife on their wedding day?

He was a powerful person at the company and she needed her job. Would he get her fired and then blacklisted at every place else in town? With massive credit card bills, she couldn't afford to go back to work at Starbucks. Distraught, she locked her office door and plopped into her chair.

Looking over email accumulating in her inbox, she couldn't concentrate. The characters on the screen wouldn't coalesce into meaningful words. She cried. Silent tears streamed down her face and her shoulders shook.

Someone wiggled the doorknob and knocked.

"I know you're in there. Let me in."

Gerusha was not ready. It was Paula, Walter Crowley's executive assistant. Because Walter was the president of the company, she *had* to open the door. While standing with her hand on the knob, she dabbed her eyes with a tissue and took a deep breath. She unlocked the door and Paula rushed in like a windstorm.

"Gerusha, you haven't answered my calls. Don't be all mysterious. Tell me everything. Have you been crying? I knew it; Glen is a brute, too rough for a nice girl like you, dear. What did he do? Everything, I'll bet. Are you sore? He made you take it in the rear, didn't he? Men are shits, all of them, treating a nice girl like a meat-market whore, putting their thing where it wasn't meant to go. They don't care how much it hurts us and you can't say no on your honeymoon, can you? Not until later. And those erection pills? They go for an hour and tear a girl up, a nasty business invented by men, of course, to torture women. There should be an international law or a United Nations civil rights committee, but there isn't."

Paula seated herself in Gerusha's guest chair.

"I'm doing all the talking. Let's hear it. You'll feel better once you've shared and all the dirty little details are in the open so the psychic wounds can heal. Gerusha?"

Gerusha did not know what to say. She shifted uncomfortably in her chair.

Paula continued. "I shared my secret histories. When I had an abortion, I didn't clam up like a sphinx, did I? You're my friend, we tell each other everything." After a moment of silence, Paula relented. "Okay, I understand, you don't want to talk about your husband's nasty urges, I get it. I can wait until you're ready. Take as long as you want, but I'm free for lunch. Let's go somewhere nice and quiet where we can chat." Paula stood and walked to the door. "Oh, by the way, Walter wants to see you; he said you should stop by as soon as you're in, as in right away. See you at lunchtime, dear."

Toxic Shock Syndrome

Walter… The first time she'd met him, she worked at Starbucks and he asked for an espresso with nicotine and belladonna. Was it only a year ago? She looked up belladonna in the dictionary... A deadly poison in high dosage, but a hallucinogen in lower doses. Walter's idea of a joke. Odd tales about him were rampant. Now he wanted to see her and it was too late to call in sick. Besides, there was work to do. Vendors needed to be managed and supply contracts needed to be negotiated. Standing by the door, she practiced a confident smile. She wasn't ready, but it was time to face the world.

Waving to fellow employees along the way, she weaved through the cubicle maze toward Walter's office. Some made eye-contact and smiled back, but most focused on their work. Soon she stood in front of Paula's desk.

"Just go in. He's waiting," Paula said. She motioned Gerusha closer. "If you've been damaged, you know, down below, don't be brave about it. Go see a doctor, okay?"

"Okay," Gerusha replied.

Walter was tall and thin with snow-white hair swept back from his face. His nose, a beak, protruded majestically below icy cold eyes.

"Ah, my dear Gerusha, come in, sit down. Should I call you Mrs. Wilson? How was your weekend?"

Gerusha had no intention of telling him anything, but under his penetrating stare, everything poured out. The scene at the wedding chapel, waking in the limousine, everything. Walter listened intently and hardly moved. When she was done, he stared at her impassively before tilting his head back and emitting a single bark of laughter.

'Gah!'

She had a brief view up his wide nostrils before his head tilted back.

"I spend half my time thinking Glen is an absurd and hopeless fool and the other half admiring his bold, unconscious genius. The truth, as always, lies somewhere in between. He introduced me to Bennie and for that I will be eternally grateful. He dares to command me and for that, I will be forever resentful."

"What should I do?"

"Great question. Let me think…" He leaned back in his chair and unconsciously patted his pompadour to assure its perfection. "You are married to a notorious, mysterious company executive. While navigating company politics, use that to your advantage. Your marriage will be unusual. Roll with it. Easy to say, but hard to do and I don't mean to trivialize the paradox, but see if you can relax and enjoy the chaos. Did he give you a cash card?"

After unclipping her handbag, she produced a paper sleeve holding a shiny new platinum debit card. The PIN was scribbled on a sliver of sticky note. She held up the card.

"Go spend some of his money," Walter said.

CHAPTER TWO

Glen

Not knowing anything about the musicians, Glen surfed the Internet and brought himself up to speed. He downloaded videos from YouTube and listened to projects the bass player and drummer played on. Steve Morse Band and Toy Matinee. Most of the performances were busy and technical. With too many notes, it sounded like monkeyhouse noise. However, he appreciated the skill it took to play the complicated stuff.

Raz wanted to test the new record on an audience, so he booked a club. The marquee said James and the Little Peaches, but rumors spread on the Internet and they sold all 500 seats in a day. Glen's job was to collect and tend the money. The manager was a Japanese man with dirty fingernails wearing an expensive Armani jacket over a dirty wife-beater t-shirt. They met in a stamp-sized office an hour before show time. After counting the money slowly, Glen stuffed it in his fanny pack with his .45. Just over two thousand dollars in cash. He gave Murphy the thumbs-up. The show would go on.

"Tell Mr. Razorblade he's welcome here anytime."

Glen snorted. Effortlessly, the guy sold 500 tickets at $20 a pop which did not include revenue from the evening's liquor sales.

"I'll be sure to let him know," Glen said.

Except for guarding the money with his life, Glen's job was done and he could relax and enjoy the show.

From backstage, he watched. How would Raz get up for the performance? Hours spent cloistered in the hermetic studio was one thing, performing live in front of a greedy audience something else. Most performers needed a boost for public appearances. Glen was sure there'd be something: a snort, a drink or a pill. However, as Glen watched, Raz meditated for an hour and then was ready.

Murphy ran the security team, large men wearing yellow t-shirts that said, creatively, SECURITY. The place was packed. Glen studied the crowd. Mostly, they were what you'd expect—young flash-mobbers dressed in black, endlessly tattooed and pierced. Also present were a contingent of nerds and scattered pockets of long-haired musician-types.

The room was a dump, but Raz filled it with high-end sound equipment bearing JBL, Mackie Rane, and Lexicon logos. Over the stage, the nimble crew swarmed like pirates on rigging, adjusting elaborate stage-lighting equipment for maximum effect. Two camera crews wandered. This show was not intended to be profitable, it was just a dry run for the tour and a way of gauging the crowd's response to new songs.

On schedule at 9:58, the house sound faded and the lights dimmed. The club manager walked to the front of the stage.

"I'm pleased to present, for your rocking pleasure, Toxic—Shock—Syndrome!"

The noise level crested and then quieted. A single spotlight illuminated a corner of the stage. Smoke machines belched clouds carved by bright laser beams. Raz, statue-still, slowly played a long, sinuous line over and over, from low to high, faster and faster, until his fingers were a blur and the amplifiers screeched. Glen tapped the technician running the sound board on the shoulder and pointed to his ears. The tech looked exasperated, but tossed Glen a plastic bag filled with foam ear plugs and then turned back to his work.

Raz strolled to center stage and shouted into the microphone.

"Hello, Houston! Let me introduce my friends helping out tonight. On drums, it's Stix McClot."

Stix plopped down on the throne and bashed out a riff.

"On electric bass, Jazz Berlin."

Jazz played a snappy line ending on a low note that pounded Glen's chest like a heart attack. Loud.

They played and the crowd ate it up. The new material went over well, particularly a slow song called Brownout, but when they played the hits, the place throbbed as the audience shouted along. Glen recognized some of the words and tapped his foot with the beat. It was not his type of music, but he could see the attraction. Raz played with his eyes closed and swayed like a cobra possessed by demons. The show did not use Raz's typical horrorshow theatrics; it was all about the music.

Two hours later, with looped feedback echoing, the band took a bow and scooted off the stage.

Afterward, Glen waved his backstage pass and pushed into the green room. Raz, with Jazz pinned against the wall, talked a mile-a-minute while the bass player scribbled notes. Glen worked through the mob until he was close enough to hear Raz shouting instructions like 'second chorus, 3-4 time, mid-tempo'. It meant nothing to Glen, but Raz was intense and serious. A Raz girl stood behind him and wiped his neck with a towel.

After guzzling a cold bottle of water, Raz was ready to traverse the crowd waiting in the back alley. Teenagers pressed CD J-cards on him; he scribbled on them with a Sharpie pen and passed them back. Eventually, the entourage arrived at the van's cargo door. While Glen watched, a young girl pressed herself on Raz and shouted in his ear.

He put his hand on her back and guided her into the van. This was it... Raz already had a girl on the van. Glen expected her to react. To scream and make a scene, but she was passive. In fact, settled on the van's rear seat, the girls sat together and clasped hands.

Did they already know each other?

With eyes closed, Raz perched on a jumpseat and paid no attention to either of them.

Two girls at once, that took a manly-man. I thought about offering my assistance, but remembered: I'm married. I don't do things like that any more. Not while I'm sober.

Gerusha

Gerusha was in her office when the call came through. Noting Glen's number on the phone's display, she took a deep breath and rubbed a hand over her face.

Enjoy the chaos, Walter advised.

"Hello, Glen," she said coolly.

"Hey, babe."

Silence stretched: one beat, two beats, three.

She broke first.

"I'm sorry, Glen, I don't know what happened. I woke up in the limo. The last thing I remember is sitting in the casino trying to stay awake while you played roulette."

Glen grinned.

I wake up in a hotel room with two whores and she apologizes. The Gods, again, smile on their humble and grateful servant.

"That's okay, babe. I don't expect you to be perfect. These things happen. It means we have unfinished business to look forward to. Intimate husband and wife business, the horizontal ballet—"

Gerusha closed her eyes and took a deep breath.

Damn, this man can be irritating.

She blurted the only thing she could think of that might shut him up.

"During my lunch break, I spent two thousand dollars of your money on shoes."

Does she think I care how much she spends on shoes?

"Damn it, Gerusha, two grand for shoes? Are they made of endangered Italian muskrats? I'm upset. Two grand! Well, I'll think of you modeling them for me, just wearing the shoes, if you catch my meaning, wearing your shoes and nothing else while dancing for me in candlelight..."

"Glen?"

"Yes, my sweet?"

"Shut the hell up. I need to get back to work. Is there anything else?"

"No, but I will be thinking of you and dreaming of the day we get together."

"Yes, Glen, you're a pig. I get that. Good-bye."

"Hold on Gerusha, before you blow my bankroll on shoes, buy us a house, will you? Something nice. Tell Walter to work out the financing."

She pressed the end-call button on her phone.

Buy a house? Like there was time for that...

On the other hand, the idea had merit. She might need more room now that she could afford to buy shoes.

She could stall no longer; she had to appear in public and feed the rumor mill. After a big promotion, she'd married a legendary company figurehead, so what she did was news. The insatiable appetite for company gossip would devour her. The narrative might go wrong unless she fed the beast. Spin control, that's what was needed. She couldn't tell the truth, so she rehearsed lies in her head until they held together. For morning break, she met Paula in the lunchroom.

"Okay," Paula said, "how is he in bed? He's an older man—does he pump you for a minute, shoot a dribble, then fall asleep? Does he have trouble achieving and maintaining. Need I say more? I had an older lover once, a college professor if you must know, so I know the drill, or the lack of drill, but the woman always suffers for love. So, tell me."

In a conference room off the cavernous employee lunch area, they nibbled items selected from the breakfast bar and sipped cans of Diet Coke.

"We didn't have much time together. He was very sweet. We enjoyed our first time in the limousine. Glen sent the driver to have a piece of pie at Denny's, so we were alone. With champagne and soft music, it was very romantic. He has great, gentle hands and I came twice, once from his fingers and once from his, uh, thing."

"Was it a big one, dear?"

"A little bigger than other men I've dated. I'm not much of an expert..."

"Well, I am, dear, big and small, I've seen them all, and bigger is better if you ask me, but my current boyfriend, well, let's just say he does the best he can with what little God gave him, if you catch my meaning. Nothing against him, not his fault, but you're lucky. I miss a man who can fill me up, if you follow. You are the luckiest girl in the world. And he has money? Big money? Endless piles of cash? We're in a community property state, dear. Half is yours. Half. How much are we talking? Six figures? Seven? Eight? My boyfriend works for Adobe and makes one-hundred and forty-five thousand plus bonuses and stock options. Not so bad. Enough to scrape by, but it would be nice to have more. So it goes; a woman does what she can. As long as he pays my credit-card bills, then I can deal with his mini. I'll get a little on the side if I have the appetite; that's not just a man's game anymore. If you need to get out and party some night while your old man's away, then let me know. I'll steer you right, no bums, just well-groomed yuppies on the prowl; they are the best, believe me. So, let me guess—another pop or two in the hotel room, drinks and gambling, then a sad farewell at the airport. Until we meet again, my sweet, I'll be thinking of you constantly and call you every day? How did I do?"

"You nailed it."

"So, tell. How much does he have?"

"Money? I don't know. He gave me a debit card, and I know there is almost two million in that account. We're going to buy a house, but I don't know what the budget is, at least four or five-hundred thousand..."

"Honey, you can't buy a crackerbox for five-hundred thousand. And, even then you'd have to live in backwoods like Monroe or Duvall or worse. That will not do. I have an ex who is an agent—large cock, small brain—but a hell-of-a real estate guy, he can get you a deal. I'll give you his card, tell him I said to give you a cash rebate on the commission. Plus, he's good for a casual hook up, if you like his type. Not afraid to dive the—"

"Please don't say it. That's crude."

"Okay, sure, but he's a master of many tongues if you know what I mean."

"Stop it."

"Okay, don't get your panty liners in a twirl. I'm trying to help a girl out. Real estate? Mr. Wilson can't live anywhere; he needs a proper neighborhood—close in, but established and high-end. Perhaps Mercer Island or Sand Point. I know, one of the old neighborhoods on the bluff in Magnolia completely refurbished with granite, hardwood, and tile with a hot tub on the deck for entertaining. It must have a nice view of the Puget Sound, that goes without saying. Don't worry about a thing, quick as a jiffy, we'll get you fixed up, no problem. Is there anything else you want to tell me?"

"No, I've told you everything."

Paula patted her belly.

"Does he want to plant one in you? Some men want to tie a girl down with brats. They don't care because they don't get all swollen up and covered with horrible stretch marks."

"The subject hasn't come up yet."

"Well, you're young, there's plenty of time for that; don't let him rush you. Can you imagine? Enslaved for eighteen years while the ungrateful offspring grow up? Fat and tied to the homestead? If you want kids eventually, that's fine, I understand, though you can import one from China and avoid the nasty side effects—the baby-growing-inside-you-like-an-alien-parasite thing. Adoption, that's an option to consider. Is there anything else I can help you with?"

"I can't think of anything. I have to get back to my desk."

"You're lucky to have a friend like me. I'll guide you through things proper-like."

She was still talking when Gerusha, juggling her snack tray, worked the door handle and escaped. By the time the door was completely closed, Paula, anxious to feed the company's craving for rumors, gossip and innuendo, punched numbers into her cell phone.

CHAPTER THREE

Raz

They planned to do the interview in the hotel coffee shop, but it was too noisy, so Raz and interviewer Barlowe Sexton slipped into a vacant meeting room. The tables were set up for a seminar. Raz's girl poured glasses of ice water from a carafe. Raz kissed her neck and gestured toward the door; the girl left them.

Sexton was a chunky man in his mid-thirties; with buckled, yellow teeth, he had a perfect face for the printed media. As a former road manager for Rasputin's Twisted Shadow, Sexton knew something of the music business. He set up his microphone and video camera and thumbed through questions scribbled on yellow paper.

"First of all, I would like to thank you for making time in your schedule to chat. What got you first interested in playing the guitar?"

"As a kid, I was exposed to all the pioneers. My dad had an extensive CD collection and I downloaded a lot from Russian rip sites. I worshipped Jimmy Page, Blackmore, Hendrix, Dunnery, Eddie Van Halen and was drawn to the technical masters like Vai, Satriani, Morse, Holdsworth, and Malmsteen. Also, I was inspired by the theatrical rockers like Alice Cooper, Frank Zappa, Insane Clown Posse, and Marilyn Manson. I mixed all that up and tried to come up with a new twist."

"Do you read music?"

"No. I should, but I don't."

"I'm surprised. Your arrangements and lead guitar lines are very complex."

"I started like everyone else, by using a computer to slow down the lead solos and picking them apart note-by-note. I developed a sort of color sense of the notes available on the fret board, and the guitar became a palette. Like a painter, I pick the colors to illustrate the mood I'm seeking."

"The song that put you on the map, so to speak, was *Stalin is Laughing*. The video is very disturbing and there were rumors former Russian President Vladimir Putin was not amused. How much of that video was CGI?"

"None of it. Everything is from film archives from the gulags and Kremlin torture rooms."

"Are you worried about retribution?"

"When the former head of the KGB is angry with you, you tend to avoid meetings in dark parking garages, if you catch my drift. Beyond that, I'm not scared. I have very good security."

"I don't want to misinterpret your work, but your second video seems to mock the prophet Mohammed. Several Islamic clerics sentenced you to death. Any comments?"

"I could not purchase better publicity for the video."

"And you're not concerned? You insulted over a billion Muslims."

"Well, this is just my opinion, but those people are backward and stupid, so I don't care what they think. Besides, they don't consume rock music, so they are not a significant demographic in my marketing strategy."

"Excuse me, I need to replace the battery in my camcorder," Sexton said as he leaned over and dug through the contents of his backpack.

Murphy

Murphy peeked into the coffee shop and saw the security guard sitting at the counter eating a plate of scrambled eggs while reading a folded newspaper. She grabbed his arm and spun him around on the stool.

"Where's Raz?"

"He's in a meeting room doing an interview."

"You're not supposed to leave him!"

"He dismissed me. I didn't get breakfast. What's the big deal?"

Murphy jogged out of the restaurant and into the lobby. Raz's girl hovered by the conference room door. Murphy pointed at the room and the girl nodded. Murphy pulled out her revolver and rushed through the doorway. Raz sat with a tight smile, looking up at Sexton who had drawn a large curved knife from his camera bag.

"God is great," Sexton said just before Murphy fired.

Sexton flew backward and sprawled across a table. Glassware arced through the air. Raz picked up the video camera and panned across Sexton's face, making sure to capture blood splattered on the table cloth. Murphy nudged the knife away from Sexton's hand. He was dead, but his fingers still moved.

"Goddam it, Raz, go up to your suite before the cops show up. You'll have to come down and make a statement, but I want you out of here for now."

"Good. That will give me a chance to download the video. We'll film the police interview too."

"This is not a photo opportunity."

"Everything is a photo op, Murphy." Raz patted Sexton on the cheek. "There is no God but God," he whispered.

The hotel security team pushed through the door with cans of mace at the ready.

With unnecessary roughness, Murphy pulled Raz up and shoved him toward the door.

"Go now," she said.

Gerusha and Walter

Gerusha and Walter had a regular table at Julia's. She ordered a Cobb salad and Walter ordered a tofu-turkey sandwich on rye bread with chipotle mayonnaise.

"I always enjoy our lunches together, Gerusha. I'm glad you suggested this. I will be traveling more and more in the coming months, so we'll have to grab our time when we can."

Unsure how to broach the subject, she blurted it out.

"Glen wants me to buy a house. Something nice, he said. And that you'd work out the financing."

Walter chuckled and sipped his water.

"We can get five million without much trouble. If you're thinking of something more extravagant, that will take creative accounting. Is that all that was on your mind? We could have dealt with this via email. We'll make up a notarized letter of credit and the real estate agents will eat you alive. With regard to dealing with realtors, I will not assist you; you're on your own. You'll have 25 business cards by the end of the week, I'll wager."

"What? Excuse me? Pretend I have five-million, run out and buy a house?"

"I didn't say anything about pretending, Mrs. Wilson. Are we still talking about real estate? I hope not. That would be dull."

Toxic Shock Syndrome

Noticing a quiver in her hand as it held a forkful of lettuce, she felt disconnected. Everyone in the restaurant went about their business. The earth did not quake. The sun did not fail. Stalling, she took a sip of water and a deep breath.

"To where will you be traveling?"

"The usual places. I have to meet money people in San Jose and Atlanta. Then I will supervise the completion of our lab facility in Brazil."

"How are Angela and the baby doing?"

Walter's face lit up. "Marvelously. The baby grows like unconstrained streptococci in a Petri dish."

She found the image disturbing, but that feeling was common when talking with Walter. He existed in an odd version of reality.

"Do you mind if I ask? What exactly do we do at Immortality?"

"Beyond raking in a lot of money from a select group of wealthy clients? Haven't you read the company manifesto? We're advancing the state of the art in longevity science and pushing back frontiers of medical technology."

"Yes, I know, but how exactly are we doing that? What do we actually do for people?"

"Ah, Gerusha, you place your figurative finger on the centrality of things. On our highly-classified company trade secrets... When you need to know, then all will be unveiled. Until then, I must say nothing more." He made a gesture indicating his lips were zipped. "How is your Cobb salad? Good?"

That afternoon, Gerusha tried to make sense of a stack of quotations. Was it better to accept a higher purchase price and lower monthly maintenance expenses or save money up-front and pay more per month? It was a complex problem. No one could help her; she had to figure it out on her own.

To get peace, her phone was disabled, but the receptionist could override the programming. Gerusha tried unplugging it from the wall, but a maintenance technician wandered in a few hours later and plugged it back in. He gave her a stern look and waggled his finger.

How did they know?

Phone systems were smart these days.

The phone gave a priority chirp, so Gerusha picked it up.

"Hey, sweet-meat."

"Glen? Is this important? I'm busy."

"Hey, I'm busy too, baby doll. I'm calling to invite you down for the weekend. We can make up for lost time. Enjoy a leisurely breakfast in bed, know what I mean?"

"Unfortunately, I do know what you mean. I'm working this weekend. Besides, you asked me to buy a house, remember?"

"You haven't done that yet?"

"Glen, it's been two days. Something like that takes time."

"Is Walter giving you a hard time about the money? I can call him…"

"Money is not the problem. Finding time is the problem. Is there anything else?"

"How about kinky phone sex to hold me until we meet?"

She didn't bother to reply before hanging up.

With fingers still on the handset, she thought about what she'd just done. Rudely hung up on a company vice president. Did the personal trump the professional? He could have her fired in a microsecond. She toyed with the idea of calling back and entertaining him with a sexual fantasy stolen from a cable TV show. His crude suggestions were demeaning, but maybe she should humor him… Was maintaining some dignity worth losing her job? Then she noticed e-mail accumulating up in her inbox and forgot this train of thought.

She concentrated on a spreadsheet pivot table while chewing on a wooden pencil. Flecks of wood stuck to her lip gloss. The phone rang and, unconsciously, she picked it up.

"Gerusha, Vendor Management. Speak," she said.

"Hi Gerusha, this is Paula. Remember when I told you about my friend, the real estate agent? We had dinner last night, a late one with drinks and a sleep-over if you must know. My boyfriend is in Santa Clara, so it was girl's night out and boy's night in, but you don't like crude talk, do you? Irregardless, I was talking to Bobby—that's his name, Bobby Bobb, with three B's in the first name and the same in the second, as he'll tell you. I talked to Bobby about your real estate problem and he's in the lobby ready to meet you and talk about things, so head down when you get a minute, no rush, he'll wait all day if necessary. Being a real estate man requires patience. No brains, just patience, so let him stew down there for a half hour if you want; he does this for a living. Okay?"

Gerusha was unsure what the question was, but said "Sure," and racked the phone.

She counted business cards she'd collected so far. Seven, and now a realtor waited in the lobby.

All her life she dreamed of owning a nice house. Now, the reality was upon her. Money was available, but the pressure of responsibility was a pain in her ass.

Buy us a house, will you? Something nice.

Right. Like it's the simplest thing in the world.

Buy a house, will you?

Just like a man to devalue finding the time to do things right.

Appalled, she realized what she was doing to the pencil; it looked as if it had been through a wood chipper. She dropped the pieces on the desk. She'd been biting her fingernails too; they were ragged and raw. Stress was killing her. She picked up a hand mirror and looked at herself. With bloodshot eyes surrounded by dark circles, she looked like a gulag prisoner.

She suddenly realized who she resembled. The software staff worked nonstop for weeks, sleeping on couches in their offices, drinking Jolt colas, cranking out code and eating junk food all day. With matted hair, thousand-yard stare and bits of yellow paint on her lips from demolishing pencils, she looked like the overworked nerds in the engineering department. She thought about going to the restroom and running a brush through her hair—washing her face and refreshing her makeup, but decided to hell with all that. If Bob Bubb didn't like her appearance, he could sit on a pool cue and twist for all she cared.

Too impatient to wait for the elevator, she walked down the stairs and popped through the door into the front lobby. Four lobby lizards lurked, all wearing neckties and jackets. Sales people of various flavors. She recognized two of them. One was her friend, Paul Butler, but she held out her palm in warning.

Stay away.

She addressed the other three.

"Which of you is Bubb?"

The man who raised his hand was young, perhaps 26. With sad realization, she remembered she was 26, too. She felt as if she'd aged 10 years in the last six months. Bubb was dressed formally in a crisp, long-sleeved shirt, cuff links, a splashy necktie, creased slacks and shiny black shoes. She remembered, with fondness, the days when she had time for precise grooming. Waving for Bubb to follow, she led him into a vendor meeting room. She shut the door and locked it. Bubb looked startled. He placed his valise on the table and extended his hand.

"Bobby Bobb, that's three B's for the first name and—"

A wave of strong emotion swept through her.

"Let's skip the small talk and get to the meat of the matter, okay, Bubb?"

What happened? She used to be a nice person. Patient and pleasant. Everyone liked her. Now she had enemies. She was abrupt and cold like the successful business people she hated when making them coffee at Starbucks. Now, she was one of them.

How had this happened in such a short time?

Too much work and too many people wasting her time, that's what happened. Would she be able to relax and enjoy life or was it a one-way street? Was it already too late?

She sighed.

"Here's the deal. I need a house. 'Something nice' is the only instruction my lousy husband gave me. I don't have time to screw around. The budget is five million, not a penny more, and I want a good deal. I want it close in and I want it quiet so I can sleep at night. You know what? Make the seller a quick and easy package deal. They can leave it furnished and I'll throw out anything I don't like. If you waste my time or try to screw me, my husband will cut out your liver with a rusty pen knife and feed it to your dog. Do you know who he is? Glen Wilson. Sales Director."

It occurred to her that she didn't know if Immortality, LLC actually sold anything.

"He's one of the founders; you probably noticed his bronze bust in the lobby. He'd gut you and enjoy it. Is any part of this transaction unclear?"

"I have a couple of properties in mind. Take a look at these photographs…"

"You're talking, Bubb, and I don't have time for talk. I will not look at any pictures. One shot. Pick one that knocks my pantyhose off. If I don't like the house, the price, or the deal, then you're fired and I'll use someone else. It's agreed? Fine."

She stood up.

"You'll need to sign a contract…"

"Let's consider for a moment. I don't really need to sign anything, do I?"

Bobby Bobb looked queasy.

"No, of course. Your word is good. Shall we shake on it?"

Gerusha waved his hand away.

"There's no time for formalities, Bubb, so get your butt in gear. Time marches on and waits for no one. Don't call me until you have the place. Then I'll go look at it. Bing, bang, boom. Easy."

Gerusha walked out in the lobby and swiped her badge in the lock. In seconds, she was gone.

In the lobby, Bob sat down and picked up where he'd left off in a conversation with one of the other salespeople. The salesman's name was Paul Butler and he worked for the Wavefront Sales Group.

"Wow, is she always such a stainless steel bitch?"

"She's not a bitch. She tells you what she wants and she's willing to pay for it. The checks don't bounce. Efficient, that's what she is. Six months ago, this was the only company in town buying anything. Things are better now, but this is still a great customer."

"She called me Bubb."

Paul laughed. "All you should care about is how accounts payable makes out the checks, Bubb."

"Is everybody a wiseass around here?"

"Pretty much," said Paul.

CHAPTER FOUR

Glen and Raz

Raz wanted to complete one last music video before the tour. The song was called My Backworld Girl and the music was gentle and sweet. Raz played acoustic guitar and sang plaintively about his Muslim sweetheart, but the video images were disturbing.

> I'll never forget the day we met
> At an Amsterdam teahouse, I could not ignore
> Your pretty brown eyes alive under veil
> I wished to explore the world under your chador

In the video, Raz sat on the edge of a pier. It was actually filmed on an abandoned dock in Galveston, but computer graphics crowded the image with digitized Dutch buildings. The girl, selected from a pile of photographs sent by a talent agency, was lovely, but dumb. She had no concept of the sociological landscape in Raz's video.

Her eyes were blue, but Raz's CGI tech turned them into a luminous golden brown. It was tedious work, hours for each few seconds of completed video, but the result was vivid and realistic.

> In a room by the canal, we invented a world
> Where east met west in our passion

Ken Coffman

I worshipped at the altar of your soul
In the timeless night we merged into one

They spent hours arranging mirrors in a small room so the cameras could not be seen. Fans blew streamers of pastel cloth and they filmed the scene over and over. The girl danced and removed layers of clothing until she was dressed only in a chaste bra and panties. She unclasped her long hair. It was achingly sexy. In the chorus, Raz sang his heart out and played quiet chords on the guitar.

All I ever wanted was to love my backworld girl
In the day, in the night, by candlelight spent
I offered my hand, and a wedding band
But I was a kaffir and her family would not consent

The camera lingered on the lover's hands before she ran out of the room. Outside, she swept through crowds on the street and crashed into her brothers; scary-eyed, dark-skinned men in casual western dress. They shouted at her. The camerawork was disjointed and unclear, but implied one of the brothers picked up a stone and hit her on the head. Her body fell into the canal. Raz sang the final chorus as her body drifted under his feet. The final image was Raz's face, crying. They did a CGI and changed him into Mohammed, bearded and turbaned with tears streaming down his face.

All I ever wanted was to love my backworld girl
In the day, in the night, a candlelit blur
I offered my hand and a wedding band
But she knew her family would kill her

Glen scouted and found Raz in a room noodling on an acoustic guitar.

"That's a powerful little film."

"Thanks. I'm pleased with how it's coming along."

"On the other hand, are you nuts? The Mullahs will come completely unglued."

"Let them," he said.

"You can't possibly expect to get airplay; the networks won't touch it."

"The networks are obsolete. We'll put clips on YouTube and sell downloads on our website. There will be a media shitstorm. I'll make a lot of money."

"Yes, but will you live to enjoy it?"

"Keeping me alive is Murphy's job. She's good. I'm not worried."

A girl came in and handed Raz a hot cup of tea. She leaned over and kissed him on the cheek, and then walked away. In the doorway, she looked back at Glen, but her expression was blank. He couldn't tell what she was thinking or even if she *was* thinking. It occurred to him that he hadn't seen the previous girl for a while. He pondered these girls. They were pretty, but not stunning like the model agency model. Normal, healthy young girls without a lot of makeup... No high heels. No elaborate hair styles. Blue jeans and sneakers. Quiet girls.

"What happened to the other young lady?"

"She's staying at my compound until the baby is born."

"Do you mind if I sample your groupies?"

Raz laughed and put down his tea. "Sure, Glen, take your best shot. I don't mind sharing if they'll have you. Good luck."

Raz played a skittering, acrobatic riff on the guitar.

"Wait a minute—aren't you a married man?"

"Oh, yeah," Glen said. He brandished his ring. "I keep forgetting."

Raz and Murphy

In the middle of the Sheraton penthouse front room, Raz smoked an elaborate hookah. A central bowl, bubbling with water, fed into coiled hoses. Murphy looked at the smoking bowl with suspicion. Raz removed an ivory stem from his mouth and chuckled.

"It's Turkish tobacco, Murphy. It relaxes me and helps focus my thoughts. Try a snort?"

Murphy shook her head. Raz pointed at a vacant pillow and Murphy eased herself onto it. It took a moment for her to settle in and get comfortable.

"You saved my life."

"You were lucky this time. The way you're antagonizing the Islamic people, you're going to have to be more careful. There is another Fatwa against you, this time from Iran. Is it necessary to be so provocative?"

"Do you think all cultures are equal and deserving of respect? I don't. The Islamic world is backward and obsolete. Do they have great technology? Science? No. They need a reformation, a separation of religion and government. I will not run and hide. I will point at their medieval ways and laugh."

"Is that why you're doing all this? You're waging a one-man war against Islam?"

Raz laughed. "No, it's just something I'm screwing around with. For each Fatwa, I get a lot of free publicity and make a few dollars, that's all. I didn't ask you to join me to talk about that. I want to tell you about my newest fan club."

Toxic Shock Syndrome

He gestured with his hookah mouthpiece and Murphy was startled. She hadn't noticed the quiet Raz girl in a darkened corner working on a needlework project. Setting aside her needles and fabric, the girl handed Murphy a card. It was like a thick credit card with photograph, complex multidimensional bar code, and a smart card connection. The symbol on the front was the Toxic Shock Syndrome logo. The card bore a stylized AEF graphic. Advanced Evolutionary Force.

"What's the nature of this fan club?"

"Ah, good question."

"But not one you'll answer?"

"'Fraid not," he replied. "Any girl who carries this card has full access. Backstage, on the tour bus, even my private restroom, no problem."

"I don't like it; it's a security risk. How many cards will be issued?"

"I don't know—tens, hundreds, thousands? We'll have to see."

"Will I be issued one?"

Raz chuckled. He held out his hand until she returned the card. "You already have full access, so you don't need one. But, to answer your question, you would not be qualified for this fan club."

"Why not?"

"Another question I will not answer, Murphy, my friend."

"I can't assure your safety with thousands of these cards floating around."

"You can't assure my safety anyway, just reduce my risk. Don't get me wrong—I greatly appreciate that reduced risk. But, please don't worry; any girl that carries the card has been carefully screened. What's the word for a background check?"

"Vetted?"

"Vetted. Yes, I like that word. The girls are carefully vetted."

"I still don't like it."

"Duly noted, Murphy."

Raz puffed on his hookah, staring passively at Murphy until she gave up. Before leaving the room, Murphy stopped to look at the girl who had returned to her needlepoint. In the dim light, the girl's pupils were wide ovals, like an owl's.

Glen

Glen wandered around the arena during rehearsals. The stage show was elaborate. A song called *Bermuda Triangle* featured three Raz's playing harmony lines. The guitarists were the same size, wore the same clothes and hairstyle and played the same style of guitars. From the audience, even close up from the front row, they looked identical. Raz had worked with them over and over until the fast melody lines were executed perfectly.

For another song, *Flames of Jihad*, the stage was filled with dancers dressed as red flames. They pranced in elaborate sequences. Glen counted, but couldn't determine an accurate number. At least thirty. Other songs included leaping devils, Raz suspended over the audience in a wire harness, 3D video projections, fighting alien armies, a robotic python, Raz fried in a giant electric chair with sparks flying, and other spectacles.

The first big show of the US tour—at the Houston Astrodome—sold out in two days. There were still tickets available for the second show, but not many. Glen shot glances at his wristwatch. He had a date with over $300,000 at precisely 5:00. If Raz did not get confirmation the cash was in hand by 5:30, the concert would be cancelled and all hell would break loose.

Toxic Shock Syndrome

Outside, ten thousand ticket holders milled, chanted and stomped their feet. The crowd was in a good mood. Buskers, playing guitars and beating drums, did lucrative business. While wandering, Glen noticed a Raz girl in a quiet corner of the arena's nosebleed section working on needlepoint. Puffing from exertion, Glen climbed the stairway and joined her. He sat and looked out over the bustling activity in the massive facility.

"I don't believe I ever caught your name," Glen said, holding his hand out for a shake.

The girl raised her needlepoint.

Can't shake right now.

"Charity," she said.

"Where're you from, Charity?" Glen asked.

"Buffalo."

The girl seemed shy. There was a calm stillness to her. Quiet. Smart. Glen felt protective of her. She was dressed in blue jeans, tennis shoes and a TSS t-shirt.

"Have you known Raz very long?"

She looked at him coolly. "You saw me get in the van for the first time."

"Yes, I remember," Glen said. "I just wondered if you knew him from before."

"No," she said, "not in person."

"You know him from his music?"

She did not respond. Machine-like, her needles dove in and out of the fabric.

"If you don't mind me saying, you're not the typical type of road girl…"

"I don't mind anything you might say, Mr. Wilson."

"There was a girl before you, a girl in a—how should I put this?"

"Pregnant is as good a word as any, Mr. Wilson."

"I was going to say 'in a delicate condition' or 'with child'. I guess she's gone away."

"I know."

"I thought you might be jealous."

"No, I'm not. Her name is Jenny. We don't compete."

"There's plenty of Raz to go around, is that what you mean?"

"No."

Years prior, Glen spent a memorable evening with a Van Hagar tribute band after a concert on the Sunset Strip. The guys were mediocre musicians, but had a laser show and perfect rockstar poses. Jack Daniels flowed like water and a lot of coke went up greedy nostrils. The girls weren't A-league talent, but they weren't half-bad either. There were many platinum-haired starlets vying for the attention of the faux Sammy Hagar. Underneath garish mascara and lip gloss, they were sweet farm-country girls; willing, acrobatic and enthusiastic. All degrees of debauchery went on in corners, hotel hallways, and the pool. Glen was only a tag-along guest of the coke dealer, but that was enough to get him near-band treatment from two fleshy girls: Jane from Sioux Falls and Patty Anne from Austin. They were athletic girls in short skirts who worked hard to please him.

From direct experience, he knew how rockers acted backstage and in their hotel rooms.

Raz's thing was different. Glen could not understand it. Drugs and alcohol were *not* abused. Stix drank a solitary can of ice-cold Fosters after a long rehearsal. Raz drank nasty hot drinks from Starbucks and smoked imported tobacco in his hookah. Jazz was into a Scientology thing and did not consume alcohol or caffeine in any form. As Murphy said, the scene was odd. Despite the violent and disturbing onstage mayhem, the behind-the-scenes action was calm and disciplined.

Glen stared at Charity. She did not glance his way; her attention was on the needlework. He noticed a necklace tucked into her shirt. It supported a pendant, but he couldn't make out the design.

"That's a pretty necklace," he said. "Is it a gift from Raz?"

She flicked her eyes at him. "Don't you have work to do?"

He checked his watch.

Shit, she was right. It was time to collect the money.

"Yes, of course, it's time to fly. It was a pleasure chatting with you, Charity."

Almost imperceptibly, she nodded her head in reply. He was dismissed. Not rudely or coldly; this girl was calm and at peace. He didn't sense trouble, but something burbled under the surface. Something that felt new in his experience. He'd been to Vietnam, run drugs from Bolivia, and won a congressional race in Alaska. He'd been around the world and experienced many wonders. At his age, he felt like he'd seen nearly everything.

What is this?

The concert promoter was built like a fireplug. At 175 pounds, he was short, maybe five-foot-three; a Jewish man with dark-olive skin chomping a thick cigar stub. With a Queens accent and sweat-stained shirt, the guy was a living stereotype of a Jewish money changer.

"Okay, Lambchop, you're the money guy?"

Lambchop? Glen looked around.

Yes, he was talking to me.

"Come on, Cupcake, let's get this business done."

"Okay," Glen replied.

"It's all there, Teacup, three-hundred and seventeen grand, cash. You guys are killing me. Do you know how hard it is to get cash? Seven-eighths of my receipts are credit card transactions and you guys want cash. I could do a bank transfer, but no, the artist wants cash. Well, sign the flippin' form, slap your thumbprint on the receipt and let's get this show going, okay, Sugar-pie?"

What was with this guy and his thick-accented endearments?

Glen's plan was simple. Carrying a black sports bag, he'd grab a cab and go to a Walmex branch office where the money would be deposited in Raz's account. As long as Glen didn't look like a courier carrying a huge amount of cash, he'd be fine. That was the theory. Murphy was unsatisfied.

"I don't need a damn baby—"

"Jesus is going to watch over you," Murphy said without irony. "If everything goes smoothly, you won't even notice him. If there's trouble, you'll be damn glad he's nearby. I'm the boss on this gig and I'm not debating with you."

"You know what, Murphy? You've devised an excellent strategy and this is an excellent opportunity for Jesus to learn a few things about doing things properly with style and panache. I—"

"Shut your yap and get going," Murphy said.

Glen shoved bundles of bills in the bag and heaved it over his shoulder. He had 22 minutes. After taking the employee elevator, he walked through the loading dock. On Central Street he hailed a cab. With professional aplomb, Jesus stayed on Glen's tail.

At the bank, the manager was ready and escorted Glen to a private room. Automated bill countering machines were attended by two young clerks. One of the girls wore a pink silk blouse with round, overworked pearl buttons. Glen smiled. She shook her head as if knowing his thoughts. The bags were unzipped and the bills were run through the machines. Click, whirl, thunk; the bills were banded and logged. In minutes he held a deposit slip for three-hundred and seventeen thousand dollars. With the manager's phone, he called Murphy.

"It's done," he said. "Green lights across the board."

"Okay," Murphy replied before breaking the connection.

He put his hand on the padded shoulder of the attractive girl's blouse and drew her close to read her nametag. *Cheryl.*

"Hi Cheryl, my name's Glen. Would you like to come backstage and meet a rock star? Toxic Shock Syndrome?"

There was a flicker of interest in her eyes.

"You know Raz?"

"Know him? Of course I know him; we hang out together and stuff. We could have a few drinks and I could introduce you after the show."

"I don't drink, Glen, and neither should you. I'm a Baptist."

"What an amazing coincidence. I'm seriously considering converting from the Church of the Nazarene to become a Southern Baptist. We can get together and go over Bible verses."

I'm not sure how I ruined the mood, but her eyes went dead.

"It was nice to meet you, Glen," she said.

She walked away. Glen pointed at her mousier coworker wearing a brown smock with white leggings and a large Calvary cross around her neck. She wasn't exactly flat-chested, but didn't have the *curva pellagrosa* of her coworker.

"You?" he asked hopefully.

She shook her head just a few degrees left and right, but Glen got the message.

The baker's kids get fat with left-over donuts and a cop's kid gets off on a traffic stop with a warning. Were there no fringe benefits in this job?

59

"See you ladies tomorrow," he called after them.

Jesus smirked.

"I heard you're a smooth one," he said.

"Kiss my pimply white ass," Glen replied smoothly.

Erik

"That's a pretty blouse," Erik said. "Did you make it yourself?"

The blouse was not particularly pretty. A sickly tangerine color, it was covered with a repeated pattern of green geckos. The girl was not particularly pretty either. Plain and overweight, her figure strained at the blouse's large buttons. The roll around her waist was as prominent as her chest; she seemed to be built in layers like a pile of truck tires. She hid a shy smile behind a chubby hand.

Erik discovered the craft store to be a perfect place to meet lonely women; this time he loitered in the dried flower section. The girl, shopping alone, did not wear a wedding band, and she seemed to be in absolutely no hurry. In Erik's experience, these were the easiest girls in the world. Pay a little attention to them and they'd give up everything they had, though it was often not much. When they had nothing left to give, he'd move on to the next one.

"No, it's from the Target store. They were on sale and I couldn't resist. We had geckos all over the house when I lived in Albuquerque."

Erik proffered his hand for a shake.

"My name is Erik, with a 'k'," he said.

"Sherene Bailey, but folks call me Sherie, 'cause it's easier," she said.

"Sherie, I don't mean to freak you out, but I'm all alone. Would you be willing to join me for lunch? We can walk across the parking lot to Denny's for a milkshake."

The milkshake seemed like a safe bet... With her figure, she surely enjoyed them.

"I don't walk much on account of my disability and all, but I can make it over there. Because of my leg, you see, I'm on 70 percent disability from the state, but I get around without a cane. It's not like I'm crippled. I do okay."

"Great, I'll meet you outside."

There was no way he wanted to get stuck spending what little precious money he had on buying stupid dried flowers.

She came out and looked around as if she didn't expect to find him. He hid behind a bank of payphones in case a former girlfriend happened by. Seeing her, he popped out and waved enthusiastically.

He took her package. "Let's drop this off at your car," he suggested.

She led him across the parking lot. They headed directly toward a massive powder-blue Chevy Caprice. He hoped this was not the one, but it was.

"I love these old cars. They're classics," he lied.

"Will I need my purse?" she asked while arranging her purchases in the back seat.

He did not blame her for asking; it looked like a twenty-pounder.

"Better bring it, just in case," he said.

At Denny's they ordered burger baskets and chocolate milkshakes. Generally, due to all the Buddha he smoked, he didn't have much appetite, but he couldn't remember his last meal. He ate every scrap with relish. Like most large women, while in public, she delicately picked at her food and pretended to be a light eater.

The conversation covered the most important topics. Her favorite daytime shows were Dr. Phil, Oprah, and The Young and the Restless. She made dried flower arrangements and delivered them to old-folks' homes. She lived alone with a cat, but it spent most of its time outside. Her disability check, received via direct deposit to her checking account on the fifteenth of the month, was $461. She'd never heard of Toxic Shock Syndrome which suited Erik fine.

After they finished their lunch and her half-eaten burger was carried away, the bill was placed on the table. Erik picked it up and studied it. $19.34. He had a grand total of eight dollars and change in his pocket.

"Sherie, I hate to ask, but I'm a little light in the wallet right now. Could you help out with this bill?"

Eagerly, she dug through her purse.

"Don't think anything of it; I'm happy to pay my share. I'm not one of those women who expect a man to pay for everything."

"You get this one and I'll get the next one."

She only hesitated for an instant.

"Sure, Erik. Let this be my treat. It's no problem. I enjoyed talking with you."

"I've asked too much already, but could you give me a lift home? I've been riding the bus since my car broke down."

"I can run you home. I haven't had this much fun since I don't know when, so I'm not ready for our day to be over yet."

Erik almost vomited up the rich food at the 'our day' comment, but choked back his bile.

"I'm having a great day too," he said. "Rather than give you directions, let me drive. It will make things easier."

"Okay," she said.

She pulled a massive collection of keys from her bag. Her key ring had a large silver porpoise hanging on it.

"Oh, I like porpoises too," he said. In the car, they settled into their seats. "I can't get over how we stumbled across each other. It's like God guided me to the rubber stamp area to find you."

"Wasn't it the dried flower section?"

"That's what I meant. Do you mind if I give you a little kiss on the cheek to thank you for lunch?"

While staring straight ahead and gripping her handbag tightly on her lap, she flushed a deep, bright crimson.

After a moment, she spoke. "I guess that would be okay."

He leaned over and brushed her cheek lightly with his lips and then started the car and drove across the shopping complex parking lot to a secluded spot. Across a chain link fence and berm, highway traffic raced by. Rain drifted from the sky in a fine mist.

"What are we doing?"

"This may seem a little odd, but I'm on doctor's orders. You know how doctors are. I smoke a medicinal herb for mood swings. It also helps me control my weight. My doctor is a naturopath and the herb is 100-percent organic. Do you mind if we sit here for a minute so I can take my medicine?"

She plucked her lower lip in consternation and decided.

"Not at all, go ahead."

Erik pulled a baggy of Buddha, onyx pipe and plastic lighter from his jacket pocket. Soon, he was engulfed in a cloud of aromatic smoke.

"Can I roll down the window a little bit?"

"The doctor says it's better if you don't."

"Okay. It's good for your weight? You're so skinny, I envy you. Do you think it could, possibly, help me too?"

Score, Erik thought.

There would be no turning back for her now.

"Sure, take the smoke deep into your lungs and hold it as long as you can. You'll cough at first, but don't worry, you'll be used to it in no time."

After a few minutes, she seemed to melt through her car seat and into the earth.

"Wow, love. Love is everywhere," she said.

"I know," Erik replied.

"Why doesn't my doctor know about this medicine? What's it called?"

"Weight Control Seven. Some people call it W-C-7. Maybe you heard about it on talk radio commercials?"

"I don't listen to much talk radio. I mostly watch TV."

"That's why you don't know about it."

"Okay," she said. "I like it."

You'll spend the rest of your life trying to feel as good as you do right now, but it doesn't work that way, Erik thought with a guilty twinge. He stifled the thought.

He started the car. He'd stashed his overnight bag behind the craft store garbage bin. They rolled up the back alley to retrieve it.

"How do we get to your place?" Erik asked.

"I thought I was going to drop you off at your place?"

"You can take me home later."

"Okay." She drifted in bliss for a minute while Erik waited patiently. "Head out on Highway 2 toward Stevens Pass. I'll tell you where to turn off when we get close. Would it be okay if I took a little nap now? I'm awfully sleepy."

"You go right ahead," Erik said.

The terrain got more rugged and remote as they traveled east.

"Watch for a turnout and a maibox. I painted it blue with flowers."

Toxic Shock Syndrome

The turnout was obscured by tangled blackberry vines. He turned the car down a long gravel driveway which curved under leaning alders. At the end of the driveway, her home came into view. It was a corroded and mildewed Airstream trailer standing on blocks. With thick trees blocking highway noise, the place was the very definition of isolation.

"My auntie left it to me when she passed on. It's not much, but it's all paid off. Twenty-two acres, mostly bog and blackberries, but I don't care, on account that I don't like mowing much. I made a sign. Can you see it? It's my Pixieland. No one ever comes here. I hope you like it."

Embarrassed and misty-eyed, she shifted away from him in her seat to look through her window. He massaged the roll of fat on her shoulder.

"Don't worry, Sherie, I like it just fine," he said.

CHAPTER FIVE

Bubb

Bobby knew of a house for sale but wanted to buy it cheap and flip it back on the market himself. It was brick, nearly a mansion, with a remarkable view of the Puget Sound from the top two floors. Filled with antiques, the grand entry held a massive crystal chandelier that would go for big money on eBay. He wanted it so bad he could taste it, but there was competition. The house appraised at 5.7 million, but after the contents were sold off, the house could be sold (after paint and repair work in the bathrooms) for at least 7.5, maybe 8. Denise from Windermere and Charlene from Century 21 were onto the deal and trying to work their angles.

Two weeks earlier, the ancient matron of the house died, leaving behind a stale, nasty smell of old flesh and medicine. Her top-floor bedroom was still equipped with an oxygen system, hospital bed, and racks upon racks of monitoring equipment. The house was inherited by two daughters; one was married to a Boeing Vice President. They'd moved to Chicago and didn't care about the house and wanted a quick, trouble-free sale. The other daughter, Rose, was the problem. She wanted to keep the house, but her meager trust-fund income didn't even cover the property taxes. Living on the first floor of the house in a converted sun room, she had never married and led a sheltered life.

Toxic Shock Syndrome

Rosa was an artist who painted acrylics on huge canvasses; dark and disturbing collages that included alien creatures eating human flesh, rows of severed heads dripping blood down a wall, and the like. Finished paintings were stacked against every wall. When Bobby tried to talk to her, her eyes constantly flicked to the corners of the room as if hungry creatures lurked. It was hard to get her to concentrate on the task at hand. She wore paint-drenched overalls. With lurid streaks of dried paint on her forearms, she looked diseased and mad.

"Rose?" Bobby said. "We need to talk about this. A property tax payment is due in April and you will lose this house if you don't pay. Do you hear me, Rose? It's twenty-seven thousand dollars."

It took years for the state to foreclose, but Bobby didn't mention it.

"Why are you hounding me? Papers, papers, papers, always with your papers. If I sign the papers, will you go away? Okay, I will sign."

She picked up a paper left behind by the Century 21 real estate agent and signed the top sheet with the fine-tipped paintbrush bearing Winsor & Newton Indian Red.

"No Rose, stop, please."

He snatched the contract from her, folded it up and slipped it into his overcoat pocket. No one needed to see that signature.

Bobby's credit score was 521 from maxed-out credit cards and too many late mortgage payments. He needed a few more days to get his own deal worked out, but this house would not stay on the market for two more days.

Thinking furiously, he took her hands and tried to ignore the slimy feel of damp paint and perspiration.

"Rose, suppose I could make things like they were before your mom passed away? Suppose you could live here after the house was sold?"

"Oh, Bob, is that possible? I would love you forever."

Rose was a large woman, running about 235 pounds. Her hair was a tangle and she didn't have much acquaintance with the toothbrush. Forever-love from a fat, deranged lady was not his heart's desire. He could be an almost-instant millionaire if he could flip the house on his own, but his split of the 6% commission on a five-million-dollar sale was better than nothing.

"I'll be back in one hour, so don't talk to anyone else. Don't answer the phone and don't answer the door. Rose, do you hear me?"

With her expansive back to him, she painted intricately-detailed ravens pecking a dog's living eyes. Bobby couldn't look. After leaving, he locked the main entry door securely with keys lifted from a foyer table.

Unable to sit still, Bobby paced the Immortality, LLC lobby from the potted plant on one side to the potted plant on the other while nervously working at a bloody hangnail with his teeth. He glanced at the Glen Wilson bust, but did not like the way the bronze eyes seemed to follow and stare through him. The ever-present Paul Butler looked on with amusement. Paul wanted to remind Bobby that desperation sells not, but held his tongue. After twenty minutes, Gerusha appeared.

"Gerusha," Bobby nearly shouted when she appeared.

She waved him into the adjoining vendor meeting room.

"This better be good," she said, "I'm in the middle of something."

"I found the place for you. If you act quickly, you can get it for five million."

"It's a good deal?"

"Yes, it's a monster deal."

"It's nice?"

"Very nice."

"I don't have time to look at it today. Can it wait until tomorrow?"

"No!" Bobby had a vision of his large commission check flying away on raven wings. "Sorry, no, we have to do this quickly."

"All right, Bubb, if I sign now, is that quick enough?"

"Without seeing it?"

"I just said I can't go today and you said it has to be done quickly. How slow are you? My husband will deal with you if this deal stinks, so that's not my problem. Show me where to sign."

Bobby whipped out a blank contract and marked signature locations with X's. She scribbled quickly and stood up.

"Let me know the closing date. My husband will be in town in a couple of weeks. Try to get it done by then. It would serve him right if this place is a turd."

"There is one detail I should mention."

"Does it detract from the investment value?"

Bobby shook his head no.

"Then I don't have time for it," she said.

After paying the brokerage, his share of the commission would be just over $200,000. On the way back to the house in Magnolia, he dreamed up $500,000 worth of things he could spend the $200,000 on. Pulling up to the house, he noticed a car in the driveway. A burgundy BMW M5. It was Denise from Windermere.

Damn it, Bobby thought.

"I have an offer letter in hand, so don't even think about it," she said, while pounding on the door with the flesh of her fist.

"Okay," Bobby replied. He got back in his Lexus and drove around the corner. After a brisk walk down the sidewalk, he peered around a hedge. While Denise pounded on the door, he slipped down the driveway and hustled around back. With shaking hands, he fumbled with the purloined keys. He'd be screwed if the back door key was not on the ring.

Bingo!

The neglected back door screeched loudly on rusty hinges.

He shut and relocked the door, then tip-toed through the dimly lighted house. Denise peered in the window, but he was sure she couldn't see him. He found Rose in her painting room and took the brush out of her hand. He handed her his Pierre Cardin pen and showed her all the places to sign. When he got his pen back, it was covered with paint. He looked at it with distaste before putting it away. He let himself out the back door. On the front porch, Charlene from Century 21, waving her paperwork, had turned up. While Denise and Charlene argued, he nearly reached the sidewalk before Denise noticed him.

"Hey!" she shouted.

Bobby sprinted to his car. After unlocking the doors with his key fob, he jumped in and got the car rolling. In his rearview mirror, Denise and Charlene, red-faced, gestured and yelled at him. Not out of the woods yet, he needed to get the papers faxed to Chicago, signed, and then faxed back. Then he could relax and stop worrying about the other vultures.

Though he still owed over forty thousand dollars on his current Lexus, he could kick in a few thousand and trade it in for a new LS430 with navigation system, Bose stereo, and moon roof.

Life would be sweet.

Dave and Erik

After being fired by Raz, Dave could no longer afford expensive equipment, but he liked to look at drum kits, shiny and full of promise under bright music store lighting. Trailing his fingers across a frog-green-sparkle Boom Theory Micro Bop drum set, he choked back waves of despair. He could sell more of his stuff—equipment and memorabilia collected over the last couple of years—but money, being a finite resource, would run out soon.

He had a high burn rate. Condo rental. Car repairs. Cocaine, condoms and beer. It added up. When the money in his checking account was gone, then what? Take a job selling insurance or writing up mortgage applications? He owed thirty-three thousand dollars on maxed-out credit cards and worse yet, there was a paternity suit filed by a woman in Buffalo with a brain-damaged kid, grotesquely high hospital bills and a persistent Jewish lawyer. Unfortunately, the DNA test was positive: the drooling mutant was his.

He almost remembered the girl; she'd led him into a sidestage restroom, jumped on the counter top and spread her legs. This was the kind of subtle seduction he could not resist. If he recalled correctly, she had a crude, self-inflicted tattoo of Jesus on her belly. Disturbing. In her last email, she'd mentioned saving up tip money from her job at Denny's to buy a Greyhound bus ticket to Seattle so she could marry him. How would he explain this to his current live-in girlfriend? It was a living nightmare.

Maybe Raz would call him back, but until then, he had high hopes for his new band, The Rain City Screamers. The bass player had done a mini tour with Heart. The singer, a former part-time roadie for the notorious Seattle band Critters Buggin', owned the PA system.

The guitar player had played with Poison Pill Theory, a historic Seattle hair-metal band that once opened for Foghat at the Tractor Tavern. Despite questionable resumes, they were talented players.

Their hastily-assembled set of Toxic Shock Syndrome songs went over well at clubs in downtown Seattle. Sometimes Dave cleared $75 at the end of the night, usually less. The club provided dinner, chicken wings and watery Budweiser. Life was filled with tough options. He could scale back spending or bring in more money. He craved the adulation of fans and playing big shows. Had he known the TSS experience would be so short, he might have stayed sober-enough to remember more of it.

Dave was well known in the historic American Music store in Seattle's Fremont district. He offered lessons to beginners impressed by his role in Toxic Shock Syndrome and ignorant of his limited playing ability. Clearing thirty-five bucks an hour (after Randy Fader chased him down and extracted ten dollars for the practice room rental), he'd sign Toxic Shock CDs and tell stories of drugs and roadies after suffering arrhythmic teen-aged wannabes ratattating on snare drums. Worse were twelve-year-old robokids with intense attitudes asking detailed questions about contracts. Skinny grade-school kids already better than him.

Did they pop out of the womb with drumsticks clutched in their slimy fists?

Dave patiently waited for Matthew, one of his students. At fourteen, Matthew was old to be taking up the drums, but seemed to have good sense of internal time. He could maintain a rock-steady rhythm while pounding out primal 4/4 patterns.

His girlfriend, Terri, disturbed Dave. Her ghostly face peeked from under a snowstorm flurry of bleached hair and thick makeup. She was a teaser, touching, always touching and working her fingers up the inseams of Dave's jeans, inch-by-inch, session-by-session.

Toxic Shock Syndrome

Always leaning over so Dave could see plump, creamy breasts hanging loose under her satin blouse. His hands itched to touch them. The way the law worked, fourteen-year-old Matthew could freely screw Terri all day, but Dave would go to jail forever for doing the same. He wanted to peel off her tight jeans and explore the nooks and crannies of her fresh, taut, teen-aged flesh, but he dared not.

"Dave, cocksucker, great to see you, man."

This was a day Dave dreaded. Slowly, he turned. Erik, the former TSS bass player, looked bad.

How long had it been?

Thin and bony with gray streaks in his sparse, greasy hair, Erik had aged beyond his time. He was ghostly, wan and emaciated with yellow teeth and sunken eyes.

A decade before, as pre-teens in Erik's garage, they'd smoked weed in a bong and listened to Nirvana, fantasizing elaborate pipedreams. *It is now my duty to completely drain you[1]*. They spent many hours figuring out rhythms, riffs and chords on Erik's dad's equipment and watching David Smith transform into Rusty Razor Blade while practicing fluid exotic scales on the electric guitar. He remembered writing their first song together, a rip off of Tad's Nipple Belt[2]. Fond memories.

Dave put out his fist for a boxer's fist bump, but Erik pushed it aside and threw his arms around him.

"You started a band and you didn't call me, motherfucker. What's with that batshit, man?"

"I'm jamming with friends—it's no big deal."

---

[1] From Drain You, Kurt Cobain, from Nevermind.

[2] *I need some anti-freeze to keep my girls young.* Tad, Nipple Belt, inspired by deranged killer Ed Gein.

"You're making money. Don't blow me off, I know what's what. I'm tired of eating shit and having to smile about it. One day... Well, never mind that, you're looking good, still getting a royalty check? Raz throws you a bone now and then? Woof-woof, give me a kibble. We get pennies while Raz gets fucking filthy rich off us. All that old stuff still sells. I should have insisted on more writing credits, like the bass riff on Bloody Discharge he stole from me. Asshole."

Dave clearly remembered Raz coaching Erik for an hour to get the timing on the riff locked in. E-bumpa-bumpa-G-bumpa-A. When they recorded it, it was easier for Raz to do the overdub because Erik shot up a hot load of heroin and nodded off in a corner with his head on Moshi's lap. Raz carried Erik longer than he needed to, even after the ugly scene in Alaska with Moshi.

Mush, Dave thought with overwhelming guilt. *I should have stood up and said something. I should have done something.*

"How've ya been?" Dave asked, cringing as he asked the question. He didn't want to know. The answer was written in the loose, fleshy folds of Erik's face.

"Erik," Matthew said. "I can't believe it, we have the backbone of Toxic Shock Syndrome. You guys are radical, awesome, bangin-phat. I brought my practice snare. Let's plug in a bass and you guys can jam it out. Play Road Kill Rhapsody, that's my favorite."

Oh no, Dave thought.

Road Kill was in ¾ time and the long bridge section had syncopated cross fill patterns. Erik never learned the bass line properly. In concert it was played by one of the keyboard players as a left hand pattern on a little M-Audio Oxygen MIDI controller. Erik played a boring root note, bomp-bomp-bomp, while, around him, keyboard bass notes swirled.

"Yeah, let's do it," Erik said eagerly.

Erik reached up to take a shiny Ken Smith bass from a wall rack but the store clerk intercepted and handed him an inexpensive Squire Jazz bass.

"This one is tuned up, plugged in and ready to go," the clerk said.

"Thanks man," Erik said. He played a repetitive two-quarter-note pattern. "Recognize it, kid? Unsanitary Field Surgery. I wrote it and Raz stole the writing credit."

Only Erik would claim to have 'written' four beats of G followed by four beats of A used in hundreds of rock songs.

Matthew held out his Pro-Mark sticks as Erik thump-thumped his primitive G to A pattern. Dave waved them away.

"You play it," he said.

"For real?" Wielding drumsticks with enthusiasm, Matthew slammed through a meaty, deafening two-fisted double-time beat. It grew boring after the first few seconds, but they kept it up. A-A-A-A, G-G-G-G for a minute, then two.

"I'm jamming with Toxic Shock Syndrome," Matthew said with glittery excitement in his eyes.

Cooly, Terri toyed with the top button of her blouse. With Dave's eyes on her, she swiveled her hips and thrust her pelvis in time with the crude rhythm. They were small movements, magnified by lust.

Oh Lord, Dave thought.

"I gotta go," he mumbled.

Erik unslung the bass and dropped it on a stand.

"Where are you going? Too good to jam with your old friend? Listen up. We can make real money, man. I have it all worked out. The Shocker System? Get it? TSS. Fuck Raz. We get a new guitar player and play the old stuff, write new tunes, get a big recording contract and get back on top. Leave Raz in the fucking dust. He never liked my songs anyway. We were the soul of that band and I can sing lead. Slap on makeup, make everything brighter, louder, bigger than big. We'll go right to the top. Get amped on all the candycaine you can snort. We'll swim in booze, babes and weasel dust and teach Raz a lesson for dumping us."

In that instant, Dave saw that Raz was right. He should have practiced more. He should have worked on his craft and grown as a player. Still young; he could learn. If he got good enough, Raz would give him another chance. He knew it. There was no time to waste.

"I'm talking to you, man. Don't look through me like you're superior. We go back; we popped our nuts in the same little bitches, smoked tasty puff from the same bowl, and borrowed *my* old man's pickup to bring home your first garage sale drumset. We share history. We're the same."

"No, Erik, I'm sorry, I can't do this."

"Yeah? Well, fuck you man. I don't need you anyways, I can always get another drummer, a better drummer. Someone who doesn't fucking suck!"

Yes, I suck. So I'll work my ass off until I get better, Dave thought.

Erik was so angry, he vibrated. He followed Dave out of the store.

Outside, the wind kicked up a notch and a misty rain fell. Erik watched Dave march north on Fremont Street.

"Erik? Homie? Can I get an autograph?"

Erik turned. Matthew held out a copy of the first Toxic Shock Syndrome EP.

"I charge five hundred dollars for personalization."

"I don't got anything like five hundred."

"What *do* you have?"

While Matthew looked through his pockets for money, Erik looked Terri over. His eyes moved from her powder-blue-suede Sketcher boots to fluffy blond hair.

"Want to get low with a rock star?"

"I believe I'll pass, thank you," Terri said.

"Eighteen dollars and change," Matthew said while holding out a palm filled with crumpled bills.

"Okay. Do you want me to sign for Raz too? I'm pretty good at his signature. The stuff I sell on eBay goes for more money with all three signatures."

"Sure," Matthew said eagerly.

With a sour look, Terri tugged on Matthew's arm. "Tell him 'no thank you'," she said.

"Suit yourself." Erik scribbled on the CD J-card with Matthew's Sharpie.

"Gotta bounce, I'm ghost."

Matthew opened the J-card.

The inscription said: "Fuck you, cheap ass kusutare[3]."

Erik walked down Fremont Avenue toward Lake Union. Thirty minutes later, he was on a Metro bus. He had to change busses three times, and then hitchhike five miles before he got home. His feet were wet and muddy from hiking the quarter mile driveway. Home was the mildewed single-wide trailer parked under a monstrous oak tree. He threw open the front door.

"Sherie? Do we have any beer?"

She didn't answer. He kept forgetting that he'd killed her a week before.

---

[3] 'Shithead' in Japanese

Glen

There was no opening act and the TSS show started precisely at 8:00. Glen watched from a skybox while mayhem was unleashed on stage. Raz would throw his guitars and it would be the job of a backstage tech to catch it while another tech quickly slipped another around Raz's neck. After suffering through endless rehearsals, Glen was amazed at how smoothly the complex show was executed.

He made another attempt to engage Charity in conversation.

"What are you working on?"

She held up a partially completed needlework. It was a neckerchief adorned with the TSS symbol and old-fashioned cannons firing a volley.

"Pirates of Power?"

She nodded.

"Okay."

Unbidden, a few lines appeared in his head.

Blackheart President with saber in hand
Launches a volley of hate on the land

"A gift for Raz?"

"Merchandise prototype."

Merchandise prototype. Glen sensed the magnitude of the TSS juggernaut, but could not fathom it. A conglomerate multimedia empire with CDs, DVDs, music and video downloads, licensing agreements, concert ticket sales, and merchandise designed and micromanaged by a 25-year-old kid. Regardless of how smart Raz was, it seemed impossible.

He decided to take a walk, so after stuffing foam earplugs in his ears and making sure his backstage passes were visible around his neck, he merged into the crowd. The music was physical, pounding like an earthquake shredding air molecules. In sputtering lighting, he tried to get a sense of the audience. Mostly young, they wore torn jeans and Toxic Shock Syndrome t-shirts. The song, blasting through the sound system, was *Famines and Fascists* and the kids, screaming lyrics at the top of their lungs, knew every line.

> Clap your hands for our blessed leader
> Clap your hands for his holy war
> While we march, march, march to victory
> In a bloody twenty-first century crusade

The north-side merchandise booth was protected by sound-deadening panels, so Glen could remove his earplugs. T-shirts $25; baseball hats $15; and tour guides $20. Business was brisk. A Raz girl showed off the stuff.

Raz had his own comic series. Surreal.

"How much for the comic book?"

"We prefer to call them graphic novels."

"What's' the difference?

"About twenty dollars."

Glen laughed.

He bought one to read later. Catching a glimpse of her medallion, he lifted it to look at it in the intermittent light. It bore a golden oval with embossed TSS logo. She took it back gently and tucked it back in her shirt.

"Not for sale," she said.

There was more to be said, but she didn't share.

He looked her over more carefully. With a slender figure in a modest, knee-length dress, she had a pretty smile and dimples. No spandex, no high heels, no lurid makeup. A wide, cheerful face with creamy skin. A typically-nice Raz girl.

How many of these girls were there?

There were three others behind the tables stacked with swag.

They weren't identical—blondes, brunettes and redheads in all shades of fair and dark. The girl dragging a backstock box covered with Kanji characters appeared to be Thai.

The concept was overwhelming. He felt dizzy. It was the vortex of a money-sucking magnet, but there was more to the story. Due to an inexplicable underlying current, the air vibrated with subtle power. A motive force. The comic book was slipped into a black plastic bag with the lurid TSS logo emblazoned on the side in large ragged letters. Glen gripped it tightly as if it was a flotation device.

Murphy

Murphy assigned herself a floater role and wandered through the pandemonium and watched for the unusual. After the last encore, the crowd dwindled, but a mass gathered at the left side of the stage. Raz signed everything put in front of him, but, when Murphy got close, she realized it was one of the fake Raz's. She turned away with disgust.

Where is the real Raz?

A crowd gathered on the other side where girls, one-by-one, were allowed backstage access. Murphy walked over. The girls clutched the elaborate Raz Girl identification cards decorated with picture, bar code, thumb print, and TSS logo.

She walked to join the last girl in line.

"What are you waiting for?" Murphy asked.

"There is no Raz but Raz," the girl mumbled.

"Excuse me? What?"

"I'm sorry. We get a private audience with Raz."

The girl was alert and seemed blissfully happy. Murphy looked her over. She appeared to be a normal girl skipping one night's homework so she could come to a concert and see her bedroom-poster hero. Nothing wrong with that. Physically, these girls were similar. Wholesome girls with slight figures and healthy skin. Nothing pierced or tattooed. It was like a receiving line at a Christian High School.

Murphy moved to the front of the line. Jesus and another beefy security guard examined the cards and scanned them with a handheld terminal. Every few minutes, at an unseen signal, another girl would be allowed to pass.

Murphy spoke to Jesus.

"Everything under control?"

"Looks good to me," Jesus said.

"Can I slip by and see him?"

"Oh, sure, sorry." With his palm, Jesus guided the next girl back to clear a space for Murphy to pass. *"No problema."*

She followed a passageway and pushed through a heavy curtain. Raz sat on an oversized chair, almost a throne. He turned and puffed on his hookah, then placed his hands on the girl's face and caressed her cheeks. He whispered and looked deeply into her eyes. He lifted her hands and she rose to her feet. Raz patted her gently on the butt as she left the chamber. Murphy took the girl's place, settling on her knees on a spongy silken pillow. The room, created by thick hanging carpets, was small and close.

Raz sucked on the hookah mouthpiece. Wisps of smoke came from his mouth as he spoke.

"Murphy."

"Hello, Raz."

"Everything peaceful outside?"

"No problems. What are you doing?"

Raz tilted his head back and laughed. A puff of smoke came from his lungs.

"The Raz girls get a brief private audience. How many are left out there?"

"Ten or so."

"Okay. Ten of my girls patiently wait for a minute with me... What can I do for you, Murphy?"

"What do you say to them?"

"I tell them exactly what they want to hear. That everything is going to be okay."

"For that, they spend their money and join the fan club?"

Raz laughed again. "I like you, Murphy. The girls don't pay."

"I don't understand."

"I know, but don't worry, everything will be okay."

His breathy words were gentle and persuasive.

"You tell them just like that? I can see why they like it."

"Yes, just like that. Is there anything else on your mind?"

"A lot."

"I know. Can it wait?"

"I suppose. If you pat me on the ass I'll break your arm."

Raz snorted with smoky mirth. He doubled over for an instant and his shoulders shook. After dabbing at moisture in the corners of his eyes with a TSS logo'd towel, he said, "Of course, Murphy, don't worry."

She followed exit signs to a metal door and pushed through to peek outside. The door opened on an alley. The previous girl settled in the backseat of a large car; it looked like her parents picked her up. Murphy waved and the girl watched with minimal interest. Murphy made eye-contact with the driver. He was about 50 and well-dressed in a suit and tie. He shrugged and smiled as if to say: *daughters, what are you going to do?*

CHAPTER SIX

Glen

On the next night, the situation with the promoter was different; there was a mad, greedy gleam in his eyes Glen had not noticed the night before. Whenever money is involved, inevitably, people get crazy.

With lots of money on the table, larger risks are justified. That's the way the poker game of life works.

"Well, sweet-roll, here we are again," Fireplug said.

There was an extra muscle-man in the room. Glen didn't like him. His eyes were not precisely aligned and it was disturbing. Glen looked around the room more carefully. It was tastefully decorated with a photograph of Fireplug shaking hands with George Bush the elder. They stood in front of a garish Christmas tree, a photo-op receiving-line for big donors. Glen tossed his black bag on the desk.

"I'm not such a stupid man," Fireplug said.

"I never thought that for an instant, chili pepper. An ugly little midget, but not dumb."

Fireplug leaned back in his chair and emitted a sharp laugh, like a bark.

"See that, my friends? The man has a sense of humor. We like that don't we?"

He gestured and crazy-eyes pulled a pistol out of his jacket pocket. It was not a large pistol; a .25 caliber automatic. It looked like a toy in crazy-eyes' beefy hand.

Pointed at my head, it's enough to do the job, if puréeing my brain is the job, that is.

"Peanut, we know the routine. It occurs to me that I can save myself— how much, Quentin?"

"Two-hundred and sixty-six thousand," Quenton said.

Quenton had been in the room the day before. He was an older man with a thick chest. Slick with oil, his thinning gray hair swept back from his face. He looked like a constipated badger.

"Tax-free, that's nothing to sneeze at, Snickerdoodle. We wait a few minutes, then you make a phone call and tell them the money's been deposited. Then, after the concert, we let you go and you run away. Easy and no one gets hurt. Otherwise, we shoot you in the head and your body gets dumped in a landfill. However you disappear, they'll assume you ran off with the money."

Glen laughed. That was it? They would shoot him in the head? He didn't believe, after all he'd been through, it would happen this way. He was chosen by the Supreme Being for greater things.

"Go ahead and shoot me, Mini-bar, you'd be doing me a favor. I have shit in my head I'm sick to death of living with. I'm not making the phone call."

There was a muffled noise from outside and Jesus poked his head in the room.

"Is everything under control?" he asked.

Fireplug sighed. "We're just having a little fun, no harm done," he said. "Am I right, Blueberry?"

"Yeah," Glen said to Jesus, "just a couple of wiseguys clowning around."

Glen gathered the bundles of money and stuffed them into his bag.

Outside, one of Fireplug's guys sat on the floor with his hands and feet bound with flexcuffs. He had a nasty bump swelling on his head.

"I thought it was taking a bit too long," Jesus explained.

Glen handed him the bag and he tucked it under his arm like an over-sized football.

"Let's use a different exit this time," Glen suggested. "Let Murphy know we're running a little late, but we're okay."

While Jesus talked into his radio, they walked briskly across the concert hall and out through a security door into an alley. The door said an alarm would go off, but if it did, it wasn't something they cared about. They crossed at a crosswalk and walked an unnecessary block before hailing a cab. At the bank office, Glen watched while Jesus supervised the count. After he waved, Glen made the call. Jesus handed Glen the deposit slip.

"Tell Raz to use a different promoter the next time he's in Houston."

"Good idea," Jesus said.

A rock band enjoying this level of success lived in a bubble. While the equipment was loaded onto semi trucks for an overnight run to the next stop, the band and entourage flew on a chartered 727 painted with the TSS logo. Thus, they avoided baggage claim, security lines, and being herded like cattle in the public terminal.

Raz had a master suite at the back of the aircraft that held a double bed and private bath which could be isolated with heavy curtains. The curtains were pulled back and he sat on a leather couch talking quietly with two girls while Charity, still working on her needlework project, watched over them.

Did it bother her? Was she jealous? If so, there was no sign of it in her eyes.

Glen found a plush leather seat at the front and, wrapped in a blanket, slept. He dreamed of a janitor running a carpet cleaner over and over in a futile effort to remove a stubborn stain. When he woke, he was alone on the plane with Charity's homemade TSS neckerchief arranged on his lap. He looked it over. It was a crude, but the design was intricate and interesting.

He shoved it in his pocket and found the plane's exit. The sun peeked over the horizon. They were in Dallas and the plane was parked next to Mark Cuban's, all smart and shiny with his Dallas Mavericks logo. Glen was in no hurry, so he grabbed coffee and a breakfast sandwich at the terminal and read through the morning paper. When he was ready, he caught a cab and headed to the Dallas Convention Center.

Gerusha and Walter

In a pink, satiny, color-coordinated athletic suit and wearing iPod earbuds, Gerusha ran. She'd put on ten pounds from eating bad food and neglecting her exercise. Stress made her seek comfort foods like fried potatoes and sweets. If she was not careful, she'd get fat and that was not what she wanted. She ran to the Ballard Locks and back. When she got back to Immortality, she showered in the company-provided locker room and blow-dried her hair. After an initial few days of soreness, it felt good to work her body; the release calmed her throughout the day. After leaving the locker room, she stopped by Walter's office to ask about the house paperwork.

"Do I need to do anything more about Glen's house? I haven't picked out a mortgage company or anything."

"No, don't worry. Immortality is your mortgage company. The earnest money is on deposit and we'll cut a check for the balance.

We'll deduct payments from Glen's paycheck and then pay off the balance with an end-of-year bonus. Easy."

"I had no idea it could be done that way."

"Well, don't mention it to the IRS. They frown on this sort of thing, but it gets buried deep in the balance sheet. As long as a lot of money is coming in, no one will notice. How is the place? Nice?"

"I haven't actually seen it yet. I'm going tomorrow."

"You'll be living there too, I assume."

Oh my.

She'd been busy and distracted. This idea had not occurred to her. Would she leave her little apartment in Belltown? She twisted the wedding ring on her finger, thinking. Glen told her to buy him a house and she did. But, this would be her home too? All of a sudden she was more curious about what it looked like. She had a vision of a doublewide trailer on flat tires, but five million bought more than that, even in Seattle where houses were over-priced.

"Did you forget you're married to Glen, dear? The house is yours too."

"No, of course not. That would be absurd and silly. What a suggestion. You're such a kidder."

"Right," Walter said with a bemused smile on his face.

"Work calls, gotta run," Gerusha said.

When she got back to her office, she dialed Bubb's cell phone. She almost smashed the handset when he didn't answer, but she calmed herself and left a message.

"Bubb, when you were here last time, you mentioned a *detail* about the house I should know about. I'm curious now, what *is* that detail? Call me back right away."

Deep in thought, Gerusha absently stared at the phone when it rang. What could be odd about a five-million-dollar house? That it's pink?

That it's next door to a sewage processing plant? That the neighbors are Jehovah's Witnesses? What?

"Bubb! Where have you been?"

"Gerusha, it's 8:30. Give me a break."

"Okay, spill it."

"Um—, it would be better for you to see for yourself. Our appointment is tomorrow, then you'll know."

"You said the *detail* would not affect its investment value..."

"Right, don't worry, it's not like the house is pink or something."

Surprised at herself, she felt an odd relief.

"Okay, tomorrow. How's the deal coming along?"

"The deal is nearly done. We close in two weeks."

"I thought this would take a month or more."

"You're paying cash, which knocks out a lot of delays."

"Wow."

"Look, Gerusha, if you know anyone else who needs a house, please pass along my name. I'll leave a stack of business cards in the lobby and cut you in for a rebate if I close on a referral. Even if they are just thinking of looking, this would be a great time—"

"Bubb!"

"Yes."

"I will see you tomorrow."

Holding the phone at arm's length, she could still hear him chattering as she pressed the button to end the call.

Glen and Jesus

Glen stirred creamer into his coffee. The meeting room was small and the walls were covered with whiteboards and pinned-up architectural plans for the Dallas Convention Center. With colored highlighter pens, they mapped out various routes out of the building.

"We need to mix things up. Never the same thing twice," Glen said.

"I agree," Jesus replied.

Murphy stuck her head in the door.

"Goddam it, Glen, if you wore a damn radio or answered your damn cell phone, I wouldn't have to run all around the place looking for you." She looked them over and studied the drawings they'd decorated with garish shades of orange and yellow high-lighting ink. "I'm glad to see you lovebirds working together."

"Can't you see we're busy? What do you want?" Glen said.

"Oh, it was nothing," she said before easing the door closed.

"That woman is a genuine pain in the ass," Glen commented.

"Aren't they all?" Jesus asked rhetorically.

Glen gave him a high five.

"Damn right," he said.

They collected the money in a small office filled with gray metal filing cabinets. This time, they had two identical backpacks; one stuffed with telephone books and the other stuffed with the cash. The concert promoter, Mr. Toles, was tall and thin with a reedy voice. His security people waited outside.

"What about this Razorblade guy—is he a big jerk like the other rockers I've met?"

"No, he's alright. Smart. What do you think, Jesus?"

"He pays us okay and doesn't treat us like shit. I worked for Hillary Clinton once. She's a real piece of work. Always screaming and putting on an attitude."

"You used to work a security detail for Hillary? That's cool."

"I couldn't wait to get out of there. Those Clintons are creepy."

"My daughters love the Razorblade." Toles shook his head as if to dislodge the thought. "Guys, I don't like dealing with so much cash; there's more security in a direct transfer. What's the deal? Nobody uses cash any more. Even the dopers use off-shore accounts to shuffle their money around."

"The boss is old-school," Glen said.

However, he'd noticed for all three transactions so far, the money went into different Walmex accounts. There was some sort of tax dodge in play, but Glen didn't need to understand it to do his job.

They mixed the bags up so even they didn't know which was which. After exchanging a Mexican palm-slapping handshake, they headed for alternate ends of the building. In a loading zone, a Honda scooter waited. Glen strapped on a helmet and merged into traffic. He beat Jesus and waited inside. Jesus had his money ready and paid off their bet. It turned out that Jesus had the money and Glen had the phone books. The cash was quickly counted and Glen made the call. The concert was a go.

Glen and Gerusha

After arriving back at the convention center, Glen found a payphone and called Gerusha.

"Hey babe, how are they hanging?"

"I call one Droopy and the other Flabby; does that answer your question?"

"No matter; I can't wait say hello with Mr. Flicky McSticky."

"You're gross. Did you call to ruin my day?"

"I love you too, honey-bucket."

"Did you just call me a portable toilet? Don't ever do that again."

"Now pretty-pants, don't be contrary."

"Why did you call?"

"I'm checking in. Did you buy us a house?"

"Yes, the deal closes on Friday next."

"Cool, tell me about it."

"You spent five million on a little pink house next to a sewage treatment plant. I hope you're happy."

"Perfectly happy, dear, you read my mind. I always wanted an expensive pink elephant next to a reeking cesspool. Please tell me the neighbors have a Pit Bull puppy farm and the dogs get loose and maul the 'tards from the special ed school across the street.

"For only five million, you can't have everything."

"If we need more money, I can talk to Walter about it."

"No, Glen, everything is fine. Don't trouble your little-pea brain; I have it handled."

"Fine. Hey, babe, I'm looking for a girl. Late teens or early 20's, slim, smart, a nice kid, not a goth or a stoner. Do you know anyone?"

"You're one sick piece of shit. I'm nearly thirty and that's too old for you? Men like you make me want to gag."

"Gerusha…"

"Pervert."

"Gerusha, are you premenstrual? Get a grip and listen. I'm not there to comfort and sate you, so your mind gets mushy and paranoid. I apologize for that neglect. Listen up. Raz has an odd fan club and I want a girl to join up and tell me about it. Do you know someone or not?"

"Why don't you look up the details online or just ask Raz himself?"

Glen sighed. "If I could, I would. It's not going to be that easy. Disengage the bad engines in your brain and find me a girl."

"A spy?"

"This isn't World War Five or industrial espionage, just a rock music fanclub of some kind. Find me a girl."

She already thought of a candidate. Paula had a younger sister, Karla. A sophomore at the University of Washington, Karla liked rock music, bands like TSS, Green Day and Radiohead. "I'll ask around."

"That's all I'm asking, for the love of the Prophet. Are you always so difficult? The tour hits Seattle in a couple of weeks. Until then, give Droopy and Flabby a sloppy kiss for me and tell them I'll see them soon."

"Pig," she said as she broke the connection.

She missed his response: "Ball-breaker."

Childhood fantasies of a *good* marriage lingered in her mind. Her husband would be slim, handsome, caring, loving and handy around the house with a pipe wrench and screwdriver. He would enjoy quiet evenings at home and paying for expensive meals in exotic locations, like Paris or Monte Carlo. Barbie and Ken, dancing in the gentle light of the moon. Roses and candles and soft, fluffy beds...

"Gerusha?"

Startled, she twitched violently in her chair.

"What were you thinking about?"

It was Paula.

"Nothing," Gerusha said. "What's up?"

"I'm going down for a latté. You need a break, come down with me."

Break?

Gerusha had not accomplished a single useful thing all day.

"Sure, that sounds good," she said. "Let's go."

93

Legendary people roamed the hallways of the young company. Corporate royalty. Walter, the company president, was king. He had a mysterious air and wielded unchecked power within Immortality's walls. If he said you were out, you were out. No more stock grants, no more quarterly bonuses, and no more paycheck. Most people knew Walter had an alter-ego, Dr. Zalooq, and that he had once been a famous magician and sorcerer (if rumors were to be believed). Many were afraid of him. With white hair and piercing eyes, he seemed diabolical and dangerous. Whether this image was a carefully-cultivated and useful persona or represented a harsh reality, no one cared to get close enough to find out. Rumors abounded.

Bennie Jackson was a thin, black eighteen-year-old kid; brilliant and playful as a puppy. He was the main researcher of the company technology (whatever that was), so smart no one understood him much of the time, but friendly and popular with the staff.

Elke was often around and worked with Walter, but her role was unknown. She was rumored to be a lesbian, but there was no outward evidence.

The most popular member of the inner circle was an Inuit named Emma. She was Bennie's girlfriend and attended the University of Washington. Always baking, she brought goodies for the employees in the lunchroom. Engineers from far corners of the building ran when the rumor mill broadcasted that plates of Emma's cookies were available. Whether she was on the payroll or not was unknown, but she was often seen in the hallways.

Gerusha was a new member of the inner circle. Recently, she'd been the receptionist in the lobby after Walter hired her away from a downtown Starbucks. Now, she managed vendor contacts, restricted vendor access to the technical staff, and negotiated contracts. This was a key company position. Enough on its own to earn her top-tier status at the company, but her boyfriend/husband was Glen Wilson.

Toxic Shock Syndrome

Who Glen was and what he did were unknown, but rumors abounded. Glen's bronze bust sat in a corner of the lobby, that was all many knew. He appeared briefly at the company, but no one was impressed with what they saw. Everyone assumed there must be more to Glen than met the eye, but even Gerusha was unsure about that.

All eyes were on Gerusha when she and Paula entered the lunchroom. Paula waved and made small talk, but Gerusha was oblivious. She ordered a nonfat latté with a sugar-free scone while Paula found a vacant table. They sat.

"Gerusha, you're buying a house. The hallways are abuzz. You must be very excited. Is it a McMansion in the suburbs? Does it have a swimming pool and hot tub and wine cellar? I'll bet it's nice, all cedar shakes and granite counters with marble tile in the bathrooms. How many bathrooms—four, five, six? When can I come see it? We'll organize a house-warming party; get a guest list together and set up a registry at the outlet mall so you can get dishes and stuff. I'll help with all the details, don't you worry about it. Tell me about the house. Will I be jealous and busted-down with envy? Tell me."

Gerusha sipped her latté. "I don't want to talk about the house. How is Karla?"

"Karla? Didn't I tell you? She dropped out of college and ran off with a hemp-growing anarchist from Eugene. We're heart-broken. She had such great potential."

While Paula pattered on, Gerusha was deep in thought.

Karla is out. Who did she know that was young, sweet and innocent who would meet Glen's requirements?

At that instant, Emma walked in cafeteria with a large platter of Tollhouse cookies. She wore a cable-knit sweater over long-sleeved shirt and blue jeans with embroidered green vines climbing the sides. She walked over with her platter. When Gerusha reached for a cookie, it struck her. Emma could do it.

She'd be a perfect choice.

Gerusha and Paul Butler

Paul took her to dinner at nice places, this time the rotating Space Needle SkyCity restaurant. Uncharacteristically, the late afternoon was crisp and clear. Bright white new snow could be seen on the Cascades. A cloud cap hovered over Mount Rainier.

"Since this is a business meal, let's talk business first and get it out of the way," Gerusha suggested.

"If you insist."

"Number one, we want the mass spectrometer due—" she shuffled a sheaf of papers, "—in four weeks, to be delivered in two weeks..."

"You're killing me, Gerusha. We already expedited the shipment—"

"Let me finish. We're willing to pay a two percent premium for early delivery and will pay the invoice in 10 days."

"Okay, I'll see what can be done."

"We need another magnetic resonance imaging machine, delivered by the end of the year and we want to pay five percent less than we paid for the last one. You in?"

"We cut the price to the bone on the last one."

"The GE guy wants this order. He called me twice today. Shall I make his day?"

"No, I'll submit the quote. How about four percent?"

"I was thinking five."

"Okay Gerusha, five percent it is. When did you get so tough?"

Toxic Shock Syndrome

"I don't know. A year ago I was trying to figure out how to fit a new pair of shoes into my budget. Last week, I bought a house for five million and I felt nothing. It's weird."

"You should have told me. I know a good real estate agent."

"Doesn't everyone? I'll tell you what—I'll pick up the lunch bill if you can guess how many realtor business cards I collected in the last week."

"You're on," Paul said. He thought about it a moment. "Plus or minus three?"

"Plus or minus two."

"Okay. I'll say thirty-four."

Gerusha picked up her purse and pulled out a card case. They counted them out together. Twenty-seven.

"You lose."

"Slackers. I met a big-talking blowhard in the lobby, did you buy through him? Bobby Boob?"

"I call him Bubb. Yes, he was the agent I used."

"For five million, it must be a nice place."

"I don't know. I haven't seen it yet. I'll tell you next week."

"Ah... But you bought it."

"We close next Friday."

"Interesting."

"Is it? I'm too weary to care."

Paul ordered a Kobe top sirloin and Gerusha ordered an apple, huckleberry and blue cheese salad. They sipped iced tea and looked out over the Seattle skyline. Far below, the monorail train hissed by.

"In a lot of ways I was happier as a barista at Starbucks. Life was simpler."

"Happiness is overrated. I think people ask the wrong things from life."

"Like what?"

"Well, happiness comes to mind. You're leading an interesting life."

"And that's what I should settle for?"

"Most people don't..."

"Lead interesting lives?"

"Yes."

"So, you're the famous salesman-philosopher from Seattle..."

"If you can't be happy with what you have, then you'll never be happy with what you're going to get."

"That's too long for a fortune cookie. Where did you get it?"

"I made it up."

"Bullshit."

"Your point?"

"No point, just an observation."

"We could talk about magnetic resonance imaging machinery instead," Paul suggested.

"Yes. If you're so smart; help me with this. Bennie said something and I wrote it down." She fished a piece of paper out of her purse. "Here it is. 'Magnetic flux is an illusion created by imbalances in wavespace resonance'. What does that mean?"

"I have no clue, but suddenly, I don't feel so clever."

"Me neither."

They ate their lunches and, through plate-glass windows, watched SeaTac-bound planes pass by. After a few minutes of silence, Paul told a long and involved story about his vacation in Cabo San Lucas. It started with Cuban cigars and shots of mescal at the Mango Deck beach restaurant and ended in front of Margaritaville with an angry, injured pelican, two mariachi musicians and a fistfight between competing timeshare canvassers. It wasn't that amusing of a story, but Gerusha appreciated the fact that it did not include discount-store philosophy, magnetic resonance or any mention of her real estate transaction.

CHAPTER SEVEN

Glen

The next show, on Friday night, was in Austin, Texas. The small concert hall on the University of Texas campus was a blocky, prison-like concrete building called the Bass Concert Hall. It had only 3,000 seats, but Raz had friends in Austin, so he slipped the venue into the schedule. Even at $115 per ticket, the place was sold out. Tickets were scalped on eBay for two to three hundred dollars. Through the limousine's tinted windows while driving to the concert hall, Glen saw his first protesters—a group of thirty led by an old man with a long white beard waving a sign that said *Down with Devil Music*.

"I suppose it's partly true, there are devils in some of my tunes," Raz mused, "but I'm not sure what they mean by 'devil music'. Most of my songs have a subtle Christian foundation."

"Well over half of all people have below-average intellects," Glen said. "I think that explains a lot."

"If average means adding all IQ scores and dividing by…"

"He knows the difference between median and average. He's attempting funny," Murphy said.

"Oh," Raz said. "I'll make that poster into a song. *Down with devil music, the flames of hell will roast you, below-average masses, the devil will toast you,*" he sang. "What do you think?"

"I think it needs work."

"*I* was trying to be funny," Raz said.

Toxic Shock Syndrome

"Some things are best left to professionals," Glen said.

Murphy watched to see how Raz would take this. He laughed cheerfully. Whistling through his teeth, he gazed through the tinted window. One of Raz's new girls sat with her hand resting on his knee. She glared at Glen. He grinned at her and, in the dim light, his teeth glowed like a wild animal's.

The promoter met them at the Capital Marriott meeting room. The Marriott Hotel was a block from Austin's famous Sixth Street-Warehouse music district. The meeting room looked over the terrace restaurant.

The promoter was a pock-marked Mexican wearing a string tie and a giant turquoise belt buckle. He wore striking cowboy boots, all lumpy and leathery. He exchanged rapid Spanish with Jesus. Glen understood most of it, but did not let on.

"He says he doesn't like dealing with so much cash and wonders why a direct bank transfer won't work."

"Tell him we hear that a lot," Glen said. "Ask him what his boots are made of."

They exchanged a few words.

"I speak English." His English was very good; crisp with a hint of south-Texas drawl. "My boots are made from the bull alligator."

"*Muy bueno,*" Glen said.

The take was lighter than usual, just over two-hundred-and-forty-thousand. The bank office was only eight blocks away. While Glen waited for a taxi, Jesus walked briskly through a suspicious-looking alley. He beat Glen by a minute or so and Glen paid off the wager with a twenty dollar bill they'd been trading back and forth. Both carried phone books in their backpacks; the bicycle courier arrived a few minutes later. The courier was a pale-faced college student with snaky dread-locked hair wriggling around his face. They paid him with cash and hauled his backpack to the counting office. Soon, the transaction was complete and they made the phone call.

"I still think it was a stupid idea to trust that hippy bicycle guy with all that cash."

"Thank you for your input," Glen said solemnly. "It worked, so stop busting my balls."

Raz signaled for a third encore and fake Razs, playing keyboards, appeared at each end of the stage. In hippy psychedelia mode, they wore long-haired, side-parted wigs, droopy fake mustaches, flowing shirts and bell-bottomed pants. Raz dedicated the song to Vincent Crane[4].

The faux Razs played modern synthesizers with realistic Hammond Organ patches that howled with ghostly precision. This final song was a cover. *Fire* by Arthur Brown. About halfway through, Arthur Brown came out. Thin and balding on top but with long hair cascading over his ears, he wore a silver suit and a large Maltese cross hanging from a heavy chain.

Fire, I'll take you to burn
Fire, I'll take you to learn
You gonna burn—burn—burn—
Fire, I'll take you to burn—

The show ended with Raz on his knees bowing before his hero while flame videos played in the background. When the last echoes of music dissipated, Raz, holding hands with Arthur, raised his guitar and left the stage. After he was gone, the house lights were turned on and the

[4] Vincent Crane, 1943-1989, progressive rock keyboardist for the Crazy World of Arthur Brown and Atomic Rooster. Talented but troubled, he committed suicide in 1989.

auditorium slowly cleared. In lines on both sides of the stage, young girls waited for their private audience. They were dealt with quickly.

After servicing the receiving line, Raz washed off his makeup and pulled back his long hair. He changed into black jeans and sandals. With his long hair bunched under a baseball cap, he looked like a Mexican college student. In this disguise, he was going club-hopping with friends. Glen and Jesus tried to join the entourage in the van, but Raz waved them off.

"Too many hangers-on will ruin my anonymity," he said. "Murphy is coming. I'll be fine."

Murphy gestured for Glen to come closer before she climbed in.

"I don't like this either. He's hitting Doc Brown's. See if you can catch up with us there."

"Check," Glen replied.

Jesus wandered over.

"Murphy gave me a clue. Fuck this, let's get a drink," Glen said.

They pressed their fists together.

"You're right. We've been dismissed so we're off-duty," Jesus said. "I like the way your mind works."

Outside the concert hall, they flagged down a cab.

They walked through Doc Brown's. Onstage, the band energetically thumped up-tempo rockabilly on stand-up bass and drums. The guitarist played a fat, single-cutaway Epiphone Emperor. The room, except for two drunks morosely guarding drinks at the bar, was empty. Glen chatted with the manager and slipped him $200 in cash. They roped off twenty chairs in the back corner. Glen ordered a shot of tequila.

"What kind?" the waitress asked.

"Cabo Wabo," Jesus said. Glen lifted an inquiring eyebrow. "I did a tour with Sammy and got a taste for it."

"I'm not being critical. Bring us the bottle," Glen said. "I'm in the mood to howl at the moon. And bring a cigar."

"Make that *dos*," Jesus said, raising two fingers.

"Smoking is not permitted," the waitress said.

Glen glared at her.

"Everything is permitted. Talk to your boss. This is now a private party."

She considered arguing, but instead crossed herself and scurried away.

"That was funny," Jesus said, while repeating the crossing motion.

"God's not on our guest list," Glen said.

On break, the guitar player wandered over. He had short hair and looked like a prep student in Dockers khaki pants and a polo shirt.

"Care for a drink?" Glen asked, waving the bottle.

"Sure." He drained a neat shot and rubbed tears from his eyes. "I heard a rumor. Are there going to be VIPs in the house tonight?"

"I'd be fired if I told you Raz from TSS is stopping by with friends. Don't tell anyone. It's an after-hours private party."

"It will be our secret."

The kid walked away.

"Why'd you do that? He'll be on his cell phone calling everyone in town. The security situation will go to hell."

"Don't give a shit; I'm off-duty."

"You're pissed because Raz wouldn't let you in the van."

"They're making shit money playing a place like this; let the kid rake in a little cash. Okay? The bible-thumping protesters are all in bed. We'll be okay."

Jesus tapped his shot glass against Glen's. "Your ass, brother."

It was 1:30 when Raz and his posse swept into the bar. By then it was packed. Glen and Jesus aggressively protected their roped-off corner. At one point, Glen showed a drunk his .45, which quickly settled the argument over the reserved chairs.

"You're an ugly drunk," Jesus pointed out. "Ever pull the trigger and plug anyone?"

"Dead men tell no tales," Glen said.

"Why do I almost believe you?" Jesus asked.

"Because you're not quite as dumb as you look."

When Raz saw Glen and Jesus, he gave Murphy a stern look.

"You told," he said.

"I'm doing my job the way I see it," she replied. "Fire me if you don't like it."

A slow grin worked across Raz's face. "No problem, Murphy."

The entourage included a gaggle of Raz girls picked up along the way, three by Glen's count. Arthur Brown, wearing a long velvet coat and fully inebriated, was present. In the audience, two men in suits, looking like insurance agents, staked out a table with three preppy college girls decked out in short skirts and fluffy hair. The rest of the audience was an assortment of goat ropers, barflies, pimply nerds, passed-prime hippies and skateboard slackers.

The band finished their set and wandered over to shake hands with Raz and Arthur Brown.

"The guitars are still plugged in and the amps are warmed up if the mood strikes you," the guitarist told Raz.

"We'll see how the evening goes," Raz replied.

At three in the morning, Raz and Arthur mounted the stage and played blues; slow songs with Arthur howling like a banshee to music by Screaming Jay Hawkins, Willie Dixon and Robert Johnson. Analytically, Raz watched the college kids slow dance with the girls;

they swayed and clung to each other as if drowning in the somber music.

And I went to the crossroad, mama,
I looked east and west
I went to the crossroad, baby, I looked east and west
Lord, I didn't have no sweet woman,
Oooh well, babe, in my distress...[5]

With acoustic bass thumping and the drums pattering, the music was sparse and slow. Raz restrained himself by inserting a stab here and there, interleaving a few abrupt notes from the fat guitar to accent the music. Only at the end did he let go with long, flowing lines that hissed and writhed like neurotoxic nightmares. For the finale, he played quietly, backing the volume to near silence—throwing out angry chords that faded into the night.

"Thank you all," he whispered.

Exhausted, he held the microphone stand and stared into the crowd. He noticed a thin young man wearing a Pabst Blue Ribbon trucker's hat.

"I know you," he said. "Is your Stratocaster out in the car?"

The man nodded.

"Go get it," Raz said.

The young man weaved out through the crowd.

In the microphone, Raz said, "I'm not going to pretend to be humble. I study, practice long hours and God gave me a certain amount of talent. It would be stupid to deny the result. However, there is always someone in the crowd who makes me look like I'm playing

---

[5] Cross Road Blues, Robert Johnson, 1936

with five thumbs. Tonight is no exception. Please give a warm welcome to Mr. Josh Zee."

Josh pushed through the mob and snapped open the latches on his guitar case.

Raz put the Epiphone on its stand and handed the end of the guitar cord to Josh.

"What's the name of your band, Josh?"

"The Mothertruckers."

"Can you find a way through Crawlin' King Snake? Big Joe Williams? Old school?"

Josh played a sinuous double-picked riff and nodded.

"I can handle it," he said.

Raz grinned.

"Not too fast, okay? I want some foreplay."

The drummer clicked his sticks, but Raz waved for him to stop.

"More like 90 beats per minute."

The drummer started again, slower, and Raz nodded in approval.

The bass player thumped sparse quarter notes. Josh played moody, slippery, multi-stop chords that dotted the musical landscape like old fence posts. Raz, with his eyes closed, listened and waited for the quiet mood to settle before singing.

> You got me crawlin' baby
> When the grass was very high
> I'm just gonna keep on crawlin' now baby
> until the day I die
> 'Cause I'm a crawlin' king snake and I rule my den
> I don't want nobody hangin' around with my lady,
> I'm just gonna use her for myself.

After he sang the final verse, Raz grinned at Josh.

"Okay, now give me a guitar lesson."

Josh motioned for the band to pick up the tempo. He started with simple lines accented with shimmering harmonics which hung in the air like audio rainbows. Then, rocking his head like a mad pigeon, he unleashed a flurry of fast acrobatics which covered all the notes on the fretboard and many more beyond. He ended with a jazzy cascade and let a final chord echo in the air.

"Always leave them wanting more, am I right?" Raz said.

Josh nodded and bowed to Raz and the crowd. He unplugged his guitar.

Raz held his hand over his heart.

"Thank you, Josh, that was amazing. Let me savor it."

After a long minute, he came from his trance. He looked over the mob. There were a hundred screaming people crammed into the tiny bar.

"And now, we have one more special treat." He made eye contact with Glen. "My friend Glen will come up and show us how things are done."

He picked up the Epiphone and wove through the crowd.

"Here you go, Glen," he said.

Glen was drunk and in a bad mood. Jesus was right, he was pissed off after being barred from the van. Then tequila; he was always angry when drinking tequila. He'd had a massive amount, so was awash in a massive fury. In his distorted vision, the room appeared splattered with red paint while speckles of wrath dripped from the walls.

Raz, one of the world's finest rock guitarists, threw down a cruel challenge to an amateur with a crippled hand. Glen should have congratulated him on pulling a good practical joke. That would have been the mature thing to do.

Unfortunately, the Glen Wilson way is often not the mature way.

Toxic Shock Syndrome

He had a card up his sleeve. In the years he'd spent in a prison-like North Dakota facility, he played endless hours on a battered nylon-string acoustic with five strings. An intern helped him tune it and showed him a few simple chords.

In deference to Glen's mutilated hand, the intern urged him to play left-handed, but that was hopeless. He *could* play a few simple chords and work his way around a 12-bar blues sequence. With malformed finger stubs on his left hand, he could only reach a few notes and the damaged, hyper-sensitive skin hurt like hell, but he learned to tap out right-hand patterns on the fretboard, playing it like a hammer dulcimer.

He took the guitar. Raz, with a mocking smile, offered his pick, but Glen waved it away.

He told the band what he wanted. *Devil Got my Woman*, the 1931 Skip James[6] version, played in A-minor. They started by playing it too fast, but he cursed, threatened and waved his hands in tempo until they settled into a glacial pace; a dirge to suit his mood. He held the guitar to his chest like a lifesaver before starting to sing.

> Must have been the devil,
> Believe that woman has gone mad…
> Must have been the devil,
> Believe that woman has gone mad…
>
> Nothin' but the devil change my baby's mind
> Nothin' but the devil change my baby's mind
>
> Laid there last night, laid there last night,

---

[6] Skip James, Nehemiah Curtis "Skip" James, 1902-1969, early-era Delta blues musician.

Ken Coffman

Tried to take my rest
My mind got to ramblin' like wild geese from the west

Must have been the devil,
Believe that woman has gone mad…
Must have been the devil,
Believe that woman has gone mad…

Woman I love, woman I love
Took off with my best friend
Woman I love took off with my best friend

He held out his deformed hand so everyone could see it and then picked out notes and multistop chord fragments, pinching and plucking with his right hand. Like foreplay with a woman he cared about, he started slow and teased the audience. He was in a zone. When he hit a bad note, he bent it up, up-up-up until it screamed in pitch. The main thing was to show no fear—to let the night and alcohol feed his arrogant confidence. This confidence was based on an unfiltered hatred of the audience. They were not remotely worthy. If they were too dumb to appreciate what he offered, they should fuck off and die.

It didn't matter that he could not play well—he could make the audience *feel*. Channeling the Reverend Nehemiah Curtis James, the spirit was drawn from the cold grave. Seeking comfort, dancers pressed together. Drinkers stared into their lonely glasses. In tribute, Arthur Brown raised a sloshing bottle of Jack Daniels and grinned like a ghoul. Josh raised a bottle of Budweiser and howled.

Glen twiddled knobs and turned the guitar down low, and then walked to the amp and cranked every knob to the right as far as they would go.

Must have been the devil,
Believe that woman has gone mad...
Must have been the devil,
Believe that woman has gone mad...

With his right hand on the frets, he played wild vibratos. Tortured notes screamed from the overheated amplifier. Then he played the few patterns he knew as fast as he could; arpeggios filled the room like a flurry of black leaves. The band caught the spirit and pounded their instruments with hot fury. He rubbed the guitar neck on the microphone stand and feedback howled like a hungry wolf.

I believe that woman has gone mad...

He whipped the guitar off his neck and smashed it against the amp. It died with screaming white-hot feedback echoing endlessly in his ringing ears. He was left holding the pickguard with ragged pickup wiring. He weaved through the dancers and tossed the pickguard at Raz. Murphy made ready to jump in the fray.

"That's the last free lesson you'll get from me, kid" Glen said.

"Impressive," Raz said. He held up the mangled guitar pieces. "I might have been in the mood for a few more songs."

"You didn't want to follow that performance," Glen said.

The bar band's guitar player, looking ashen and angry, grabbed Glen's arm.

"I liked that axe, man," he said.

"Shut the hell up. It was a Korean knock-off, not a real Gibson. Besides, Raz will cover your cost."

Competing emotions washed across Raz's face, but his face settled on a wan, thin smile.

111

"Okay," Raz said while gesturing to Murphy to hand over money.

When the pile got high enough, the guitarman grabbed it and stomped off. Raz signed a few autographs as the place cleared out. Real people needed a few hours of sleep before going to work.

Raz, drinking a Snapple, stared with piercing eyes while Glen and Jesus puffed rekindled cigars and passed the nearly-empty Cabo Wabo bottle back and forth. The night ended for Glen when he passed out. The next day started with a massive hangover.

Again with the game.

Where the hell am I?

A Raz girl sat on the edge of the bed holding a Styrofoam cup of black tea. Out of place in his messy room, she looked fresh and utterly wholesome. Glen searched, but there was no sympathy in her eyes.

"If you don't get up now, you'll miss the plane," she said.

His head was filled with fractured images; looking-glass fragments smashed and embedded in his brain.

"I'm not sure tequila is your friend," she continued.

Wisdom from the mouth of a babe. Tequila? She was right; I should be smart enough to stay away.

"Are we still in Austin?"

"For another hour, then we move to Denver."

"What do you have for pain?"

She thought about it.

"Midol."

How low had I descended?

"Okay, give me three or four."

After slowly sitting up, he washed the Midol down with hot tea. He was still dressed from the night before. Politely, she'd thrown his dirty clothes into a travel bag. Once he could move, they rolled out.

Gerusha and Emma

Emma's black hair had grown out; she tied it back with a woven leather lash. She was 17, but appeared younger. Her dark skin seemed to radiate solar energy. Gerusha felt old and worn out in comparison. They sat in the holistic meeting room paneled with split bamboo. Water trickled into a drain over a channel lined with river rock. Faintly audible, new age music whispered in the background. The room was called Tranquility. In the dead center of the building, it was rarely used.

"How do you keep your trim figure?" Emma asked. "You're so lovely."

Gerusha laughed bitterly. She felt ungroomed, bloated and flabby.

"I started running again. You could join me in the morning."

"Running is not something I've ever seen a native Alaskan do," Emma said. "How is Glen?"

A tough question. How to answer?

"Glen is Glen, I guess."

"A lot of people hate him, but he's always been kind to me. You know Bennie worships him." Emma whispered, "That's why Glen's bust is in the lobby. Bennie had it made. I think it's over the top, but when Bennie sinks his teeth into something, you can't deflect him. What are you going to do? It is what it is."

Gerusha couldn't argue with that logic.

Emma continued. "You're lucky. I'm sure you've seen Glen's tender side. I have. He loved a girl in Alaska. Moshi."

Tender side? Glen? Gerusha almost laughed, but held the impulse in.

"He never mentioned her. What happened?"

"Glen, being who he is, has enemies—"

I think I'm one of them, Gerusha thought.

"—and Moshi was shot. She died in his arms. It was sad."

"Was this in the news? What happened to the killer?"

Emma shifted uncomfortably in her seat.

"Her naked body was found in a motel room. Strangled."

Glen showing more of his tender side?

"A girl? I assumed it would be a man. Was she a jealous lover or something?"

"I never got the full story."

"And that girl's killer?"

Emma nervously picked at her teeth with a fingernail. "The police didn't arrest anyone. I'm a city girl, but I know Nature's Way. It includes beak, fang and claw and the rending of living flesh into meat. This can be man's work too. Can we talk about something else? I'm dancing in a graveyard. The murderer reaped what she sowed and there's no profit in digging any deeper." After taking a deep cleansing breath, she visibly brightened. "I'm sitting with Glen's wife. This is so exciting." She gathered Gerusha's hands in hers. "Tell me everything. How has it been so far?"

"Ummm. Unusual is the first word that comes to mind."

"Of course, and I'm babbling away about Glen's ancient history and you're his wife. I'm a silly girl. You probably know him better than anyone else by now."

Don't bet your mortgage payment on that one, sweetie.

"Glen doesn't tell me much," Gerusha said. "Anything that pops into your head, I'm all ears."

"Great!"

Apparently, nothing popped into Emma's head. They sat and listened to the trickling water for a long minute.

"You're buying a house. You must be overjoyed. Walter told me about it."

"Ecstatic. Do you like rock music?" Gerusha asked in order to change the subject.

"Yes! You must be thrilled that Glen is working with Toxic Shock Syndrome. Raz is so cool."

It occurred to Gerusha to download TSS music and see what it was like. She had a vague impression of it being loud and brutal heavy metal. She couldn't get her mind around the concept. Glen was on tour with TSS. What was his role? Raz wore makeup and bit the heads off bats or something. The overwhelming tangles of thought made her head spin. Feeling hypnotized, she trailed her fingers in the burbling water. It was bitterly cold. She raised her finger and looked at a drop of water swelling at the end. She carefully transferred the drop to Emma's button nose.

"What are you doing?"

Gerusha shook her head.

What was she doing?

She had a job she didn't fully understand and bought a five-million-dollar house, unseen, without even seeing pictures. She married a maddening cipher of a man. Her unspent paycheck piled up in her bank account. Life, a long time prior, was a simple thing.

Any instant, I'll wake up in a padded room, or worse, back at Starbucks making iced mochas for fussy soccer moms saying 'Are you stupid? I said organic non-fat milk and extra whipped cream.'

"I'm sorry. I don't *know* what I'm doing."

Emma dabbed the drop of water on her nose.

Gerusha, grasping at straws, changed the subject.

"Toxic Shock Syndrome. Glen is curious about a girls' fan club. Would you join up and give us the details? How it works and stuff?"

"Fan club? I've been busy with school and baking. I don't know about any fan club. Why is Glen interested?"

The asshole didn't say why.

"Explaining does not appear to be a Glen Wilson thing," she said.

"Why doesn't he talk to Raz or Murphy about it?"

"I don't know."

Emma laughed. She leaned over, dipped a finger in the water and flicked it at Gerusha.

"I can join up, poke around, and tell you about it. No problem." She jumped up, leaned over the table and kissed Gerusha on the cheek. "You're so pretty and I love you so much. We're going to have great fun together."

Standing by the door, she pointed her finger at Gerusha and spoke with fake scolding. "But I'm not jogging; that's out," she said before bouncing out of the room.

CHAPTER EIGHT

Erik

He played the same CD over and over. The first full-length TSS disc, recorded in a warehouse-like studio in North Hollywood. The sounds brought back great memories. The sessions were financed with money Raz borrowed from his parents. For Erik, it represented the last of the really good times.

While sitting in the listing Airstream, Erik ate Lucky Charms from a box and nodded his head in time with the music. Only memories of resin were left in the bowl of his bong, but he fired up the lighter and tried anyway. Moving the flame around the edges of the bowl, he got a hint of smoke. Sherie's direct deposit would magically appear in her bank account in two days, so he had to wait before he could use her debit card.

His credit was poor with the Cambodian gang that served the area. On payday, they would give him a ride to the bank and sell him smoke for cash. Buddha Bud, pot laced with opium, was the only thing that got him off. He craved the peace and safe harbor he found in the smoke. Sadly, this bliss had to wait until payday.

After running out of propane for the furnace, the trailer was cold. He wore all of his clothing, layers and layers of sweaters covered by a wool army blanket with a hole hacked out for his head to poke through. On the table, surrounded by empty beer cans, lay the Thompson Contender pistol he'd shot Sherie with: a single-shot .30-.30 with rubber grip and a fourteen inch barrel.

He couldn't recall why he'd shot her. She was bitching about something or the other, and, just as surprised as she was, he'd found he'd pulled the trigger. She lay on her side with the question etched in her eyes while blood pooled in a large, messy puddle on the carpet. Laid to rest in the cramped bathroom shower stall, she smelled so putrid he didn't go in there anymore. Even with frigid temperatures and covered with twenty pounds of corn meal he found in a cupboard, she still emitted a nasty reek. Something climbed in the window and ate at her. Eventually, he supposed she'd be only gristle and bone, and easier to carry. Then, perhaps he'd bury her proper-like.

Her cat missed her and meowed constantly, so, as an act of compassion, he shot it too. Its body was easy to deal with; he swung it around his head by its tail and lobbed it deep into the woods. Problem solved. Disposing of Sherie would be a larger problem.

Sometimes he thought about loading the pistol with one of the cartridges lined up on the table and shooting himself in the head. One easy pull of the trigger and it would all be over. Then Raz and the other assholes that hated him and stole his life would be sorry. The cold world would be deprived of his genius. Usually when he felt this way he'd smoke a bowl and lose himself in the music and dream of the day he'd kill 'Razorblade' Smith. He'd shoot Raz in the heart and enjoy watching life fade from his eyes as he died.

He selected a bullet and loaded the long pistol. It was hard to move under all the clothing, but he waddled down the hallway and pushed open the bathroom door. Sherie looked like a melted wax figure. The overwhelming smell of decay was sweet and sickening. He couldn't stand to look at her closely, so he pointed the gun in her general direction and fired. Her body jerked and moist flecks of her flesh speckled his face. With ears ringing, he pushed the door closed and tried to forget they way she looked splayed out in the shower stall.

Restless and hungry, he looked through the cupboards. He was tired of Lucky Charms, but there was nothing else. He stabbed sweet marshmallow bits onto the points of the cartridges and admired them lined up like little soldiers with funny hats. Stars, moons and what were these things?

Horseshoes and balloons.

It was better than having no food in the house, but not much.

Gerusha and Bubb

On Saturday morning, Gerusha, propped up on a pillow, sat in her bed and read through the Seattle Times while sipping from a bone china cup of black tea. Idly, she flicked a fingernail on the delicate cup. Ting! She had not looked at the china set inherited from her grandmother the same since Glen told her real bone was used in the clay. Human bone, he'd said, but she knew that was untrue.

Unbidden, Glen's bullshit drifted through her thoughts. Looking around the room, she admired the tall ceilings of her apartment and the bright morning sunlight that poured in from the southwest windows. Solar radiation. Visible, ultraviolet, infrared and x-rays, photons of many energies dying in her apartment after traveling from the sun's nuclear furnace.

Glen! Get out of my head!

Why did he ruin her simple pleasures? She tapped her forehead as if a secret reset button was hidden there. The solitude of her Saturday morning was ruined by toilets flushing and doors slamming. The upstairs neighbors walked around sounding as if they wore hob-nailed logging boots. She heard the insane Jesus-freak on the street. He wore a sandwich sign bearing passages from the Bible. With

119

nightclothes billowing in the breeze, she opened the sliding door and called down to him from her little balcony.

"Take it uptown, Reverend."

"There is precious little time to repent, harlot," he said.

However, there were sinners at the Seattle Center that needed the word, so he ambled toward his usual daytime spot by the Elephant Car Wash.

Am I ready to leave this place?

There was a pang in her belly.

She'd miss living here.

And what am I buying?

It's one thing to punish Glen by spending an insane amount of money to buy a dump, but everyone would expect her to live there too.

Can I pretend to live there and keep this apartment?

That would avoid the whole 'sleeping-with-Glen-who-is-a-disgusting-and-perverted-pig' thing she dreaded. Regardless, that left the 'Glen-is-my-husband' thing that needed to be faced.

"What have I done to my life?" she groaned.

She looked at her face in the mirror. This would never do. She patted Crème de La Mer onto her cheeks and rubbed it in briskly.

I have to rise and embrace the day.

She tried a cheerful smile, but it looked false. Her eyes were tired and sad.

She studied the selection of shoes arranged on a long rack in her closet. Glen didn't know it, but his debit card had bought her a pretty pair of Versace sneakers flecked with ruby-colored jewels. That was what she needed to get the day off to a good start.

While looking for a spatula to turn her French toast, she found one of Glen's dirty socks in a drawer. She was always finding his dirty underclothes in odd places, but today? Today, she would let it slide. This would not ruin anything. After picking up his sock with a pair of salad tongs and throwing it off the deck, she put the salad tongs in the dishwasher.

That's better.

After breakfast, she put the dirty dishes in the sink to soak. Bubb was supposed to pick her up at nine.

Could that be him outside honking?

She poked her head over her deck railing. It was a powder blue Lexus. Bubb.

"I hear you," she shouted. "Knock it off with the honking already. I'm coming down."

When she appeared on the street, Bubb opened his passenger door for her with a flourish.

"Adjust the seat anyway you like, m'lady. It goes up, down, left, right, and sideways. Would you like the seat heaters on? Women love the seat heaters. Isn't it a great morning? Should we swing through a coffee place? I'm buying, so you get whatever you want."

"Okay," Gerusha said, "there's a Starbucks drive-thru on Queen Anne."

She ordered a short double non-fat latté with lots of room, an eighth-inch of foam and no straw. Bubb ordered a grandé Americano with cream and sugar and they were on their way. They had to backtrack down Queen Anne and circle around to get to the Magnolia District, but it was early and traffic was light.

All the way, Bubb chattered.

"The neighborhood is very quiet, class-to-the-max. Old-money Seattle, if you catch my drift. Trees everywhere, so it's nice and green, but your view from the top floor is incredible. If I could figure out how to finance the deal, I'd buy it myself. You're one lucky lady, that's for sure."

"How many bedrooms?"

"That depends. There are rooms galore and some can be bedrooms or a sewing room, craft room, storage, what have you. You could have five bedrooms, or you could have nine or anywhere in-between, depending on how you arrange things."

"How many square feet?"

"I'm not sure. There was no time to measure it. The owners had it a long time, so there's no record with the county. At least six-thousand square feet, maybe sixty-five hundred."

Bubb rubbed his mouth nervously. The deal was closing in a matter of days and was as solid as they come, but, in his experience, there was always something that could come between him and a commission check.

"I'll warn you, the curb appeal is not up to snuff. The place is rough around the edges. It never made it to the market, so the landscaping needs sprucing up and the house can use a good cleaning, but there's no major problem. Pressure wash the moss here and there, give the lawn a good mowing and thatching, prune and shape the hedges, that's about it. There are no structural problems I know of."

"Did you arrange for an inspection?"

"No, there was no time to slide it into the quick schedule. The owners weren't accepting contingencies and other offers were coming. We needed to move quickly or lose the deal."

"What's the appraised value?"

By this time, Bubb mumbled.

"We didn't do a formal appraisal. It wasn't necessary. Since your company is writing a check, there's no bank to satisfy."

"So, that means the only estimate of its value is your word."

"Yes, that's true, but I assure you—"

"Bubb, I'm getting tired of hearing your voice. Drink your coffee and get us there—"

"Yes ma'am."

"—in complete silence, please."

Bubb closed his mouth, nodded and drove.

The streets in the neighborhood were narrow and winding. She looked for signs of children, but there were no bicycles, Big Wheels, or skateboards abandoned on the neat front yards. They wove toward the Puget Sound and caught peek-a-boo views of blue water through the trees and between the houses. They parked in front of a large dark house.

"Can I speak?" Bubb asked.

She nodded.

"This, my dear Gerusha, is your new home."

He pointed.

Her heart thudded deep into her stomach. The house looked abandoned, as if haunted. The shutters were closed tight. Forlorn-looking trees and overgrown hedges cast everything into deep shadow. The house was at least a hundred years old. In her mind, when she visualized her dream house, it was the polar opposite of this monstrosity. She wanted something in the suburbs with modern, light-colored siding, a clay tile roof, and features like a burbling fountain or brick-accented carriage lights. Glen wanted something in the city for investment purposes.

Here's your goddam investment, jerk-off.

"Please tell me you're joking."

"I told you the curb appeal is lacking, but everything can be easily fixed," he said. There was a desperate edge to Bubb's voice.

"Can you easily fix it so I can push the reset button and start over again?"

"No, this is your house. However, you can flip it quickly. I could re-list it for you and turn it around in a jiffy…"

He had a sudden vision of collecting another large commission check. It made his penis tingle.

"If I resell this place, I'll sure as hell find another realtor."

Bubb's tingle dissipated.

"It's your house. You might as well take a look around. Give it a chance. We'll start on the top floor."

"We'll start by looking at the grounds and the garage," she said.

"Okay, as you wish," Bubb said.

Walking up the crumbling driveway, she noted more weeds than concrete. Around back, four mossy apple trees lurked with rotting fruit strewn around. The sickly-sweet scent made her dizzy. She wrestled open a heavy garage door. A car rested under a dusty canvas. The only parts visible were flat whitewall tires. The place was filled with cobwebs and mice droppings, so she was not inclined to enter and explore. In the center of the back yard, a massive fountain loomed. It was about eight feet tall and overgrown with blackberry vines. A carpet of moldy leaves covered the yard. It was impossible to tell if the ground was dirt, grass, or paved in some manner. A crow chattered in the bare tree limbs and she felt as if she'd fallen into an Edgar Allen Poe novel.

Quoth the raven, get the hell out of this miserable place before the paperwork gets signed.

On paper, she'd be half-owner. It was a living nightmare.

"Rent a leaf blower and we'd have it spruced up in no time."

"A leaf blower and 14 dump trucks might make a dent in it."

"You don't see the potential?"

"I see the potential that I'm going to kill you slowly. It's really too late to back out?"

"That's correct," Bubb said firmly. He hoped the bluff would hold. It was never too late to back out of a deal; happened all the time. Usually when he'd already spent the commission check. He couldn't afford to lose this one. "Let me take you in and show you the top floor where the view will put the sparkle back in your pretty eyes."

"Is this big flippin' mess the minor *detail* you hinted at?"

"This weekend's worth of clean-up work? This is nothing."

"Great," Gerusha said.

Bubb fumbled through his key ring and worked open the back door. The back porch opened onto a mud room. Validating the name, there was plenty of dried mud. It looked like an indoor swamp.

"This gets better and better."

Walking through a short hallway, they climbed the back stairway. Ancient grimy photographs hung on the wall, but Gerusha didn't care, so she ignored them. Most of the light fixtures were filled with dead, dusty bulbs. The ambience was dark and depressing. It smelled like a moth's grandmother's closet. At the top of the stairs, she poked her head into a bedroom. It was filled with a hospital bed and medical equipment.

"It smells like someone died in here."

"Um," Bubb said.

"Oh no, don't even say it."

After closing the door, she leaned against it. Her breathing was ragged. After marshalling energy to move, she tried a door that opened into a small bathroom.

"Excuse me for a minute," she said.

She entered and slammed the heavy door. After flipping down the olive-green, carpet-covered toilet lid, she sat. The bath area was covered in tile; large squares decorated with lurid brown Mexican designs. Hideous. An over-sized tub with claw feet had a thick layer of dust and dead spiders coating its bottom. It was all too much.

As she sobbed, her shoulders shook and tears streamed down her face. She could not stop; her sorrows cascaded. She wondered what she'd done to offend the Gods to such a heartrending degree.

CHAPTER NINE

Glen

In Denver, they were taken down for the first time. Glen blamed himself. Hung over, he was off his game. His thoughts were fractured along tectonic faults. Scattered thoughts flitted. Raz's face, bearing an enigmatic, self-satisfied grin, hovered over his temporary madness like a harvest moon.

During sound check, Glen napped. Uncomfortably sprawled across nose-bleed seats, he dosed his aching brainstem with Midol Menstrual Complete which disassociated him from his head's pounding pain. Unfortunately, there was a side-effect. He felt the urge to piss every five minutes.

He was also disassociated from himself. Eerily, his mind's 'I' floated a few feet above his head. It made him feel schizophrenic, seasick and slow.

Murphy tapped him on the shoulder and motioned for him to follow. Time to get to work.

The promoter was a former football quarterback dressed immaculately with a suit jacket over a turtleneck sweater. His hands were remarkable. Huge with mutant, monstrous fingers. Perhaps it was the drugs, but Glen did not enjoy shaking that hand. He unreasonably feared the promoter would rip off his arm and eat it. Again, tequila was not his friend. Murphy chose from identical backpacks and worked the straps on his shoulders. She looked into his eyes with no sign of motherly sympathy.

"Are you sure you're up to this?" she asked. "You're green around the gills."

"Don't bust my balls, just gimme the damn bag."

He didn't feel confident. More worrisome, he felt nothing. How many Midol had he taken? Six, all told? Too many. If he carried the money and not phone books, then he'd have four hundred and fifty-seven thousand dollars strapped to his ailing body. It was part of their strategy that he didn't know what his backpack contained.

Get the mission done and take a nap, that's all he cared about.

A direct route to the bank's office was about a mile, but he walked, shambling like a bum, following a round-about path. Jesus had a rented a huge, comfortable SUV and took off from the Pepsi Center valet parking lot. Glen didn't like the grin as Jesus, stopped at the red light, watched him risk his life crossing against traffic on the Auraria Parkway. Disgusted and angry with life, Glen walked across a soccer field. It wasn't raining, but it was cold and misty. Soon his shoes were soaked through and his feet frozen. Cursing the clear-eyed and fresh-faced students, the city, and life in general, he walked across a corner of the UC Denver campus.

He crossed 15th Street and wasn't paying attention to anything but his aching head and starving lungs (in the thin air, he couldn't seem to catch his breath), when two men wearing ski masks dragged him into a narrow alley between two tall buildings. In seconds, they jammed a wad of paper towel in his mouth and wrapped a length of strapping tape around his head to hold it. He struggled as they taped his arms together and sliced through the straps of the backpack with evil-looking hunting knives; it took about twenty seconds. Immobilized, he could not reach his .45 or his cell phone. The only things he could move were his eyeballs. When they covered his head with a paper sack, they were useless too. He could hear sawing sounds as they cut open the sport bag.

"Phone books!"

"How come they both had phone books?" the other voice hissed.

"Shut your face."

"Let's grease this slimy motherfucker."

"The boss said leave him be."

They threw the bag of books onto Glen's belly. He concentrated on not throwing up. He didn't want to expire in this alley, choking on vomit like a rock star. The men argued while walking away. Glen shivered on the cold pavement and felt sorry for himself. He tossed his head until the paper bag fell off. Then at least, he could see while dying.

Jesus and Glen both carried phone books.

Murphy.

How'd she do it?

Both Glen and Jesus were turned around when she strapped on the backpacks. Clever.

The thieves worked for someone. Mafia? What could he remember about them? White guys without noteworthy accents. Average heights and weights. Nothing useful.

If Murphy was so damn smart, then why am I freezing my ass off in this alley with only an angry rat for company?

The rat turned red, jealous eyes on Glen. As if Glen might steal the forage; the nasty, rotting shit that fell out around the dumpster.

For an hour, he lay in the alley like a homeless bum. He would never forgive the man, dressed in a suit and expensive overcoat, who darted into the alley to take a leak. He saw Glen, but refused to be drawn into Glen's drama. He shook his dripping dick and walked off.

Fucker.

Toxic Shock Syndrome

While cold seeped into his bones, Glen had nothing else to do but think.

He didn't preplan his route, so how could the thieves know? He watched and knew he was not followed across the University of Colorado campus. Student foot traffic was light. A tail would be evident. Few pedestrian bridges crossed the Cherry Creek canal; were they all watched? Was a tracking device inserted in the backpack? The way Glen figured it, luck didn't fit in the equation.

Finally, he was found. With his fat, moony face, Jesus looked down at Glen, trussed up and helpless as a baby.

One day, he'll pay for his twisted grin.

After Jesus tore off the gaffer's tape, Glen tongued out the slobbery paper towel.

"Murphy made it okay?"

"They smashed my window when I stopped for a light on 24th. Put a gun to my head. Made me drive into an alley."

"Who gives a shit about you? I know Murphy had the dough. Did she make it?"

"Yeah, she made it and called it in. She's looking for you over by Sonny Lawson Park. How'd you know?"

"I figured it out. You going to cut me loose?"

"I kind of like you this way."

He couldn't get much leverage, but it had to hurt when Glen kicked Jesus just below his rebuilt knee.

"Don't do that again," Jesus said.

"Cut me loose," Glen replied.

Murphy was inordinately pleased with herself. She smiled while delicately picking Brazil nuts out of a large crystal serving bowl. They were in a club-level suite where Glen stood in front of the plate-glass window looking over the arena while drinking another bottle of water, his third. His mouth was dry and he could not get enough to drink. He watched the last-minute activities on the stage; workers climbed the light and sound rigging like spider monkeys.

"Raz was really surprised when *I* called in the deposit."

"Was he surprised it was you or that the money actually made it?"

She quickly figured out Glen's implication and didn't like it. Jesus glanced between them, sensing, but not knowing.

"Try to be a good sport, Glen. It was nothing personal; you were both too messed up to be reliable. Give me credit for being right. Can we go back over the descriptions? White males, medium builds, no accents? That's unhelpful."

"They wore black nylon running suits and plain black ski masks. They didn't give me anything to work with."

"Jesus?"

"They pointed a gun at my head, I moved over. They didn't say anything. When they found the phone books, they ran off."

"Forget description. Any impressions?"

Jesus thought about it. "They were smooth."

Murphy turned to Glen and looked over her notes. "'How come they both had phone books?' 'Slimy mother-F-er?' 'The boss said let him be?' That's what they said? They don't sound so stupid. Most criminals are dumb-heads. Slimy implies foreknowledge of you. Is that troublesome?"

"Yes, Murphy, it troubles me."

They didn't act like random muggers... A boss steered them.

The stakes were increased. They would have to work smarter. With ten more stops on this tour, there were ten more chances for things to go askew.

Yes, I was troubled.

130

Emma

Far from the peaceful tranquility of the executive offices, Emma staked a claim on a cubicle near a software support group. By a stairwell, it was rarely quiet, but she grew accustomed to the racket of doors closing, headphones whispering, telephones squawking, and loud hallway arguments over arcane algorithms. White noise, piped over the public address system, helped, but her mind needed to tune out distractions or no work would ever get done. Her doorway was delineated by a woolen Inuit blanket draped over a shower curtain rod. This provided a small measure of privacy. In addition to routine clerical work for the company, she did most of her University of Washington homework there.

Bored, she surfed the Toxic Shock Syndrome website and clicked around the site map. She found the typical fare: tour schedule, music and video samples, a shopping area for downloads and merchandise, fan forums, Raz's tour blogs and the band history/biography. She could sign up for access to the forum and updates, but she found no special girls' fanclub. She had homework for her UW Biostatistical Methods class—applying the Kaplan-Meier survivor function to epidemiological datasets—so there was no time for trivialities like joining rock band fanclubs. Being busy all the time was frustrating.

Bennie poked his head through her blanket-door.

"Whatcha doing?"

He had stringy strands of gray fuzz in his hair.

Cobwebs?

"Oh Bennie, what have you been into?" She rubbed his head and worked out the worst of the fibers. "I'm fighting with this dog-blasted website."

"Have you tried entreating Nunaliuqti for assistance?"

131

"Don't mock my ancestor's Inuit shamanism. Nunaliuqti, the Earth Maker, will curse you."

"No, that's what I'm calling my new synthetic-intelligence search engine." He scratched his nappy head. "Maybe it's something easy. Try uploading your profile. Perhaps a private invitation will be issued if you match a personality contour. If that doesn't work, I'll run Nunaliuqti for you. Gotta scoot."

She pursed her lips for a kiss, but Bennie was gone, leaving her feeling silly.

"I love you too, sweetie," she muttered.

Earlier, she'd skipped through the profile section and loaded only enough information to get full web access. She went back, uploaded her photograph and filled out all the optional data fields. There were many. The site asked intrusive questions about family history, education, allergies, height, weight, marital status, number of children, and other medical information. One section appeared to be a simple psychometric IQ test. Her interest was piqued.

Why so much detailed information for a rock band fan club?

She looked at her watch. Time had evaporated. Biostatistical Methods could not wait any longer; her epidemiological paper was overdue. Minimizing the TSS website window, she immersed herself in specificity, temporality and biological gradients.

Gerusha and Bubb

After crying herself dry, the absurdity of Gerusha's situation struck her. The house was a horror. A repugnant, malignant, cancerous wart on the ass of the city. A stinking pile of shit dumped on Seattle by a squatting giant.

What would Glen say when he saw it? What would he do? Splash gasoline on it and burn it to the ground? Fall down and gnash his teeth and froth at the mouth like a rabid wombat? Maybe the overwhelming horror would drive him to suicide. Perhaps he'd run away screaming and throw himself off the Magnolia Bridge.

Whatever he did, it would serve him right. Screw him.

Rising from the toilet and brushing at the seat of her pants, she admired the toilet in a new light. The shag carpet on the toilet seat was a sickly, pukey green. Perfect.

Just what Glen deserves.

She wiggled the handle. There was no water, so the handle flopped limply in her hand.

Excellent.

Outside, Bubb paced up and down the hallway. Finally he worked up the courage to check on her.

"Is everything okay?"

"I'm coming out," she said. "There's no water in this bathroom."

"I'm sure it's just shut off."

"Right," she said. "Let's see the rest of it."

Roaming, she looked into each room. They were filled with large pieces of old furniture. The smells of dust, mold and decay were oppressive and overwhelming. The more she saw, the happier she became.

Maybe Glen's cold heart will seize at the sight of all this. 'Buy me a house, something nice.'

Jerk.

At the end of the hall, she found a large bedroom. She looked in briefly and slammed the door before anything could crawl out. As the doors closed, something caught her eye. Refracted light streamed through heavy glass French doors. The door creaked on complaining hinges as she opened it again. Moving quickly and hoping nothing would attack her ankles, she strode to the doors and worked them open.

A wrought-iron dining set, covered in rotting vegetation, rested on the deck. She walked to the rail and looked over the yard. The gutters, pulling away from the house, overflowed with black leaves and damp gunk. The only spot on the roof that was not covered with a thick moss carpet was a swath where a large branch had fallen and carved a rough gash into the lush green.

On the other hand, the view was phenomenal. The blue sky merged into the darker marine of Puget Sound. A flotilla of sailboats danced on Elliot Bay's choppy water. The view included the top of a lighthouse and mist-draped Olympic Mountains in the distance. Leaning over the railing and peering through trees, she could see the top of the Space Needle and Mount Rainier.

"All the furniture comes with the house," Bubb said proudly.

More crap to haul to the land fill.

"That's great," she said.

"The place next door sold for four-point-five million in 2002."

"I really don't care, but I might as well see the rest of the place before I kill you."

"You're funny," he said.

The second floor showcased a huge library with towering shelves filled with old leather-bound books. She pulled one down at random. *Last of the Great Scouts, the Life Story of Col. William F. Cody.* As told by his sister, 1899. Number 59 of 500. It would take a crew of ten, a fleet of large trucks and endless trips to the landfill to clear out this room alone.

Not my problem.

She took down another title. *Howl and Other Poems* by Allen Ginsberg with clumps of hand-written scribbles on the title page. She flipped through the book.

"—yacketayakking screaming vomiting whispering facts and
memories and anecdotes
and eyeball kicks and shocks of hospitals and jails and wars—"

Ouch, that's really bad.

She plugged the book back into the gap on the shelf. She heard a muffled thump from downstairs.

"Bubb? What was that?"

"Before you go down, there is something I should explain…"

"Get out of the way."

Marching resolutely, she located the main stairway. Wide enough for a parade of soldiers, it curved into a reception area landing. The thick carpet runner emitted puffs of dust as she stomped downward. Muffled noises came from a back room. Shafts of light escaped through gaps in the doorway and speared dust motes. Gathering her nerve, she threw open the door. The room was filled with blinding light from industrial fluorescent fixtures hanging from chains. A grossly obese woman sat on the edge of a chair staring at globs of paint spattered on a canvas.

"Would you mix me up a pitcher of Tang, please? We don't have any, so you'll have to go to the store. Mix it up good. I don't like the gritty powder on the bottom of the glass. It's vulgar. In the future, everything will be instant and there will be powder at the bottom of everything. That's why I don't like thinking about the future."

"Who the hell are you?"

Bubb elbowed around Gerusha. "Let me introduce you, ladies. Gerusha, this is Rose."

"That's fine but *who* is she?"

"She sort of comes with the place," Bubb said, his words spilling like dirty dishwater.

Gerusha looked around the room while blinking her eyes in the blinding light. Paintings were stacked all around. They were bizarre, stygian nightmares captured on canvas.

"Yes, thank you, this is wonderful." Ignoring danger to her clothes, Gerusha grabbed the woman in a bear hug. She tried to lift her off her feet, but could not. Gerusha's arms only reached partially around. Giving up, she raised her hands to the sky and laughed hysterically.

"Yes, perfect. Pile it on."

"I would like a glass of Tang, please," Rose said.

CHAPTER TEN

Glen

Raz, with a bath towel draped across his shoulders, paced. Damp from a post-soundcheck shower, his tousled hair fell around his face. His money had made it to the bank, so Glen expected him to be happier. Tilted back in a folding chair, Murphy scribbled notes in a spiral-bound notebook. Jesus, hunched over, studied scars on his work-coarsened hands.

"Neither of you carried the money? You were both targeted, but neither carried the cash," Raz mused, staring over a bottle of water at Glen. His mood was impossible to read. "They took you down even though you were armed?"

"They came on fast," Jesus said defensively. "There was no time to respond. I'm not Superman."

"How about you, Glen? Are you Superman?"

Still hung over, he couldn't think of a snappy response, so he remained silent. Something hinky nibbled at his subconscious, but he could not pinpoint it.

"No one called the cops?"

"Didn't see the need to get them involved," Glen said.

Murphy glanced up from her notepad.

"I don't like the guns," Raz said. "The money is important, but I don't want anyone to get hurt over it. What do they do in banks?"

Murphy spoke. "They follow the robber's instructions and hand over the money. They let the cops sort things out later."

"The banks don't like to be sued by a dead teller's family. They'd rather cough up the cash up front," Glen said.

"That's cynical," Murphy said.

"That will be our policy. We'll do what the banks do."

Leaning forward, Murphy said, "Make a mental note of everything. Height, weight, accents, tattoos, jewelry, scars, what direction they go, and get a description of their car."

"I don't see the need for you to be armed," Raz said. "Lose the guns."

"You'd be dead if I hadn't shot that nut-job in Houston."

"Not you, Murphy. Just the guys. Give up your guns to Murphy."

Raz walked out and left them looking at each other.

"You heard the man. I'll take your weapon."

Glen snorted. "Ha."

"I figured," she said. "At least keep it out of sight."

"You're the boss," Glen said.

At that, it was her turn to snort. "Right."

She left. Jesus and Glen stared at each other.

"Unless you're in on it, I don't know how they zeroed in on us so quickly."

"I was thinking the same about you. We need a new plan," Jesus said.

"I'm open to suggestion."

"Splitting up isn't working. How about the original plan? One carries and the other watches?"

Glen thought it over.

"Fine," he said.

Toxic Shock Syndrome

An hour later, the show started. Fighting the effects of his lingering hangover, Glen stuffed foam earplugs into his ears and wandered through the general admission mob on the main floor of the arena. With multiple levels of backstage passes around his neck, the security team did not bother him. The paying customers were young, stereotypical, suburban yuppie-spawn. Massive denim trousers, never touched by dirt or hard work, drooped loosely around their waists. He was long-tired of this style and imagined these kids when they were older; middle-aged men with bandanas, backwards hats and huge billowing acres of denim hanging off their fat asses.

They wore tattoos like human graffiti and everything visible was pierced; eyebrows, lips, ear lobes, nostrils, and bellybuttons.

A young man, with a smooth, bare chest and blood-red contacts in his eyes, flicked a grotesque forked tongue at him. Glen wanted to hit him hard enough to matter, but could not dredge up the energy. The punk would probably like it anyway. Looking for the thread of theme, Glen thought of the time and energy spent on hair, clothes and the cultivation of their carefree, spoiled attitudes. Mallrats, spending endless hours on skateboards and sitting in front of video games. This is how a rich country utilizes the luxury of leisure.

He shouldn't be so cynical; there were many good kids in the crowd, fresh-faced and clear-eyed. He recognized Raz girl candidates—small girls dressed in practical clothes watching him with wary intelligence, as if pre-warned. Like they could tell what he was thinking. For example, one girl stood and oscillated her hips with the pounding beat. He stopped and hefted her medallion. He did not get a good look before she batted his hand away.

"No," she mouthed in the raging cacophony of sound.

He waved the backstage passes and inclined his head in invitation.

I'm with the band. Want to go backstage and party?

"Go away," she mouthed with a faint smile on her innocent lips.

He paid no attention to the music until it died. The lights faded and Raz stood, center stage, in a tight beam of bright spotlight. He held out his hand and the guitar tech handed him a battered Gibson L-0 acoustic with patches of bare wood scuffed in the finish. He played a slow blues and it took Glen a moment to catch on. He copped Glen's performance—barring frets with a middle finger on a guitar tuned to an open-string Em. Glen was angry.

Is he mocking me?

He wanted to run to the stage and beat him silent. The crowd swayed and Raz had them breathing the chorus:

> *Must have been the devil,*
> *Believe that woman has gone mad...*
> *Must have been the devil,*
> *Believe that woman has gone mad...*

He motioned for the crowd to keep singing and waved to stage right. Helped by fake Raz twins, a middle-aged black woman came out. She stood stiffly in the spotlight, frozen and confused. Raz lowered to his knees and kissed her hand. He reached his hand backwards and a bouquet of roses was placed in it. He stood, handed her the roses, and urged her to address the crowd.

She waved tentatively at the raucous audience. Raz got up and, holding her hand in the air like a heavyweight champion, pulled her to the microphone. While she stood, shivering in nervousness, a guitar tech handed him a shiny Gibson semi-acoustic guitar. He strummed the sparkling, skeletal chords of a different song.

> Now, if I can make a half a million
> I declare, I'm gone give it all to the hoodoo man

Toxic Shock Syndrome

I declare, if I can make a half a million
I'm gone give it all to the hoodoo man
Just after he promise me that he will
Bring my lovin' Lorenzo, back home to me, again
An' I want her back ho—oh—ome, to me again.

"Ladies and gentlemen, please welcome the only known descendent of Nehemiah James. Skip James' daughter, Takeisha Lorenzo James-Schaefer. Tell her how we feel. Tell her we love her."

He led the crowd in a gentle, whispered chant.

"We. Love. You. Takeisha…"

Something swept through the crowd like a spiritual wind, something that touched Glen's bones with cold. Was it imagined? Did Raz's piercing eyes find him in the crowd and lock on?

The fact is, he beat me. Beat me silly.

Ten hours earlier, Glen had pulled the old Skip James song out of thin air.

With so little time, how did he find this woman and bring her to Denver?

Did he send his private jet to Mississippi or Illinois or wherever? It seemed impossible. Glen couldn't get his mind around the premise. Itching to strangle Raz slowly, his fingers twitched. But, he had to admit, Raz rubbed Glen's face in arrogance and provided a lesson in humility, like rubbing a kitten's face in its urine. Glen was outclassed.

The fake Razs led the woman off stage. At the far fringe, she stopped and waved. A whispering wind flowed through the swarm.

"Thank you for your patience," Raz shouted. "Shall we get back to our rock show?"

The audience erupted while the ghostly song echoed in Glen's head.

I'm gone give it all to the hoodoo man...

Emma

A day later, while analyzing and collating data from axial, cyclotron and magnetron electrode measurements developed by a quadrupole Penning/Dehmelt Barium Ion trap for her Physics 432 (Modern Physics Laboratory - Atomic and Molecular Physics) class, Emma received an instant message.

TSS: Hello Emma, thank you for registering on the TSS website. Your picture is lovely.

Emma thumbed in a reply: Thank you.

TSS: There is a very special fan club for young women. It's called the Advanced Evolutionary Force (AEF). Would you like more details?

Emma: Yes.

TSS: There are additional requirements. First off, a notarized Non-Disclosure Agreement (NDA) is required. You can download this NDA (I will email a password-enabled link), but it must be express delivered back before we can continue. Please understand that we take privacy and security very seriously. I will text you again with more details once I've received the NDA. In the meantime, I would like to send you a TSS CD of your choice as an honorarium. Which CD would you like?

Emma quickly opened a new browser window and surfed to Amazon.

How many discs are there?

She picked one at random.

Emma: Please send The Dogma of Empiricism.

TSS: Excellent choice, one of my favorites, recorded live in Madison Square Garden. We'll get it shipped out right away. All the best to you and I look forward to receiving your NDA. Remember, it must be notarized or we can't accept it. Until then...

She copied the website link into her browser, entered the password (EmmaRocks) and downloaded the NDA. Printed, it was seven pages of fine-print legalese. Immortality had an executive assistant, Doris, with notary authority. Emma walked over and, with Doris as witness, signed. Doris applied the notary stamp and countersigned.

"Does anyone actually read these things?" Doris asked.

"Not me," Emma replied.

She dropped the NDA off in the shipping department, sent it on its way, and then returned to her physics homework. Musing, she shook her head with wonder.

The Advanced Evolutionary Force.

Bizarre.

Gerusha and Bubb

While sitting in Bubb's car, Gerusha watched him kick sodden leaves in the yard. She'd asked for a minute of privacy and he didn't know what she was thinking.

He probably thinks I'm calling my lawyer to sue his ass off.

The house squatted in malevolent, gothic horror. She sat with her finger on the send button of her cell phone, dredging up the nerve to call Walter.

What did the president of Immortality, a former Las Vegas sorcerer, do with his Saturdays? Summon evil spirits? Work on PowerPoint slides for investors?

In answering the phone, Walter did not waste time.

"Who is speaking, please?" he asked.

"I'm sorry to trouble you on a Saturday, but I didn't know who else to call."

"Ah, Gerusha." His voice softened. "What troubles you?"

"This house I bought. It's indescribable. A mess."

"Please come to the point. Does it need cleaning or maintenance? You're leasing it back to the company as a remote research facility. Do what's needed and have the bills sent to the company. You're in charge of vendor relations, so vendor it out."

"It's a weird situation. I suppose I'm nervous about the deal..."

"This is Seattle, for the Green Man's sake. It's damn near impossible to lose money in the Seattle real estate market. It's only a few million dollars—"

"Five million."

"Whatever it is, you're trying my patience. How does this make us money? Do what you need to do and call me again if something important comes up. The keyword is *important*. I have to go; I'm in the middle of someone."

She sat with the dead cell phone on her lap. Bubb dropped into the driver's seat and sat with his hands on the steering wheel.

"Okay, bottom line, where are we?"

"I wanted a modern house with skylights, an island kitchen, European track lighting, Berber carpets, a hot tub and a monogrammed refrigerator. You sold me, this, this—"

"It needs a clean-up, I won't argue that."

"—monstrosity. This hideous, grotesque, putrid, steaming heap of shit. It's filled with crap I don't want including a crazy fat woman who drinks Tang. I can't believe what you've done to me."

"Now Gerusha, I don't think you're being fair-minded."

"Stop talking, please. Get workers in to clean up this mess."

"I'm the real estate agent, so I don't get involved with labor. I can recommend contractors, get you a few phone numbers, that sort of thing."

She grabbed his collar and twisted. "You still need me to sign the fugging papers, don't you?"

Bubb squirmed. "Yes," he said through clenched teeth.

"Get this place cleaned up. It's not like I'm asking you to, heaven forbid, do any of the work yourself or spend your own flipping money. Fix the plumbing, clean up the yard, have the mattresses replaced, install new appliances and get it ready to move in. Have the invoices sent to Immortality."

"It will cost…"

"I know what it will cost. Well into six figures. I don't give a flying fig. Get it done."

"Yes, ma'am," Bubb said, beaten.

"Take me home now."

"Yes, ma'am."

CHAPTER ELEVEN

Glen

Glen didn't see Raz much for the next few days. Who avoided whom? Glen was whipped like a disobedient cur. Trampled underfoot. Beaten down. He'd write a song about it, but Skip James had already said it all.

> You know I never missed my water
> till my well went dry
> Didn't miss Crow Jane until the day she died[7].

On the plane ride to Salt Lake City, Glen isolated himself with a sleep mask and earplugs. Once on the ground, he waved away the limousine, deciding to make his own way from the airport. After throwing his bag into a taxi, he watched the streets flow by his window. Ivory snow blanketed the Oquirrh Mountains that framed the city to the south and west and the Wasatch Mountains to the east.

Their rooms were booked at the City Center Marriott, but instead of checking in, he stayed outside feeling depressed and lonely. One-by-one, he tossed pennies into the Plaza Pool. Lost in his thoughts, his defenses were down, so he did not notice two teens on bicycles as they approached. When he finally noted their white shirts,

---

[7] Skip James, Crow Jane

black neckties and backpacks, it was too late. Having made eye contact, they would not be deflected.

"Brother, if you put your trust in the lord, all your troubles will be lifted away."

"You don't look like Mormons…"

"Seventh Day Adventists."

"Ah, well, you're wasting your time with me. Even if I was willing to stop masturbating, I love camel steaks[8] too much to give them up. Grilled medium with peppercorns? You don't know what you're missing. On the other hand, I'll give you guys credit. I enjoy a big bowl of Frosted Flakes[9] now and then. Anyway, if I decide to embrace religion, I will start my own and make a killing. Glen Wilson, latter day prophet. I like the sound of that."

"Excuse me, sir?"

"Never mind. Usually I see the Mormons or Jehovah's riding around on bicycles…"

"Jehovah is the Lord God. The J-W missionaries prefer to be called Witnesses."

"I know, I'm being needlessly confrontational and insulting. Hand over the Watchtower and be on your way with you."

"Sir, again, it's the J-W's that publish the Watchtower. We publish the Adventist Review."

"You seem to know a lot about the Jehovahs. You used to be one?"

"No sir."

Glen unwrapped a cigar.

---

[8] There are some that only chew the cud or only have a split hoof, but you must not eat them. The camel, though it chews the cud, does not have a split hoof; it is ceremonially unclean for you. New International Bible, Leviticus, Chapter 11, Verse 4.

[9] Dr. John H. Kellogg, the originator of flaked cereals, was an influential figure in the Adventist church.

"Do either of you boys carry matches?"

They shook their heads.

"No, that would make you useful. Boys, time is of the essence and I have more sinning to accomplish before I die. Beat it."

A scrap of song drifted through his head.

> You go your way, I'll go mine,
> and we'll get along just fine…

He could find a private-club bar, become a temporary member, and down a few drinks to help him forget how low he was on the cosmic totem pole. He wasn't himself. Generally, the Glen Wilson way was illuminated as if by spotlight. Even molesting bible-thumpers didn't raise his spirits. He puffed on his cigar and got a little lift from the way passersby glared at him.

A mother, pushing twins in a carriage, spoke to him in a scolding tone.

"Secondhand smoke kills six-thousand children each year."

"If you believe that, you're stupider than you look. And that would take doing."

Better.

Sparring with a defenseless young mother.

The smoke warmed him and cleared cobwebs from his mind. He waved the pamphlet at her. "Perhaps you'd like to read the word as passed down by the Seventh Day Adventists."

The look on her face showed she despised Adventists more than tobacco.

"Bugger off."

Wow, a 'bugger off' from a young Mormon mother.

"That was unchristian," he shouted at her expansive backside.

His soul was back from purgatory. He could reinvent psychotherapy.

Give the depressed a cigar and a soccer mom to insult and all would be well.

These days, no one used payphones except drug dealers. In this part of the city, the drug dealers were scarce, so he had a whole bank of phones to himself. It took a minute, but his revitalized mind regurgitated Gerusha's cell number.

"Hey, babe."

"Who is calling, please?"

Was she napping? Drunk? She seemed groggy.

"This is your loving husband calling from Salt Lake City. I'm checking in to see how you are. What's going on around there?"

"Um, not much? We're cleaning up your house for you. Making it ready. Taking care of minor repairs. I can't wait to see your face when you see it."

"What did you get? Is it nice?"

"It's perfect for you."

"Great." Something about her tone needed to be explored, but he refused to allow anything to disturb the delicate balance of his mood. "SLC is two hours away. You could fly down, rock my world, and have a nice dinner. Fly back and be at work like a normal drone tomorrow. What say you?"

"You make it sound so appealing... Unfortunately, I have a lot of work to do, so I'll pass. Why don't you jerk off in a sweat sock and pretend it's me?"

What did she think he'd been doing the last couple of weeks?

But she wasn't done. "Better yet, pretend it's someone else, I'd prefer that."

"I don't want to be unfaithful..."

149

"Our love is strong, we'll work through it. Look, if there's nothing else, I need to go."

She disconnected and left him staring at the handset. It made rude noises, so he ground out his cigar in the earpiece.

She needed lessons in dominance and submission to relieve her destructive passive-aggressions. Later.

He stole a glance at his watch. It was time to head inside, collect the money, and get the show going.

The rendezvous was in the Marriott. In the lobby, Glen admired the Beehive Hall of Fame and the plaque for Philo T. Farnsworth.

Philo was a pioneer in motion pictures, who knew?

Glen walked up the stairs and greeted the impatient Jesus at the top. In the small, plain meeting room, the clean-shaven promoter stared at the world with mad eyes. A true believer wearing an old-fashioned haircut. A wave of greasy black hair swept across his skull like a curling breaker. He wrinkled his nose at cigar smoke clinging to Glen's clothes.

"I hate dealing with so much cash," he said.

"We know," Jesus said.

The room had one window hidden behind a heavy curtain. From habit, Glen lifted the curtain to see what was outside. It was an ugly view of a loading dock. A group of heavyset Hispanic maids with hips straining for freedom under cute uniforms perched on benches under a small shelter, smoking and chatting. The window was painted shut, but Glen worked his knife into the seams and forced it open. Jesus watched with a crooked smile.

The promoter, tight-lipped, scowled at them. "You guys are crazy. 'Yea, a very cunning people, delighting in all manner of wickedness and plunder...'[10]"

---

[10] The Book of Morman, Book of Mosiah, Chapter 24, Verse 7.

"'Jesus I know, and Paul I know; but who are ye?'[11]" Glen said.
"You'd better get out of here before they blame you for the damage."

The promoter glared and pointed a finger. "You..."

Glen waved him off. "Scuttle away, little man."

He gestured for Jesus to climb through the window, then followed. Outside, he stopped to talk to the maids. They had sad eyes, as if they'd seen everything. Jesus stood at the edge of a concrete wall and waved at Glen to hurry up.

"*Me van las chatis con dos buenas peras. Grande agarraderas.*" It was imperfect Spanish slang, but they got the idea...

I like a girl with big tits.

Most of the women giggled. They were mothers, probably Catholics with mean-tempered men at home sharpening switchblades.

And me, a married man with no time to slow down and enjoy life. So it goes.

One of the ladies was offended. The sadness in her eyes was replaced with fire.

"*Castrozo chilito y dos albondigas.*"

Me, an annoying person with a little dick and two fish balls? That was a good one. Her eyes blazed with Latin fire and there was sexual promise in the aggressive set of her ample hips. Glen grinned at her.

"*El horno está listo para uno bollo.*"

The suggestion that her oven was ready for a bun brought a faint smile to her luscious lips.

"*Vete a freír espárragos.*"

He should go fry an asparagus.

Oh, the sadness of having so little time for banter.

---

[11] The Acts of the Apostles, Chapter 19, Verse 15.

Glen scurried. Jesus, carrying the suitcases filled with cash, was almost a block ahead. The trip from the Marriott to the Wells Fargo bank office was short and sweet. They'd mapped a route by the Mormon temple square. Jesus carried the money and Glen, feeling much better about life, watched the pedestrians. Wispy clouds swept by the tall church spires. The streets were filled with neatly-dressed people, all busy as bees. He sensed nothing awry. Smooth. The Mormons were a curiosity[12]. They had great families and responsible habits.

If they want to wear funny underwear and leave all the alcohol, tobacco, random sex and gambling to me, how can I argue? What's wrong with kindness, charity, virtue, forgiveness, patience and integrity? Not my style, but who am I to judge?

Glen noticed he was too far behind. He could only see Jesus in glimpses between weaving pedestrians on the sidewalk. On Second Avenue, near B street, Glen saw the trap form. A Ford Crown Victoria, with heavily tinted windows, shadowed Jesus while two bangers on foot eased up behind him. Had he been closer, he would have missed the setup. After taking a picture of their license plate with his tiny digital camera, Glen hurried and caught the car stopped at the next traffic light. He stepped off the curb and quickly removed the valve cap and unscrewed the core from the rear tire. It took five seconds. The tire hissed like an angry serpent. As they pulled across the intersection, Glen walked up to the passenger side and smashed

---

[12] And thus he [Korihor, an Anti-Christ preacher] did preach unto them, leading away the hearts of many, causing them to lift up their heads in their wickedness, yea, leading away many women, and also men, to commit whoredoms—telling them that when a man was dead, that was the end thereof.
- The [Mormon] Book of Alma, Chapter 30, Verse 18.
Korihor has a bad end. He is struck dumb by God, is cast out, begs for food door-to-door and finally "is run upon and trodden down, even until he was dead."

the window with the butt of his .45. He jammed the barrel into the passenger's neck.

"Give me half a reason, scrappleface."

The passenger's neck was covered in ugly acne boils. Glen felt he'd be doing him a favor if he blew his head off.

"They're not supposed to have guns," the passenger said.

"Shut your fucking yap, Mr. Smith. I need to use the radio," the driver said.

"My name isn't…" Not the brightest man, he figured it out and clammed up.

"Okay," Glen nodded.

"Abort," the driver barked into the microphone. Addressing Glen, "Unfinished business," he said.

"Bring it," Glen replied.

He took their picture.

Around them, Glen could see upstanding Salt Lake City citizens dialing 9-1-1 on their cell phones. The two bangers tailing Jesus turned around. Glen grabbed their photo as Jesus rounded the corner of C Street. He was almost home.

Glen stuffed the .45 in his jacket and ducked into an alley. After coming out in the crowd on Third, he walked briskly toward the bank office. Jesus was already in a back room. Glen loitered in the lobby and chatted up a pretty Asian girl behind the information desk. Her name was Lya and she was from Hong Kong. With mixed British and Chinese heritage—Glen found her accent enchanting. Unfortunately, she was completely uninterested in him or a backstage pass to Raz's show. She liked Kenny Chesney and didn't believe him when he said the country star would be there.

"I looked at his website this morning. He's on tour in Australia," she said.

"Must be my mistake," Glen said.

153

Jesus was unamused. He turned on Glen when they got outside.

"What the fuck, man, do I have to do everything? You're supposed to watch my back. Instead you chat up every slit in town. Why don't you hire a professional girl and get your mind right so you can focus on your job?"

Glen laughed. He'd saved Jesus' ass, but the dimwit didn't know it.

The thug in the car had said 'They're not supposed to have guns.' They needed to work through this. Jesus needed to know, but Glen decided to talk to him later when he wasn't all wound up.

"Can it, my brother."

Jesus didn't speak on the way back, which suited Glen fine. He was sick of Raz's game show; his slick excellence was a mockery.

Glen wandered outside the arena and watched the kids line up for the show. His mind was a muddle.

We weren't supposed to have guns.

The implication was obvious; either Raz disclosed they were disarmed to someone else, or he was behind the attempted robbery.

Why would a man steal his own money?

That's easy, what's the tax rate on uncollected revenue? Zero. They were supposed to act like a bank teller... Turn over the money and call the police. An easy transaction.

What could Glen do with this knowledge? He would never fault a man for trying to protect his money from rapacious government thieves. But, Glen *could* find fault with a man who jerked him around. Accounts would have to be settled.

With backstage passes prominent around his neck, the security staff nodded and didn't interfere as Glen wandered around. He caught the eye of a young man, huddled and freezing inside the thinly-insulated nylon jacket typically issued to minimum-wage security guards. His uncontrollable hair was spiky in an unfashionable manner:

154

random and asymmetrical. The entry gates were not open yet and the crowd waited—placid and patient.

"What a scene, eh?" Glen asked.

"We had Insane Clown Posse last month. This is nothing compared to that. *Those* people are nuts."

The guard was onto something that troubled Glen's subconscious. These kids, for the most part, were well-behaved. Sure, there were skateboard punks smoking weed and running their boards on stairway rails. Otherwise, they were quiet and civilized for their demographic. Rich kids. Smart kids. The cream of the crop, such as it was.

"Thanks, man," Glen said.

As he strolled, lost in thought, the lights of the city came on around him. The Wasatch peaks, stained with pink from the waning sun, decorated the horizon like jagged teeth as the air's heat vanished. His mood was inexplicable.

"Hey mister?"

Glen turned.

How old was this girl?

Studying her face, he realized she was older than he first thought. Late teens, maybe early twenties. Thin as a whisker, with a cold, pinched face peering from a fleece hood.

"Buy me a cup of soup?"

All bone and gristle; she had no figure to speak of, but Glen wasn't a man to reject a woman based on how she looked. He'd been surprised many times before. Sex appeal lives in the attitude, not the equipment. Regardless, he still enjoyed a good pair of equipments and this waif had none so far as he could tell.

He thought of JB's restaurant at the Salt Lake City Plaza Hotel. It struck him. He was hungry too.

"Okay," Glen said. "What's your name, kid?"

"Uh, Mary."

Yes, that's as good a name as any.

Mary. She'd hesitated. He couldn't tell if she'd decided to reveal her real name or not. She seemed alert, smart and undamaged. He held out his hand for a shake.

"I'm pleased to meet you, Mary. I'm Glen Wilson." Shaking her hand was like grasping frozen twigs. "Big fan of Toxic Shock?"

"Is that a band? Never heard of them."

"Perfect," Glen said. He guided her while stuffing useless backstage passes in his jacket pocket.

The waitress was an older woman pressed like a summer sausage into a gravy-stained dress. She'd seen everything and liked little of it; she made an accusation with her eyes. They had an all-day breakfast, so Glen ordered a Denver omelet. Mary could not decide.

"Order whatever looks good. I'll help you eat."

Stabbing a finger at the menu, she selected chicken fried steak, a cheeseburger, waffle fries and a Marionberry milkshake.

"How old are you, Mary?" Again, various answers flitted through her mind and Glen read the options on her face. "I'm like a human lie detector. Be straight with me or you'll buy your own dinner. Your name is not really Mary, is it?"

Her cheeks grew pink.

"Is so." Her eyes searched. "Well, okay, my name is Mary Ellen after my mother. Everyone calls me Ellen."

"That's better. How old are you, Ellen?"

"Nineteen."

"I almost believe you, but we'll get back to that later. Take off your jacket so I can get a better look at you."

She hesitated, shrinking into the fleece hood like a turtle. Glen reached over to help with the zipper and, like a robot, she shrugged off the jacket. She was layered up with a wool shirt under the fleece and under the wool shirt a green t-shirt. There wasn't much under the shirt. After a shy moment, she squared up her shoulders and straightened her posture. It didn't help. Glen had bigger pimples on his ass.

"How long have you been on street, Ellen?"

"Two nights."

"Cold, ain't it? At this elevation, the air is thin and the heat doesn't last when the sun goes down."

"I had money for a youth hostel the first night, but now I'm broke."

"Let's get down to business. How much for the night?"

The direct question threw her. Like a six-year-old trying to decide on a lollipop flavor, she chewed on a fingernail. She glanced toward the kitchen. Standing by the IR heat lamps, the waitress chewed a massive wad of gum and watched.

"For a date?"

"Yes, Ellen, for a date."

Her eyes were misty.

"Um, twenty bucks?"

He couldn't help it. He laughed.

A stubborn look crossed her face.

Like I was going after her Tootsie Pop.

"Don't laugh at me, Glen. Twenty is as low as I'll go."

The waitress dropped heaping plates on the table.

"And dinner; twenty dollars and dinner. If you laugh at me again, I'll add another five dollars."

She said the last part while stuffing waffle fries in her mouth, so the words were muffled.

"I'm not laughing at you, Ellen, but here's my problem. I don't believe you're nineteen. I think you're fourteen and you know what

157

happens to a man when he *dates* a fourteen-year-old. They lock him in a cell with an indiscriminate lumberjack and throw away the key."

"I'm nineteen, I told you."

"No problem, Ellen. Prove it and we have a deal."

Her small mouth worked at a hunk of cheeseburger.

She nodded.

Glen watched her eat like a machine. Her bony fingers flicked around her plate as she grabbed at errant pickles and hunks of lettuce. She alternated bites of her hamburger with working the straw plugged into her huge milkshake.

After a few minutes of gluttony, she slowed down.

"Let's see that proof."

Just one minute, she indicated with a greasy index finger.

She had a zipper pouch in her jacket pocket. Mary Ellen Plant, her student ID said. She was 19, though barely.

"I'm going to the bathroom," Glen told her. "It's a sit down job, so I'll be a few minutes."

He slipped out the door and walked two blocks to a row of pay phones outside the Family History Center where he quickly dialed Murphy's cell phone number.

"Murphy, there's no time to explain. I need you to do something for me."

"Glen, where are you? The show is starting. I don't have time to mess around."

"Write this down. I have a girl." He recited the information memorized from her ID card. "Track down her parents. Tell them to come get their daughter. We're at the JB's restaurant by the Temple Square. Do it now. I don't know how long I'll be able to keep her here."

"All right Glen, is there anything else? Can I iron your shirts or something? Polish your shoes? Starch your briefs?"

"Sure, Murphy, there is one more thing—", but he talked to dead, disconnected air.

She'd bust his balls—whine, moan and complain—but she'd do what he asked. He could call in favors for the rest of his life, and there would remain an unpaid debt. Without Glen, she would never have met her beloved life-partner, Elke. At the bottom of the bottom of things, Murphy would never forget that.

As Glen came back to the table, he made a point of adjusting his belt.

"You're too young to appreciate it yet, but there is nothing like a great shit to sooth a man's soul."

"Thanks for the attractive image while I'm eating." Slowing down, she mechanically worked at scraps on her plate. "What did you do to your hand?"

He rotated his mangled appendage in the light as if he'd never seen it before.

"I left one finger in Florida and the other in Bolivia."

"The stubs look funny."

"God-forsaken bioengineering. It's a long story. I'd rather not go there. Want coffee?" he asked.

"No, I don't drink coffee."

He found this amusing. Old habits die hard. She'd sell herself to a pervert for twenty dollars, but she'd still stay away from demon caffeine.

"Save room for pie," he suggested.

She looked over the menu, reading the descriptions of the sundaes and pies again and again as if this would be her last dessert. In her own way, she was pretty, like a tiny, frail fairy princess. She concentrated with a sliver of moist tongue appearing and disappearing at the corner of her mouth. He fell in love with her. Her matted hair was velvety brown, short and mussed. It needed a good shampooing, but he didn't care. She decided on two slices of lemon meringue pie.

This exhaustive selection process took a long time. Long enough that her parents had time to appear in the reception area. They brought the whole posse, four or five kids and grandpa wearing a suit and overcoat and carrying a leather-bound Bible.

Ellen looked at Glen with horror. Her eyes flicked about, seeking an escape route, but there was none. Her mama, large and round like a beetle, wrapped her up her arms and they cried. Her father had a round fleshy face with thick tangles of nose hair protruding from his nostrils.

"Could I have a word with you, sir?" Glen inquired, while guiding him away by the arm.

"What?"

"Outside," Glen said.

They walked a few yards down the sidewalk.

"I think she's going to be okay," Glen said.

"Who are you? I'm calling the police."

"It doesn't matter who I am. What's the problem in your family?"

"It's none of your…"

"I'm making Mary Ellen my business." Glen showed him the handgrip of his .45. "Don't make me get tough with you. Spill it."

Glancing toward the restaurant and the scene inside, the defiance drained out of him.

"She wants to go to college back east. Virginia. William and Mary. We want her to go to BYU after her missionary work."

"Look, I understand spoiled kids and family problems, truly I do. But, let her go or you're going to lose her." Glen squeezed his arm. "I will check in and you'd better be able to explain yourself when I do. Are we communicating?"

"Who are you?"

"It doesn't matter who I am. I'm your friend and many will be your blessings or I'm your enemy and harsh will be my retribution. Search your heart and do the right thing by this girl because I will be around and I will be watching. Do you believe me?"

"Yes," he said while jerking his arm from Glen's grip. "I'll work it out with the Elders. She can go."

"Super," Glen said cheerfully. "And, Mr. Plant, when you catch the bill, don't stiff the waitress on the tip. Give her 15 percent, minimum."

"Anything else?"

"No, that will do until we meet again."

Glen patted him on the shoulder and headed toward the concert hall. He was in no hurry and took a roundabout path which went by Spenser's Steak House. A lady loitered a few steps away from the valet station.

"Hey, big man."

"Yes, my dear?"

It was dark in the shadows. She was illuminated via intermittent headlights and a dim wash of city lights. Young, in her mid-twenties, she was a seasoned professional. Her hair appeared shellacked; stiff like brown cotton candy.

Glen admired her glossy lipstick, lurid eye makeup and high heels. Her breasts were pressed up and squeezed together like loaves. A strand of pearls disappeared down her cleft and Glen's mutilated hand itched to follow.

"What's yer name, big guy? I'm Candy. Got time for a quick one?"

"How much we talking about?"

"One-fifty an hour, all night for six-hundred."

The absurdity struck him. He could have violated a near-virgin all night for twenty bucks.

"I would, but I'm a happily married man."

"I'd starve if not for the happily married guys who come around. Pork chops for dinner, Candy for dessert."

This was logic Glen could hardly argue with.

CHAPTER TWELVE

Glen

The meet was set for a small storage room tucked away in the back of the arena. The union loading crew, on overtime, slowly rolled endless transit cases toward waiting semi trucks. Jesus was angry. From fifty feet away Glen could hear him shouting. He stopped outside the door and listened in.

"I was wide open on the street. He's fucking worse than useless."

"Believe me, I've seen it over and over. Glen has a knack for being in the right place at the right time. Don't expect him to focus on the task at hand—that's not his core competency. Knowing Glen, he's outside listening to you mouth off right now."

Good old Murphy. Why we never got married, I do not know. Oh yes, she hates me, that's part of it. Plus, she's a lesbian. The first time I saw her, smoke from a downed copter swirled in the hot and humid south Florida air. Her hair was a'tangle and a smudge of blood was smeared on her cheek.

Only at death's door would we part.

Glen entered and Jesus glared daggers. Nearly a closet, the tiny room was filled with rolls of plastic and five gallon buckets of industrial cleanser.

"Good evening, ladies," Glen said.

"Where have you been?" Murphy asked. While looking at her, Glen formulated a creative answer, but before he could speak, she said, "Stupid. Forget it, I withdraw the question."

"We need to straighten things out, jerk-off. You have a simple-enough job and you're not fucking doing it, man," Jesus said.

"Can I show you something before we get into all of that?"

Glen gestured to Murphy's laptop. She nodded. He plugged in the memory card from his little camera. The first picture showed Ellen from the restaurant. With her mouth full of food, her cheeks bulged like a chipmunk. A trickle of salad dressing lubricated her chin.

"Is that the girl?" Murphy asked.

Ignoring the question, he zipped through random images until he got to the guys weaving through the crowd on the sidewalk. He pointed at their faces. They were far way and moving, so the photo was blurred. Unusable for identification, they looked ghostly.

"These guys were prepared to take you down, but that's not the interesting part."

He flipped through more images until he found the guys in the Crown Vic. Strobe lit, the passenger had a stunned look on his face. Shattered glass was sprayed across his shoulder. The driver glowered with gloved hands clamped on the steering wheel. He'd caught both faces in clear profile. The barrel of his .45 was embedded in the oozing sores on the passenger's pimply neck.

"That's attractive," Murphy commented. "This is the interesting part?"

"No, the interesting part was when Mr. Pimples, here," he said while making a greasy smudge on her laptop screen with his finger, "said we're not supposed to have guns."

"Ah," Murphy said. She scowled while cleaning her computer screen with a tissue.

"Wait a minute," Jesus said. "How the hell would they know that?"

"See, Murphy," Glen said, "He's not as dumb as he looks."

He scrolled through the images and landed on the close up of the Crown Vic's Nevada license plate.

"Probably a stolen plate, but see what comes up, will you?"

Murphy was already thumbing numbers into her cell phone.

Gerusha

She couldn't concentrate on the bids. There were three competing proposals for centrifuges. Why did Bennie need so many? And autoclaves? Big ones, walk-in size. These things were expensive, over a hundred thousand dollars each. She negotiated a 27% discount and an additional 2% for paying the invoice in 10 days. Then they had to be plumbed and wired. More contractors and more contracts. The work was endless.

When she worked as receptionist in the lobby, she could leave at 5:00 and forget the job. Work did not follow her home. They were great days, wielding power behind her brushed aluminum desk sitting front and center in the fern-adorned lobby. Vendors she liked could get an audience; the ones she disliked sat and read old trade magazines all day and got no farther.

She was the cruel queen of the reception area fending off inquisitive sales people. They pried and probed. Where did she go to school? What were her family ties? How did she like her coffee? Hobbies? Boyfriends? The good ones were smooth and subtle. The bad ones were crude and transparent MBA robots, programmed to attack until her defenses were penetrated. One, scary and desperate for an appointment, was escorted out by security and banished from returning.

What pressure to produce sales would cause them to stoop so low?

She received a priority instant message from inside the company firewall. It flashed in red on her computer screen. Walter. The last time she'd talked to him, he seemed irritated, but that was typical.

What could he do? Fire her?

She'd be thankful. Relieved. Eternally grateful. This job paid a lot of money, but the pressure was relentless and eroded her soul.

Gerusha knocked once on Walter's door, then entered. His top-floor office had an unimpressive view to the north. Low clouds spit rain on the Wallingford district. Walter kept the top of his desk immaculate, with one silver pen and a chrome desk lamp. A pampered plant, a Venus Flytrap with lurid crimson lips, graced a table in its own little greenhouse.

Karl Timmons sat in front of Walter's desk. He was small and dainty, always formally dressed in a suit with vest and tie. His shoes were small, like doll shoes, polished to a mirror-like patent leather sheen. Karl was a junior accountant in the finance department. Gerusha did not like his smirky, self-satisfied look.

"Gerusha." Walter's tone was cold and brittle. "Take a seat."

He flicked his glacial eyes between the two seated before him. Karl, with dainty fingers, plucked a hair from the fabric of his trousers. "Fraud will not be tolerated at Immortality," Walter said. "Nor larceny. Nor brazen, stupid thievery."

Gerusha could not help herself. She laughed.

"I hardly think of these somber topics as laughing matters, young lady. Karl has audited and certified your theft. We are prepared to press charges. You will be persecuted to the fullest extent of federal

166

and state law. If you resign now and sign a binding reimbursement contract, I believe prison time can be avoided."

She glanced at Karl. He was ineffectively trying to conceal his delight.

Slimy little weasel—what does he think he's found?

"You created a special Bank of America account. True or false? What was the account and routing number, Karl?"

Karl flipped through papers in a three-ring binder. He read the numbers with a precise and stilted tone.

"Yes, I opened that account."

"And you funneled kickbacks from vendors into this account?"

"Rebates and discounts are deposited there, yes, that's true."

"And finally, you inappropriately spent funds from this account on personal goods? Where was it, Karl? Nordstrom's?"

"What? Yes, used this account to purchase the silver tea set we use in the executive conference room. And prizes for the quarterly sales meeting. Jade globes and figurines."

Walter opened a desk drawer and pulled out a silver cage filled with buzzing blue bottle flies. Using tweezers he captured a fly. After lifting the greenhouse flap, he placed a fly on a flytrap leaf. The lips slammed closed as Walter watched with fascination.

"So, you're going to stonewall and deny the inarguable facts of this matter, Gerusha. That's too bad. I was hoping to settle this quietly and efficiently without bringing in the police. I'm impressed, Karl. It took a lot of courage for you to come forward like this. Knowing what you know about Gerusha and all."

Karl shifted in his chair and leaned forward.

"Excuse me, sir, I work in accounting and don't know anything about Miss Andersen. I've only been here six months, almost. Numbers and accounts, those I know."

"You know, the leaves on these plants," Walter mused, "my own variety, registered with the International Carnivorous Plant Society, called dionaea muscipula Walter, can close in about a tenth of a second. They have little spikes, called cilia, that trap the prey. Did you know the Venus Flytrap is a type of herb? Well, that's irrelevant to our conversation." He pushed back in his chair and put his feet up on his desk. "What is the right word, Gerusha? Naïve doesn't quite get it. Innocent?"

"Clueless?" Gerusha suggested.

"That works." To Karl, he said, "Ms. Andersen is married to our Chairman, Glen Wilson. On top of that, I consider her a close personal friend."

"Oh," Karl said, as if struck. He stood up and his binder fell off his lap. "No one in accounting warned me about this."

"What does that suggest about your relationship with your coworkers, Karl? Never mind. Sit down. What to do? I can smell guilt on a person. I admit, Gerusha, this was a test. A trial, if you will. I would have been surprised and disappointed had you failed. Which, of course, you didn't. I don't mind judicious care and oversight in our accounting and I was being facetious with Karl, but still, it tells me something that he had the nerve to make an appointment and come up here to talk to me. I think, what I will do is—give him your job."

Gerusha picked at a fleck of loose fingernail polish.

"Sir?" Karl sputtered.

"No reaction, Gerusha?"

"Nah. When you're ready, you'll unveil your convoluted strategem. I gain nothing by agonizing over it."

"See that, Karl? Cool under fire. I admire that very much. I shall create a new position for you, Gerusha. How does Contract Director sound?"

Thinking, Gerusha leaned back in her chair and ran her fingers though her hair.

"I like Vice President of Vendor Relations better."

Considering, Walter sprayed a mist of water on his plants with a plastic bottle.

"Having another VP around here won't hurt anything. Done. Karl, shake hands with your new boss."

"Uh," Karl said.

"Let's get out of here," Gerusha said. She tugged on Karl's jacket to move him along.

They were almost out the door when Walter spoke again.

"Karl?"

"Yes, sir?"

"I enjoyed this. Come back and see me again soon?"

Gerusha pulled the door closed. Standing outside, she straightened Karl's necktie.

"What happened? I'm sorry, I didn't mean..."

"I know, don't worry. These things happen." She brushed a stray hair off his shoulder. "You're a cute little guy, so we'll start fresh. Perhaps we'll get along, or not. I'm curious. Do you have any further desire to chat with Walter?"

"Never again. That man scares me."

Gerusha grinned and patted his cheek.

"Perhaps there's hope for you," she said.

Emma

Emma daydreamed with the Toxic Shock Syndrome CD insert spread across her lap. The music swirled and plucked at loose corners of her mind. She looked deeply into Razor Blade's intense eyes. Like a gargoyle, he crouched on the side of a tall building with long, black hair blowing around his face. The photograph was not monochrome, but the colors were muted and flat. He wore a long black coat that fluttered in the wind against a backdrop of pregnant thunderheads. *The Dogma of Empiricism.* Was there a sliver of wisdom in this non sequitur?

There's no question about it. He's cute.

He was thin with fine facial features often covered in bizarre makeup. His image was a contradiction; alternately commanding and vulnerable. It stirred her internal organs in an inexplicable way, releasing messy, unbidden juices. Hormones. They flooded her body and she felt a yearning heat. Deep inside, there was an unexplored void Raz would fill if she gave him the chance. Unfulfilled emotions, evoked by a photograph.

How does he make this work?

It was a mystery. A Viking chorus erupted on the CD. She shifted in her chair and turned the volume up with the remote.

The power, the glory, the ancient's demise
History recorded in dying men's eyes
On a bloody field with a last feeble breath
He whispers her name and embraces death

She turned down the sound and tried to focus on her work. It was hopeless. Giving in to distraction, she scanned headers in her email inbox. Her eye stumbled on one. The Advanced Evolutionary Force. That was familiar.

Raz's Toxic Shock Syndrome fan club.

Eagerly, she clicked on the links and typed in her password. A graphic appeared on her screen; collapsing concentric circles with Raz's smiling face in the center. A glowing X.

You are here, it said.

The outer reaches of Raz's intimate circle.

She clicked on the outer circle and a matrix of faces appeared. Young women, all live and looking at her.

"Hello Emma," her computer said. "Welcome."

It was juvenile, but she wanted to be one of these girls. Wholesome, fresh-faced and pure. The essence of innocence. They were her sisters, revolving around the sun that was Raz.

"Welcome," the website whispered.

"What's this?"

Startled, Emma convulsed in her chair.

"Darn it, Bennie, don't sneak up on me."

"I knocked, but you didn't hear me. What website is this?"

"Glen asked me to join the Toxic Shock Syndrome fan club. He didn't say why."

Bennie shrugged. "Explaining is not one of Glen's strong suits. Did you notice? The website Java code is modulating your video frame buffer. You can see its artifacts in your peripheral vision if you look to the side. Something subliminal. Do a full-motion capture and send it to me. I'll analyze it with the Cray mainframe."

"Okay."

"Are we still okay for lunch? I'm starving. I must have skipped breakfast."

"Sure, give me a half hour to wrap things up and we'll go out."

"See you then," Bennie said.

Emma clicked around on the site. What did it take to get to the next level? The checklist was comprehensive. Health screening permission forms, lab test requests, a detailed medical history and Mitochondrial DNA screening for ancestry? All this in-depth personal information for a silly fan club? Who would agree to such things? On the screen, a hierarchy of beautiful young girls sought closeness with

171

an ethereal Raz in the center. Emma felt gentle pressure, like the wind, quantum gravity or hard-wired basic instinct. A hormonal imperative. For Glen and Bennie and Raz, but mostly for herself, she'd make the appointments and get the tests done.

Glen

He couldn't explain his thinking.

On the edge of control, that's where I spend my life, but this mayhem was all Raz's, not mine.

He was off-balance and unsure, as if magnetic north had changed its vector. Pulling as hard, but askew, with twisting tendrils of force making him seasick.

Raz was a successful rock guitar plucker, and me? An aging roustabout teetering on the lonely fringe of senility, decrepitude and death.

He needed to decompress, so, on a whim, instead of riding the TSS airplane, he decided to hitch a ride with the equipment crew.

Around three AM the union crew finished the load-out, the supervisor signed their time sheets, and they drifted toward the hotel parking lot. There were seven trucks to pick from, but he liked the way one slight, overall-clad Teamster, with mucho gusto, banged on the truck tires with a rubber hammer.

The face was hidden under a floppy denim hat. Glen was surprised; the driver was a woman. No beauty, but not bad. Plain, tending toward pretty in a country-fried, down-home style. She had dark brown eyes staring at the world from behind tiny, glittery eyeglasses. Untamed wiry black hair sprayed from under her hat. Glen held out his hand. Her palms were rough, like sandpaper. Her grip was merciless; like shaking hands with a monkey wrench. A tough little girl.

He waved his all-access pass, but she was unimpressed.

"If you don't mind, I'd like to hitch a ride to Vegas."

"Well," she said, "it happens I do mind. I seen you around, so I have a gen'l idea who you are. Go ride the fancy private jet where yous belong, Mister Slick."

Her accent teased him. She'd moved around some. There was flat Missouri mud mixed with some down east vector. Perhaps Vermont or New Hampshire? There was something else mixed in the way she choked the words between her teeth. It hit him, and he laughed. Black Dutch, a traveling people. Not Dutch as in the Netherlands, but Dutch as derived from Deutsch. German. She'd be Jewish, German and some flavor of native north-eastern Indian; a mixed-breed mongrel. A handful.

"Going to give me a name or should I just call you Von Donck?"

This she did not like. She spat a wad onto the blacktop.

"Clever, are ye?" she said.

"Let's start over," he said. "My name's Wilson, Glen Wilson. And you are…"

From under the brim of her hat, her eyes weighed, measured and found him marginal. The other trucks, rumbling and spewing smoke, revved up and pulled out.

"I want to get away from the jet set for a while. I won't be any trouble."

She puffed up her cheeks. "Pah," she said, exhaling rudely. "Trouble ye'll be, nothing but." She pounded brutally on the nearest tire with her rubber hammer before surrendering. "PaDutch.[13] Sylvie

---

[13] Pennsylvania Dutch, descendants of German settlers in Pennsylvania.

Schwenkfelder." She lifted a corner of her flannel shirt to show off her knife. The handle was carved from a curved section of buck antler. "Lay a hand on me and I'll split you from talkbox to peckerwood. Try my patience if you don't believe it, Mister smooth-talking Wilson. It's time to decide if we're gabbing or driving."

She stowed the hammer and waved him around to the passenger door.

The Kenworth T2000 cabin seemed 50 feet in the air. He had to climb like a mountaineer to reach his seat. She spent the first few minutes of the drive barking into the radio. He didn't know how they understood each other. The cab was noisy and the language, so far as he could tell, was something other than English.

Were all these drivers some sort of black Gypsies?

He caught a word. Trempist, a word derived from German, meaning a freeloader or hitchhiker. Or, he could have imagined it in the babble.

"How can you understand anything over that crappy radio?" he asked.

"It's not like we use a wide vocabulary," she said.

The gearbox had 18 speeds. Sylvie worked through them methodically while merging the truck in Interstate 15's southbound traffic. Hanging from a visor, a tied-bundle hung over the dashboard. Feathers, bones and a leather bag closed with a drawstring. Some sort of Black Forest magic. He flicked it with a finger of his mutilated hand.

"Don't touch that," she said.

The cabin was neat and spacious. The control panel looked like something engineers at NASA might dream up after a few shots of absinthe. GPS, rearview camera system, and a panel that displayed outside air temperature and a weather forecast. For what it was worth, they were in for clear skies, dry pavement and cold temperatures. A

174

compartment behind his seat looked like a cooler. He opened it and found a mini refrigerator filled with Rockstar energy drinks. No surprise, they were a tour sponsor. He offered one to Sylvie, but she waved it away.

"Maybe later," she said.

He eased back in his seat and planted his feet on the dash. She looked at him sideways but didn't say anything. Sipping the bitter drink, he watched the miles slowly melt away.

"Gets dull out here," he commented.

"Earn your ride by entertaining me. Talk," she said.

So he did.

"Raz is not an evil man. Under that satanic makeup, something interesting happens. Something multifaceted and polydimensional."

She waved her hand as if dissipating smoke, indicating he should stop laying philosophical pipe and get to the point.

"I recognize he's smarter than me. Game over, I surrender. He hires me to get his cash to the bank, then hires another crew to steal the money. I understand, he wants to cheat the federal income tax to save forty or fifty percent. There should be an easier way to do it, but okay, I get it. However, I was hired to get the money into the bank, and I'll die trying."

He could tell by the way she used a finger to clean grit from the corner of her eye that she didn't approve. He wouldn't expect a woman to understand.

"A man can't give up, he must complete the mission, even unto death or worse. Any other course leads to shame and ruin."

She offered him a stick of Wrigley's Spearmint Gum. Glen waved it away.

"Strip away artifice and bullshit and what's left? A messianic figure dressed in robes puffing on a hookah? Raz isn't enslaved to any vice. Girls. There are girls everywhere, but they are not typical groupies. No sloppy sluts with big boots and small skirts trading themselves for a ticket on the big bus. Raz girls do not debase themselves for a brief moment in reflected light."

"You've noticed the girls?"

"Of course," Sylvie shrugged. "Can hardly take a step without tripping over three of 'em."

"What do they think they'll get from Raz?"

"The same thing all women want—a good provider to take care of thems and their children."

Didn't Raz have a song like that? Providence?

He wracked his brain and came up with scraps.

When I raise my umbrella
To shelter us from chaos
I'll cover you with my blessing
and refill all loss

After Provo, the landscape under starlight was monotonous. He didn't think he'd sleep but, in spite of the energy drink, he was wiped out. He drifted in slumber. He woke with hail battering the roof. So much for the weather computer. Forward visibility in the storm was three inches.

"Where are we?"

"Halfway between Cedar City and St. George."

"Yes, that's wonderful, thank you very much, but *where* are we?"

"Two hours from Las Vegas, depending on how long this hell storm lasts."

Hell storm.

He knew she meant hail storm, but hell storm worked too. Hammering mercilessly, they drove another ten miles until the storm broke. The sky, almost instantly, was clear and the sun, with no shame at all, announced itself over the mountains to the east.

"I gotta pee."

"Me first," she said. "Take the wheel."

He slipped under her, enjoying the momentary cheap thrill of her warm ass pressing on his lap. She showed him the cruise control knob.

"Don't touch anything unless you have to and keep the rubber side down," she said before pulling the privacy curtain closed. Regardless of the curtain, she was three feet away and he could hear everything while she did her business. There was no privacy in these rigs.

Driving, he felt on top of the world. An occasional passenger car passed and, like the good lord above, he looked down on them through their sun roofs. He wished for one of the fine Utah farm girls to unbutton a jumper and secret garment and flash him, but none did.

"Okay," Sylvie said.

"I'll drive for a while."

She scanned the rolling hills and the nearly-vacant highway emerging from dawn's gloom.

"Fine," she said.

Like a hedgehog, she curled into a tiny ball on the passenger seat and, from what he could tell, was unconscious in seconds. As they approached St. George, he dialed back the cruise control. This woke her.

"Play time is over," she said.

"Oh, mom," he complained.

"You wait until your pa gets home."

She climbed on his lap. With his hands holding her slim waist, he forced her to sit for a moment.

"No funny stuff."

"Don't worry. I'm pretty sure I'm a married man."

This amused her. "Ha," she said. "Sit down when you piss and close the lid when you're done."

She was right; the pressure was on. He still needed a piss. As an old man, he did not have the ironclad bladder of youth. Once he was done with the portable potty, he pushed it back into its cubby hole and latched the cupboard door. She steered with her knees and cut a strip of buffalo jerky into mouth-sized hunks with her knife. The blade was so sharp, the jerky appeared to fall apart on its own.

"Gimme some of that."

She handed him a ragged palmful. They chewed and, cozy like old married folks, watched the road unfold before them. Leaning his head against the cold window, he slept.

At the Pearl Concert Theater, trucks lined up like a cavalcade. The approach to the loading dock looked too narrow for the Kenworth, but Sylvie took a quick look and backed in smoothly. After bumping the dock gently, she put on the brakes and shut everything down.

"Joyride's over," she said.

He pointed to his cheek, rough with stubble.

"How about a quick one right here to remember you by?"

She looked at him passively, trying to decide. It seemed equally likely he would get a kiss or a poke in the gut with her knife. The kiss, gentle, was barely a touch.

"Thanks for the lift," he said.

On the loading dock, Murphy and Jesus watched equipment being rolled off the trucks.

"We wondered what happened to you," Murphy said. "I suppose an explanation is asking too damn much?"

"No time for chitchat. I have a plan. Walk with me and I'll explain what we're going to do," Glen said.

CHAPTER THIRTEEN

Glen

The odd wing attached to the top of the Palms Hotel made the high-rise building appear ready for liftoff. His room on the 51st floor had windows that overlooked the garish lights of Sin City; it was one of the finest suites he'd ever camped in. After all the travel, a week in Las Vegas was a luxury. He sipped from a crystal glass half-filled with Chateau Laballe hors d'age Armagnac. Only one thing was missing...

He punched numbers into the cordless phone and caught Gerusha at her desk. Since she lived there, it was no big surprise.

"Andersen," she said abruptly.

"We've never talked about this, but I think you should use your new last name. Gerusha Wilson rolls off the tongue smoothly, don't you think?"

"Maybe you should change your name to Mr. Glen Andersen."

Did I marry a modern woman? I did that once and swore I'd never do it again.

"I suppose you could hyphenate. Would it be Andersen-Wilson or Wilson-Andersen?"

"I'm busy. What's on your mind?"

"You, that's what. I'm standing high above the city looking over the Vegas skyline like a pagan God. I could buy you a slinky next-to-nothing at the Playboy Shop. Then we could have a few drinks and loosen up our kinks. I could nibble caviar from your navel and see where things go from there."

"Glen, please. I don't want cold fish eggs on my belly. Other than distasteful imagery, is there a point to this call?"

Mental note: this woman needs remedial training on how to please her man.

"I need you to take care of banking business for me."

"I'm completely swamped. Let's talk about this later, okay?"

"Your problem is not workload, it's priorities. Perhaps you'd have more time to serve your husband if you were unemployed."

There was an elastic silence on the line. It stretched.

"What do you need?"

Smart girl. She gets it. Glen giveth and Glen can taketh away.

He explained. She took notes and read them back. She understood the plan.

"Will that be all?" she asked.

"Look, I'm sorry for pulling rank. I know this is an odd situation. On the other hand, I asked you to marry me and you said yes. Right?"

"I suppose..."

"I'll do whatever you want. Annulment, divorce, I'll even jump out of this window and leave you a wealthy and grieving widow if that's your heart's desire. But, I suggest you set aside your prejudices and open your mind. Give me a chance to be your husband. If you don't like it, then we'll deal with it how you wish. Do we have a deal?"

I could hear her breathing, so I knew she was still alive. The silence didn't bother me; she could think this through.

"Andersen-Wilson. If things go awry, I'll drop the Wilson."

Got her.

In victory, he raised his fist against the gaudy lights of the Vegas skyline.

"Fine," he said. "You're a good girl."

He pressed the end button and terminated the call. Immediately, he punched in Walter's cell phone number.

I didn't get to where I am without hedging my bets.

It didn't take long to tell Walter what he wanted.

Emma

The elaborate certificate was suitable for framing. Emma's photograph was surrounded by a two-dimensional bar code and an elaborate seal with holographic security features. After passing all the tests, she'd entered the Second Circle of Intimacy. There were only two more circles to go before—before what? As the other girls described it, the final level was a soul-fusion with Raz. Holding the certificate on her lap and staring into her computer screen, she craved that coupling. She wanted Raz to absorb and make her whole.

"It's interesting."

Emma jumped in her seat.

"Stop sneaking up on me," she said.

"I knocked."

"Not loud enough. What's interesting?"

"Theta and Mu brain wave modulation. Artificially induced autistic spectrum disorder. Electrophysiology stimulation of the diagonal band in Broca sections of the basal forebrain."

"I hate it when you talk so fast. What are you trying to say?"

"You're playing with very sophisticated technology pirated from a Google-financed research program in North Korea. Walter has been experimenting in this area too. Be careful, it can rewire your brain. Permanently."

"Bennie, I love you with all my heart, but you need to slow down and tell me what you're talking about."

"The motion video file you gave me from the Toxic Shock Syndrome web page? His programmers are hacking the cerebral cortex."

"Why?"

"Why? Why is not my department, I just figure out how it's done. You're the one playing with this stuff. Why are you doing it?"

"Because Glen asked me to."

"Well, be careful. This is unfiltered access to the prefrontal complex. Limbic-association leading directly to manipulation of your emotions and abstract thought processes. Dangerous, sure, but cool technology. If he's into this, then there's no telling what else he's doing. Is he creating a cult or is this some weird marketing ploy?"

Bennie's wrist pager clicked. He glanced at the display.

"Oh, gotta go, sweetie. A biochemical stew is overboiling."

He kissed her cheek and loped down the hallway.

To take the next step and enter the next circle of intimacy, she'd have to meet Raz in person. She could schedule a private audience at her convenience, but she felt a pull. Like a magnetic needle seeking north, she'd like to get this done sooner rather than later.

Gerusha

While chewing a fingernail, Gerusha reviewed the terms and conditions of a service contract. In red ink, she circled a clause on page 17.

"Terminate this order wholly or in part without prejudice to any other remedy. I told them to strike this," she muttered while wielding the red pen like a chainsaw. "Shitheads. They want to play? I'll show them how to play."

"Anything I can help with?"

Gerusha jumped in her seat. "Crimey, Walter. How long have you been standing there? You creep around like a cat."

"So I've been told. Just a few minutes, to answer your question. Do you need my help?"

"No, I've got it. It's just routine contract stuff."

"Did you get Glen's banking taken care of?"

"You know about that? Well, yes. It was a lot of money, but it's done. I have a transaction number if you want the details."

"I don't need to know, nor do I care. If you say it's done, then it's done. That's good enough."

Walter walked behind her. She swiveled in her chair to keep him in sight. He raised the shade and stared out the window. In the Ballard cut, a sailboat drifted by.

"I like your view better than mine," he said.

"You didn't walk over here to admire my scenery. What's on your mind?"

"I have a task for you. A site survey and contract negotiation for a property we'd like to lease. The situation is very sensitive. You'll have to unplug yourself from things going on around here until it's done."

"I'm completely swamped. Someone else will have to go."

"No. You're going."

Gerusha dropped her pen onto her desk and idly twirled it with a slender finger.

"I can guess what this is about. The property, by happenstance, is in Las Vegas where, coincidentally, Glen is hanging out."

"You're a clever girl. Travel has set up the flight for you. The company car is out front."

"I have to go home and pack a bag."

"No time. You need to scoot. Have a great flight."

"You enjoy this manipulation way too much."

"Such are the simple pleasures of my life," Walter said.

Glen

The security guards were dressed like Argentine playboys with sleek satiny jackets worn over open-collar shirts. Like Rodeo Drive manikins, they stood duty around the office door. Glen felt a flash of recognition. He looked into the man's eyes.

"I know you," Glen said.

"Good afternoon, Mr. President."

"You switched to a private sector gig?"

The former secret service agent shrugged.

"Beats working for a living," he said. "I retired... That whole thing sat poorly with me, sir. Better get inside. We're not supposed to talk with visitors."

"Anything I should know?'

The guard's shrug was a hint under his jacket.

"George is handling this himself. He likes things to run smoothly. There won't be any surprises."

"Good. Thanks."

"Great to see you still kicking around, sir."

"I couldn't agree more."

Over his shoulder, the security man rapped on the door with a knuckle.

"President of what?" Jesus asked.

"Shut up," Murphy said.

George Mool was a small man with dark, thinning hair swept back from a lumpy face. The ceiling of his office extended upward into the next floor; the room was huge and brightly-lighted like a dirigible hangar. Glen waved away the handshake and walked to the window that overlooked the pool. The view included a twenty-year-old blond, wearing a few scant square inches of bathing suit, rubbing suntan oil into the hairy back of a swarthy man.

"We own Wells Fargo Bank for Christ's sake. Why do we have to do this transaction in cash?"

Like all impatient businessmen, George liked to get to the point.

"We like the smell of it," Glen said.

The money was split between three brushed aluminum briefcases.

"It's all here?"

George sighed. "Counted and recounted. Modern casinos have world-class cash-counting machines, you know."

"Tell me, Georgie, who's the most famous hotel guest you've had?"

Glen didn't know why he tweaked him. Was it the way George's cufflink winked when he shot a look at his gaudy watch?

"Leave him alone, Glen," Murphy said. "Let's sign the papers and get moving."

"Really. I'm curious. The Oprah? The Sultan of Brunei? I bet this is Bill Clinton's sort of place."

"We don't comment on our guests."

Murphy pinched his arm hard and tugged him away from the window.

"I apologize for our poor manners, sir," she said.

She scrawled her name on the paperwork. Jesus took two cases and Murphy took one. They made it to the door before George spoke again.

"Jack Nicholson likes the ghostbar suite. He's the closest we get to royalty around here."

"Thanks," Glen said.

In the hallway, Murphy muttered rhetorically. "Why do you have to be such a prick?"

"How are we handling this one?" Jesus asked.

"Head toward the load-in dock," Glen said.

Jesus looked at Glen with curiosity, but did not comment. They took the austere service elevator and weaved through housekeeping staff assembling for their shift. Glen selected a battered flightcase on rollers. The only marking was the Toxic Shock Syndrome logo and various scrapes and dents.

"Put them in."

"We're going to roll this transit case to the bank?"

"No."

After the latches were shut, Glen pushed the case into a stack. It was nondescript among a hundred other equipment cases.

"You sure you know what the fuck you're doing?" Jesus asked.

"That would be a singularity," Murphy said.

"I transferred the money yesterday."

"What money? The money we just stuffed away back there?"

Murphy patted Jesus on the cheek.

"Jesus, Jesus. I get it. He used his own money."

"Why?"

"I've had bad luck on the streets in Vegas. That cash is mine now and I'll sit on it."

"I don't understand."

"Good," Glen said.

CHAPTER FOURTEEN

Glen and Gerusha

The limo driver, Hazrat, was a Punjabi from Islamabad. He pressed a business card into Glen's hands.

"I worked at the Best Western Hotel on Club Road. Perhaps you've stayed there? Near the golf course by Rawal Lake?" he asked.

"No, sorry to say. Nice place?"

Hazrat seemed momentarily confused by the question.

"It's very popular with visitors from the west; only fifteen minutes from the Islamabad International Airport. My cousin Irfat Khan has a fishing boat and I can get you a good rate by the day. He's the secretary of the Pakistani Game Fish Association. My sister make Tandoori carp. You let me know and I set it up. Okay?"

"Absolutely. The next time I'm in Pakistan, I'll look up Irfat. Allah willing."

"Of course, sir."

Gerusha, looking frazzled, walked through automatic doors. Hazrat took her bag. Glen tapped his cheek until she gave him a weak kiss. She wore black flats and camel-colored slacks.

"Hi honey," he said. "You look great."

"Let's get on with this," she said.

Traffic was heavy on Russell Road, but they merged into lighter traffic on Highway 515 and headed north. They soon arrived at a business park in Winchester. The building was a modern azure-glassed two-story structure adorned with palm trees and For Lease signs. Except for a handful of Mercedes and BMW sedans, the parking lot was empty. Off the lobby, in an ornate meeting room, she shook hands around the table with the team of real estate agents and lawyers. Champagne cooled in a silver chalice beaded with condensation. Silver pens were placed like tick marks around the round table; it looked like an absurd giant's watch.

"Can we get you coffee or a soft drink, Mrs. Wilson?"

"Please call me Ms. Andersen-Wilson. I'd take a bottle of mineral water, if you have it." One of the real estate agents scuttled. "Give me the highlights."

"Fifty-six thousand square feet with a three year triple-net lease and an option to buy. The first year's payments are a dollar a month."

"I want an at-will opt-out clause."

"Fine, but the accrued rent will be due in full."

"Agreed. Before we go any further, I'd like a tour."

"The inspectors have been inside and out—"

"I don't care." Gerusha stood. "Who has the keys?"

The scuttling agent, having returned, handed her the cold bottle of water and rattled a batch of keys on a ring.

"Let's go," Gerusha said.

She walked briskly to the back of the building. Shielding her eyes, she spotted the dumpsters hidden behind a chain link gate. Grunting, she heaved open the gate and flopped open the dumpster lids. The furthest back was filled with damp ceiling tiles.

"Show me where these came from."

"We had a leak, but it's been fixed."

She stood and waited.

"Of course, Ms. Andersen-Wilson. Please follow me."

They walked back into the building and followed a side hallway.

"Wait. What's behind this door?"

"It's a broom closet, Miss."

"Good. Open it."

Gerusha pushed by the agent and reached in to grab a push broom. The entourage continued until they were in a side corridor.

"We repaired the leak here," a lawyer said, pointing.

Gerusha prodded the ceiling with the broom handle. The acoustical tile disintegrated and fell to the floor with a soggy thump.

"Bring me a ladder."

"Miss?"

"Now would be soon enough," she said.

One of the lawyers stepped down the hallway. After punching in numbers, he argued with someone on his cell phone. Gerusha climbed the ladder and hauled herself into the ceiling. When she came back down, she had a smudge of dust on her cheek and her hair was flecked with pink insulation.

"The sprinkler system is leaking. A whole section needs to be repaired. Ten grand worth of work, at least. We're not interested in the lease."

"Mrs. Andersen-Wilson, we'll make all necessary repairs, of course."

"I see what your repair work looks like. I said 'no thank you'."

As they marched to the lobby, Glen slipped into the conference room and grabbed the cold bottle of champagne and a pair of crystal glasses.

"We'll be taking this," he said.

In the car, after pressing the button to lower the limo window, he fired the cork at the lawyers. They scattered like quail. One threw his cell phone and Glen plucked it out of the air as the limo picked up speed.

Through the security divider, he tossed the phone onto Hazrat's lap.

"Got anyone back home you want to talk to?" he asked.

After returning his attention to Gerusha, he pressed a glass into her hand.

"You know how to make an impression," he said.

She looked at him with open curiosity. "I assumed this trip was a feeble setup ending with my pants around my ankles. I don't care for any champagne right now."

"That would be a shame. It's Krug's Clos du Mesnil. Big bucks, but suit yourself."

She took a deep breath and stared out the window while the outskirts of Las Vegas streamed by.

"Oh, fine."

She held out her glass and he tipped in a hundred-dollar's worth.

She took a sip.

"You can go home, but that would be a shame."

"How so?"

"You're in Vegas and you've earned an evening on the town at the company's expense. But, it's your call. Go home and go back to work if you prefer."

"The last time didn't turn out so well, but..."

"Let's take that as a 'yes'," Glen said. "Take us to the strip, Hazrat."

Outside, on the Vegas strip, the evening collapsed across the city. Pale neon hinted at the night's glory. Hazrat parked by the Mirage and they poked their heads through the moon roof and watched the first volcanic eruption of the night. After the fiery show, Glen signaled to Hazrat, who eased the car back into the traffic and drove toward the Palms.

Gerusha's eyes glittered over the rim of her glass.

"What do you have in mind?" she asked.

"Let's try poker again," he replied.

"I don't know much about it. As a kid, I played a little with my dad, that's all."

"Believe me, I know, but it's no problem. First, I have to get some money."

He instructed Hazrat to drive to the Palms.

They walked to the concert hall. He showed his backstage pass and they were allowed inside. The stage swarmed with the equipment crew and was cluttered with gear and cables.

Gerusha's eyes were wide as she and Glen walked toward the loading docks.

Raz, wearing his hair pulled back into a bundle and talking with Murphy, sat casually on Glen's equipment case.

"Hello, boss," Glen said.

"As usual, your timing is perfect," Murphy said.

"Hello, Glen," Raz replied. "Who is the charming lady?"

"Where are my manners? This is my wife, Gerusha."

Raz reached out and took her hand.

"It's an immense, incredible pleasure to meet you."

"Forget it, Raz, this one's mine."

Coolly, Raz looked him over as if he'd never seen him before.

"Perhaps," he said.

"You're sitting on my money."

"It's curious how *my* money, through a mysterious alchemical process, gets transformed into your money."

"Your money is in the offshore account. Show him the transaction log, would you, Gerusha?"

She opened her briefcase and pulled out a sheaf of printed forms, which Raz studied.

"How can it be that the cash was deposited before you had it?"

"It doesn't seem possible, does it?"

"He made me go to the bank and take cash from *his* account which I then moved to *your* account. It was a major inconvenience. The banks hate dealing with such large amounts of cash."

"Thus, your payment is safely in your offshore account. Be a good little man and get off my dough; I need to stake my bride for a round of poker."

While stubbornly sitting, Raz considered the situation.

"You've said how this happened, now would you explain why?"

"Look, Raz, I get that you want to steal your own money in order to jack the feds out of the tax bite. I understand and I'd help you do it, but that's not what you hired me to do. With great risk to me, you play stupid games while I hump massive amounts of cash around town and make sure it gets transferred. How I get that done is not your concern. Now, get off my money so I can get on with my date."

Raz laughed. He spread his hands in supplication.

"Okay, Glen, you win. Let's get together and invent a new deal that works for both of us."

"No more fucking around with cash."

"You got it, Glen." He turned to Gerusha. "You'll come to the show tomorrow?"

"She'll come to the Seattle show."

Gerusha looked at him with a pained expression.

"I—"

He silenced her with a raised palm.

Raz hopped off the equipment case.

"It was delightful to meet you, Gerusha. I'd love to get to know you better, my dear," he said.

With a dreamy expression, Gerusha watched Raz and Murphy leave.

"He's charming. Nothing like the bat-eating metal-head I expected."

"He's a manipulative asshole. If you're smart, you'll keep your distance."

"The same could be said about you, Glen."

"Yes, but I'm *your* manipulative asshole. Besides, it's a tad late for second thoughts. Shall we play poker or stand around jawboning all night?"

Without waiting for her reply, he unlatched the case. He pulled out bundles of cash and stuffed his pockets, and then rolled the case back into the stack.

"Now we're ready," he said.

While hovering outside the poker room, he scribbled a note on the back of a keno form. He folded it and handed it to her.

"After an hour, excuse yourself. Go to the restroom and read this note."

She started to open it, but he clasped her hand over it. "I said, after an hour. Let's do this my way, shall we?"

She opened her mouth as if to argue, but changed her mind.

"So be it," she said.

"We're playing Texas Holdem. You're dealt two hole cards face down and you bet on them. Then, one-by-one, four more community cards are flopped with a round of betting. The first bidder can stand pat by checking, otherwise you either raise, see someone else's raise or fold. The last card is called the river. You build your best five-card hand from the seven cards. A flush beats three-of-a-kind. Hole, flop, river. Got it?"

"Sure."

"Okay, let's play."

As the room manager looked them over, his eyes lingered on Gerusha. Her hair was mussed and she had a mad glow in her eyes from the champagne. Glen palmed him a c-note and he unhooked the red rope.

"I can seat you at table five."

There were four players. Glen immediately assigned each a shorthand name. Admiral Hirohito, Pawnbroker Feldman, Oilman Carter and arm-candy, Peppermint. Apparently working on a bender, Pepper welcomed them with an awkward gesture; she lifted a brim-filled crystal glass in salute. The areola of her left nipple peaked over the edge of a loose neckline, but Glen did not stare. She wore a ring the size of a gear shift knob, but it was on her right hand.

Was she married to Oilman or a high-end hooker?

He had a feeling about her. She was, perhaps, smarter than the empty-headed bimbo image she cultivated.

"What's the buy-in?"

The dealer, a microscopic codger who looked like a desiccated cricket, said, "One thousand."

Glen tossed in two bundles of hundreds from his jacket pocket. Ten grand.

The dealer inspected the Palms-adorned bands on the bills. He looked for approval from the pit boss, then counted the bills, spread them on the table for the security camera, and then counted again. He slid colorful piles of chips across the table.

"So everyone knows up front, the lady has a redeye flight to catch, so we'll cash out about ten o'clock."

"We playin' or talkin'?" Oilman said.

The drink girl stopped by. She wore something like the Playboy bunny suit but without the ears: high heels, black one-piece pushup, and stockings. Her hair was an auburn swirl and Glen loved her liquid-brown eyes. He handed her a twenty-five dollar chip and whispered in her ear.

"When I ask for a seven-and-seven, bring me ginger ale. Got it?"

"Yes, sir, seven-and-seven it is."

"Easy ice."

"And for the lady?"

"Red Bull and Gray Goose."

"Yes ma'am."

As she sauntered away, he admired her gait. It was a marvel how graceful she was on four-inch heels. They must have been like walking on stilts. When his attention returned to the table, Gerusha gave him a sour look.

"I gotta get you into some of those heels, babe."

"Right after Sean Penn votes for a Republican."

Funny girl.

As they played, he studied the players. Gerusha, playing every hand with wild abandon, was joyous when she (rarely) won and cussed under her breath when she (often) lost. Soon, she was down over a grand. Glen played cautiously and lost a couple of hundred. It was a stereotype, but Hirohito was inscrutable. He played with no emotion as he sipped a Bud Light.

Feldman couldn't stop peeking at his hole cards as if he thought they'd change if he didn't look at them every ten seconds. Pepper giggled and stroked the thick fur on Oilman's leathery arm. He couldn't decide if she was a fourth wife or a local girl on lease. She had long nails painted white with the Lone star of Texas on each thumb. Oilman loved to talk and kept up a running commentary on the hands. Soon, he won more than his share and chips piled up. Glen wondered if Pepper folded any hand that might beat her oilman.

After an hour, he wondered if Gerusha would heed his instruction. At the seventy-minute mark, she raked in a rare win and pushed back her chair.

"Excuse me; I need to use the restroom."

"I'll go too," Pepper said. "You men play. We'll be back in two shakes of the beaver."

"Save some of that shakin' for me," Oilman said while slapping her rump.

Glen lifted his hand to give Gerusha a friendly swat too, but she gave him a stern look that made him reconsider.

It was a faster and more serious game while the ladies were absent. Glen won two pots and then got Oilman to fold when he bluffed a nine and three in the hole.

He wondered what Gerusha would make of his note.

The most important fact about poker is this. With six people playing, your average odds of winning are one in six. If you play out every hand, you will lose money. Learn to fold a bad hand, or you'll never come out ahead. Bluff every fifth hand or so to avoid being predictable. Large pots are worth taking large risks to win. Never show your cards unless someone else at the table has bought the right to see them. Play smart and pay attention and you'll win. Above all, have fun. It's just money. Money is a slave to us, not us to it.

When she returned, arm-in-arm and giggling with Pepper, he wondered if she'd forgotten about the note. However, she slowly changed her play and began winning. After she took the Oilman to the cleaners with three fours, he threw his cards down with disgust.

"I thought you had a plane to catch," he said.

Her cheeks were flushed. The winning hands and drinks fueled a mad gleam in her eyes. Glen had her; he knew it. After they cashed

197

out, she folded the wad of bills into her purse. He called Hazrat, who agreed to meet them out front.

As they strolled through the noisy, more public areas of the casino, she grasped his arm in a death grip.

"That was fun," she said.

"I thought you might get a kick. You have an aggressive, predatory nature."

"You know how to sweet talk a lady. Predatory?"

"No insult intended. I'm just sharing an observation."

Standing at the main entrance, they watched well-dressed clients come and go. Kevin Bacon, escorting his wife, Kyra Sedgwick, stopped for an instant.

"Glen," he said, "are you still kicking around?"

Glen knew Kevin from hanging around the *Footloose* movie set many years before.

"Always," Glen said. "Let me introduce you to my wife. Gerusha."

"Glen, you dog, she's beautiful." He tugged her hand and kissed her cheek. "What are you doing these days?"

"Contract work for Toxic Shock. Come by and I'll introduce you."

"I'd love to do a cameo on stage. I know how to play Hell Hounds of Hollywood."

"Say no more."

"Good to see you, my man."

Gerusha watched them disappear into the Palm.

"You know Kevin Bacon?"

"Everyone knows him, it's no big deal."

"It's a big deal to me. Look, I don't need to go home. I'd like to see the Toxic Shock show. Let's finish the champagne, wrap up the night in your room and go to the concert tomorrow night."

I wanted her. Every cell in my body craved her. But, this love affair needed to be done right.

"Airport," he said to Hazrat.

After slipping deftly through airport traffic, Hazrat parked the limousine by the curb. He jumped out and produced Gerusha's briefcase from the trunk. Though rumpled, she glowed like an emerald. Glen gathered her into his arms. They kissed and the world vibrated. Colors, formerly mute, shouted.

"I'll see you when the tour gets to Seattle."

They drove away and left her standing on the sidewalk.

"Back to the Palms, sir?"

"You got it."

"If you don't mind me saying, sir, I can't tell if you're the dumbest guy on earth or playing very cleverly."

"I get that a lot," Glen replied.

Gerusha

The plane hit the tarmac after midnight. After a long walk through the SeaTac airport, Gerusha, with grainy eyes and a growing headache, hailed a taxi.

"Miss, where to?"

She realized the Sikh driver, with a thick accent, had already asked this question several times. After giving him her Belltown address, she changed her mind. On a whim, she gave him the address to the new house in Magnolia.

It was a dreary night in Seattle, misty and cold. The city seemed waterlogged and lighted only by pale neon smears. They drove past Paul Allen's Experience Music Project (a grotesque melted Stratocaster), the Space Needle and climbed the winding, deserted streets to the bluff that overlooked the Puget Sound. A ferry hooted as it approached its dock.

She stared at the house through rivulets of water pouring over the side of the taxi. The driver eyed her in the rearview mirror, but did not speak. She needed to pay him and get out or give him her Belltown address. The massive house squatted beneath the trees. A large container overflowed with discarded roofing material; the new roof was almost completely installed. Light poured from a side window.

She handed him a wad of bills, accepted his receipt and stood in the driveway with her bag. Picking her way around construction rubble, she approached the front door. Before fumbling with keys, she tried the door. It was unlocked. She went in.

After dropping her suitcase in the reception area, she followed the sound of music and knocked on Rose's door. The music trailed off.

"Who is it?" Rose asked.

"It's me, Gerusha. Can I come in?"

Rose opened the door.

"Who are you?"

"The new owner. I bought this house."

"Yes, I know that. Come in."

Gerusha entered. Rose worked on a large canvas covered with finely detailed men, dressed in business suits, marching in lockstep over a cliff like lemmings.

"I'm thinking of calling this one 'Masters of Business Administration'. What do you think?"

Gerusha considered it.

"That's a perfect title," she said.

Rose cupped Gerusha's chin and rotated her head back and forth while staring into her eyes.

"When I feel like you look, the Doctor says I should take pills. I have lots of them—Zoloft, Zyprexa, and others. I don't take them, so I have bottles and bottles. How many do you want?"

"None, thank you."

"Well, if you're going to be miserable, you might as well be useful. I like Tang. Would you mix some up? I don't like the grit at the bottom, so mix it with warm water and then add ice. Add a splash of grenadine for the cherry flavor and to adjust the tint; I don't like the fluorescent orange of plain Tang because it looks radioactive. Okay?"

Though beyond exhaustion, Gerusha could not think of reason to refuse. Navigating the hallways, she went to the kitchen and flipped on the lights. The renovation was amazing; she stood and gaped at the room with wonder. The counters had been replaced with polished and gleaming granite slabs. An array of flush-set ceiling fixtures illuminated the room with a soft and even flood of light. The cabinets, glowing warmly with a rich finish, were maple. The microwave was still in its box and not yet installed, but the stainless steel stove and refrigerator appeared to be working.

It looked like a page from a magazine. After running her fingers over the cool, smooth counters, she opened cupboards until she found a whole shelf where bottles of Tang and grenadine were arranged neatly in military precision. After finding a hand-made blown-glass pitcher with matching glasses, she mixed up the powdered drink. After filling glasses with ice from a dispenser and topping with rose-tinted grenadine, she called out to Rose, who appeared promptly and flopped onto a dining room chair.

"The contractors did an amazing job with this room."

"Hmmph," Rose grunted. "With all the noise they make, it's a wonder I can get any work done. I had to threaten them with my shotgun to keep them out of my studio."

"You have a shotgun?"

"Sure, one of Daddy's old ones, a Winchester. Don't tell anyone. The stock has ivory inlays. From elephants. Daddy said the set once belonged to Winston Churchill's grandfather, but he told lots of stories. I'm not sure they're all true. It hasn't been fired since 1926. Do you want to see it?"

"Maybe later."

"What shall we toast to?"

"I don't know."

"Okay, though it's not really true, we'll toast to NASA for inventing Tang for the astronauts."

They tapped their glasses together and drank.

Rose made a sour face.

"Too much cherry," she said. "If we're going to be friends, you'll mix my drink properly."

This struck Gerusha as absurd. She laughed, and her laughter led to hiccups.

Between convulsions, she said, "I'll put in less next time."

"Thank you very much. Are you staying here? I think your room is ready. They brought a bunch of furniture yesterday. One of the movers, a monstrous man built like one of the Himalayas, was forward with me. I had to scold him severely."

"What did he do?"

"He told me he likes big girls. Some men do. He asked me for a date. I set him straight in no uncertain terms."

"Do you want me to call the moving company?"

"No, that's not necessary, I dealt with the situation. We're going to a show."

"You're going out with him?"

"I'm crazy, not stupid. If a man asks me, I'm going, but I made sure he knows there will be no kinky sexual activity until we get to know each other. I'm no round-heeled party girl."

Gerusha drained her Tang.

"Your paintings are… interesting."

"I studied the classical style at a conservatory in Geneva. It was nearly fatal; it took me a long time to forget what they taught me so I could be who I am." She shuddered and her ample flesh jiggled. "If someone asks me to paint another portrait or still life or landscape, I swear, I will eat Daddy's shotgun first. Though, maybe I'll change my mind and paint Marcus in the nude."

"Who is Marcus?"

"The mover. No matter how small his dangler is, I'll draw it real big. I suppose he'd like that."

Gerusha stood. "I have to sleep," she said.

The sweeping expanse of stairway terminated in the reception area. The rails, newels and banisters, carved from dense, black-like-dark-chocolate walnut, had been cleaned and polished. The filthy and ragged stair runners had been replaced with textured carpeting. The enormous chandelier, glowing with lights like scifi stars, captured her attention.

"Daddy said it belonged to the Czar, but he always told wild tales. Maybe it's really from a Parisian whore house. I don't suppose we'll ever know."

"Regardless, it's lovely."

"I suppose," Rose replied. "Get along with you. I'm painting and won't be distracted when I'm painting. My visions will not paint themselves, you know. Although, there are several… Well, never mind that. Take a little of Daddy's brandy if you can't sleep; it's good for that."

Rose waddled back to her studio. While the door was open, the hallway was flooded with blinding light, but darkened when she closed the door. The music restarted, though a little quieter. Gerusha picked up her briefcase and trudged up the stairs. She was pleased to find, in the master bath, the water was on and all the fixtures worked. After brushing her teeth, she collapsed on the bed.

This bed is huge, almost an acre.

There was no need for Daddy's brandy; she was asleep in moments.

CHAPTER FIFTEEN

Erik

Welkome Home, Amerika, the headline read. With round-tipped kindergarten scissors, Erik snipped the advertisement from The Stranger. He stabbed the ad into the wall with a grime-encrusted paring knife. Toxic Shock Syndrome one night only at The Moore Theatre. Erik could not believe the ticket prices—$350 for general admission.

Fucker gets rich while I live in a stinking trailer with a dead girlfriend, no heat and no food.

Outside, a horn tooted. He peeked through loose strips of aluminum foil covering the windows. The Cambodians had come to take him to the bank.

He didn't like the small men and their thinly-veiled insults and taunts, but they supplied the Buddha Bud he craved. Always smirking, their nasty little mouths were filled with crooked teeth held together with gold wire. He owed them money and dreaded the day when Sherie's disability direct deposit would not come through. As long as Sherie's body was not found, he couldn't think of anything that would stop the payments, but, in his experience, there was always some evil lurking to derail his plans.

They parked a hundred yards up the driveway to avoid splattering mud on the sides of their sleek, black Cadillac Escalade.

The enormous SUV had dark-tinted windows and 20-inch tires with chrome-plated wheels. The rims, still spinning, hissed.

Lo always wore a long brown coat. His hands were stuffed deep in the pockets and Erik worried about what was hidden within. It could be many things: wads of cash, a machete, an axe, a sawed-off shotgun, or simply more chewing gum. He kept the Buddha Bud stuffed in an inside pocket.

"*Ola, mi amigo. Apurate,*" Lo said.

Erik did not know why the Cambodians pretended to be Mexicans. They did not look anything like any Mexican he'd ever seen, but the pretense seemed to amuse them. Lo pointed to a patch of wild grass. Erik wiped mud from his shoes before crawling into the cavernous vehicle. He took a place between two wiry teenagers on a fur-covered bench seat.

Inside, as his eyes adjusted to the dim cabin light, he noticed a tiny girl wearing a tank top and no panties idly smoking a big log and holding Che's limp prick. Che's real name was unpronounceable, something like Mock-Law-Wing, but he always wore Che Guevara garb: an olive green army jacket, t-shirt, and a black beret adorned with a red star.

"Che, how's it hanging?"

Looking at each other, the Cambodians chattered and decided they liked his little joke. They laughed. In the murky light, the girl's spliff glowed as she took a drag.

Erik motioned for her to hand over the joint. She slowly offered it and then changed the gesture to a brandished middle finger. She said something abrasive he could not understand.

"So, it's payday," Che said. He gestured and Lo produced a plastic-wrapped bundle. When Erik reached for it, Lo pulled it away. "Not until we see the color of your money."

Erik's grand plan was to smoke half the Buddha and sell the rest to high school students and slumming yuppies with a taste for the exotic. Then, he'd have money to repeat the process. Unfortunately, the stash always seemed to disappear before he sold any.

They arrived at a strip mall. The bank ATM was attached to the end of the building. The Cambodians escorted him. He knew they tried to observe the numbers as he punched them in, so he hunched over and obscured the keypad as much as he could. He breathed a sigh of relief when he saw the deposit had been made. $461. He took out $400, which left $61 to live on until the next deposit. It was enough for Lucky Charms, instant milk, cheap beer and canned beans. He'd make it.

Lo grabbed the money out of his hands and counted it. He flipped the plastic-wrapped roll onto the ground and slipped back in the SUV. They rolled away smoothly. Hastily, Erik, scanning the parking lot with paranoia, stuffed the roll under the waistband of his jeans. It was always the same. He'd have to hitchhike or walk the four miles to get home. To fortify himself for the journey, he decided to splurge at Zack's Burger Shack.

Zack's had seen better days. The mossy roof was caved-in on a corner and patches of tenacious weeds grew in the parking lot's sparse gravel. The food was greasy, but they served big portions for the money, so the place was popular with the construction trade.

The hostess was young, perhaps 15. Her hair was spiked and she wore heavy eye makeup and lurid purple lipstick. Her nametag said Trish.

"I'll take a double-Zack and a vanilla shake," Erik said.

"For a buck more, ya get curly fries."

"Nah," Erik said.

He swiped the card through the terminal.

"Debit or credit?" Trish asked.

"Debit," he replied. While punching in the numbers, he noticed a crude TSS-logo tattoo on her hand. "Do you know Toxic Shock?"

"I liked them when I was little. Raz is dreamy."

"I'm Erik."

"Your debit card says Sherene Bailey."

"That's my old girlfriend. We broke up, but she still lets me use the card. You know me, I'm the TSS bass player, Erik, on a little break from the band, but I'll be back on the road with them soon."

She looked him over suspiciously as she offered up the receipt.

"Don't roast, you look like'a dog been dragged behind a pickup."

"If I'm lying, would I have this?" He pulled up the sleeve of his layered sweaters and showed off a garish TSS logo that crawled up his arm. "If that's not enough, if you have a car, you can take me to my place and I'll show you pictures to prove it."

"I have a piece of shit Hyundai that runs okay. How far out is it?"

"A couple of miles, that's all." He lowered his voice. "We can toke up Buddha and have ourselves a party."

"That sounds like a rip. My dad is pumping a skank from his work, so he's never home. Can you wait around until three? That's when I get off. You swear to God you know Raz?"

"Yeah, we grew up together and we're best buds. I wrote most of the hits, but he's the lead guitar player, so he gets all the attention. I play lead too, but he doesn't like competition. How come you're not in school?"

"I'm pretending to be a home-schooler. Dad signed off, so I get away with it."

The Zack-burger was ready. Erik made eye-contact with the cook when the burger basket was slid under the heat lamp. The cook looked unfriendly.

"I have a band," Trish said. "We used to be called Trash Republic, but now we're called Dik Juse, like dick juice, but spelled different. Maybe you could get us an audition. We could open a show for TSS and that would be insane."

"I have to check you guys out and make sure you have chops. You gotta be real good to share the stage with TSS." He neglected to mention that TSS had not used an opening act for several years. "I can show you a few tricks if you can afford a lesson. I get a hundred bucks for a half-hour."

"I can void out your debit transaction," Trish whispered.

"That will do it. You gotta bring your own bass, 'cause all of mine are stored in New York City."

A group of laborers pushed through the door. Erik grabbed his burger and shake and found a rickety table. He watched Trish take orders and occasionally caught her eying him while he dined. When he was done, he wiped his thin mustache with a paper napkin and pushed the basket away. After the lunch crowd thinned, he walked back up to the counter.

"Give me the key to your car and I'll wait for you out there. If you get a break, we can share a toot."

She kneeled and fished in her handbag and located a key ring, and then pushed them across the counter.

"It's out back."

He located her Hyundai, started it and backed it around soggy picnic tables to a hiding place under the cover of dripping trees. After unrolling the plastic package, he sniffed the aromatic weed. The marijuana was mixed with a pitchy black tar. He stuffed a load in the bowl of his pipe and lighted up with a plastic lighter. Soon, he drowsed.

He was startled when the car door was thrown open. The cook, bearing a large, blackened spatula, dragged him out onto the gravel.

While slapping him with the spatula, the cook said: "Leave the jailbait alone, you white-trash piece of shit."

"Don't you know who I am?" Erik protested.

"I don't give a bucket of snot,"—whack—"if you're Paul,"—whack— "McCartney, you get the fuck out of here,"—whack—"and don't come around again."

With a bloody paper napkin pressed to his face, no one would stop on the highway to pick him up. So, he had to walk home, cursing all the way and vowing to get revenge.

Glen

While the music roared, Glen traversed the backstage area and checked on his flight case. The money was still there, unmolested. He added bundles of cash from the poker winnings and re-buckled the latches. He rolled it to a freight elevator and, while leaning over, pushed it through the casino to the hotel elevator. He pressed the button for his floor.

A couple riding the elevator eyed him with curiosity. Young, they were dressed in elaborate formalwear.

"What are you looking at?" Glen asked brusquely.

They averted their eyes and pointedly ignored him.

In his room, he looked over the contents of the minibar and selected a miniature bottle of Crown Royal. Sipping, he opened the curtains and stared over the garish city while loosening his necktie. It had been a long, exhausting, but fruitful day. He thought of Gerusha's shining eyes and carefree laughter as she raked in piles of colorful chips.

He had her, he knew it.

Life is good.

Gerusha

She woke to pounding, pounding, pounding. The clock by the bed was stopped, but she peered at her watch and saw that it was almost nine o'clock. Wearing one of Glen's dress shirts over panties, she got out of bed and walked to the balcony. The morning sky was unusually clear. Frost tipped the grass. Three men on the roof installed clay tiles. A diesel truck, rumbling, backed into the driveway. The yard swarmed with activity.

"When are you going to be done?" she asked, but the workers could not hear her. "Hey!"

She shouted until one of the workers scuttled over. He stared at her nipples, erect under the thin fabric from the cold air, so she interrupted the view by crossing her arms over her chest.

"What?" he asked with his voice raised above the din.

"I said, when are you going to be done?"

"The boss says we get a thousand dollar bonus if we finish on Friday. So, we'll be finished on Friday. Okay, lady?"

Satisfied, she waved him off. Bubb, wearing a cashmere sweater over shirt and necktie and bearing a big grin, walked briskly around the recently-trimmed hedges. He stood on the freshly-mown grass and raised his face toward her on the balcony like a suitor.

"Gerusha! There you are. Why don't you answer your cell phone? I've been trying to reach you with great news."

"What do you want?" she called down to him.

"I have an all-cash offer for the house. A couple from San Francisco love the place and they're offering an even eight-mil. They made a lot of money in the social networking bubble and they're offering all cash, did I mention that? It would be a painless quick-close."

"Bubb, go fuck yourself."

"Don't be hasty. I'll take a small discount on the sales commission and you'll make a mint for doing absolutely nothing. It's free money."

Gerusha walked back to the house and shut the French doors on him. She stood for a moment admiring the prismatic light refracting through the facets of the cut glass door panels. She turned to examine the room. With an unbidden thought, it occurred to her how nice the colors of her bedspread would look against the new wallpaper and freshly-painted wainscoting.

Where is my life headed?

She had no clue.

CHAPTER SIXTEEN

Erik

He needed to do something with Sherie. The whole trailer reeked of her. Suppose he talked a girl like Trish into coming home with him? What would she say if she found a partially decomposed corpse in the shower stall? He smoked a bowl of Buddha and built up his resolve. Today, he would get rid of her.

He soaked a bandana with mouthwash and tied it around his face. This killed the stench a little. He stood for ten minutes, daydreaming with his hand on the bathroom door before remembering his mission. He pulled the door open. Shiny blue-green flies buzzed. The odor assaulted him like something physical.

If I needed to shoot her, why didn't I do it outside?

Grabbing her slimy arm above the elbow, he tugged, and then tugged harder. The limb, loose in its socket, came away with a syrupy, ripping sound.

If she comes apart this easily, this won't be so hard.

The main part of her body, even without arms and legs, was the hardest part. Trying not to look at what was left of her eyes, he wrapped her torso in a blanket and dragged her out the back door. The air was crisp and cold. Out of breath, he exhaled clouds of mist. He planned to dig a hole six feet deep, but, with hands blistered by the shovel handle, gave up after creating a rough fissure about a foot deep. He threw in the body parts and covered them with a few shovelfuls of dirt. Rubble from an unfinished roofing job was piled nearby, so he threw heaps of asphalt shingles over the crude grave. Gasping for air, he was done. It occurred to him to say a few words.

Bitch didn't know when to shut up. Rest in pieces.

With a gallon of Simple Green he found under the kitchen sink, he scrubbed and scrubbed, flushing endless gallons of filthy water down the toilet, over and over refilling his wash bucket with clean water. When he was done, the place still smelled, but not as badly. His muscles ached and his ripped-up hands stung from the cleanser. He'd earned a break.

Sitting at his fold-down dining table, he packed bud in his bowl and smoked. How long he sat there, he did not know. He roused when a car crept down the driveway. It was the black Escalade.

What?

It made a sweeping turn in the yard and nudged up against a fir tree. It idled, pressed against the tree, with steam coming from the tailpipe.

What are those fucking gooks up to?

He checked to make sure his Thompson Contender was loaded and went out to investigate. Che was slumped over the wheel. From the passenger side, Erik reached in and turned off the engine.

"Che? What the fuck, man?"

Slowly, Che turned his head and smiled through a mouthful of bloody teeth.

"Hey, Loser," he whispered.

Erik walked around the vehicle. He opened the driver's side door and Che tumbled out. The front of his shirt was soaked with blood. From underneath, purple coils of entrails were visible.

Great, another dead body to deal with.

Erik watched Che take a last shallow breath. Inspiration struck. With cold temperatures and the windows rolled up, Che would keep in Sherie's old Chevy Caprice until Erik was ready for another burial detail. Out of gas, the Caprice had not run for a while. It sat on two flat tires under a vine maple tree.

Kneeling beside the body, Erik went through Che's pockets. He didn't carry much: a gold Zippo lighter with a naked lady painted on it, a wallet stuffed with one-hundred dollar bills and a cheap, plastic Timex watch. Plus, stuffed in his belt, a silvery .45 automatic pistol with dragons engraved on its wooden grip. Erik tossed the gun in the SUV.

Slightly built, Che was not heavy. Erik worked the Caprice door open and maneuvered Che inside. He slammed the door.

You can rot in peace too, asshole.

Che's beret had fallen off. On impulse, Erik picked it up and arranged it on his head.

He went back into the trailer. While sitting at his table and counting the money from Che's wallet, he smoked a bowl and thought about the SUV and the new situation. The car would be conspicuous, but he could swap the plates with the Caprice and get a Maaco paint job. That would get him out and about without problems.

He knew, if he searched it, it would be a treasure trove of dope, more cash and weapons; he could easily afford 99 bucks for a hasty coat of paint. It was as if God finally remembered love and smiled down on him. Daydreaming, he imagined the look on Trish's face when he pulled up in the Escalade and tapped the horn. With the imagined booty, he was suddenly free; he could do what he wanted. But first, what he wanted was to smoke another bowl of Buddha Bud.

Ken Coffman

Gerusha

Sitting behind her desk, Gerusha was drowsy and distracted. She could not concentrate on contract terms and purchase orders. Hearing a tap at her door, she looked up. Walter, dressed suavely in a cream-colored suit, stood in the doorway looking pleased with himself.

"What are you so happy about?" she asked.

"We have good news from the lab. A breakthrough. Bennie is truly a genius."

"Can I ask again? What do we *do* at this company?"

"Ah, the details... In good time, we'll disclose the full nature of our technology, but for now, information is disclosed on a strict need-to-know basis. I'm sure you understand. We must protect our trade secrets with all diligence. As I said, the name on the front of the building says 'Immortality', isn't that clue-enough? May I get to the point of my visit?"

"Please."

"About the building in Nevada..."

"Signing a long-term lease would have been a disaster. I nixed the deal."

"We need to find something; Nevada doesn't have inventory or income taxes."

"I understand. Let's fire the real estate agent and start over."

Walter sighed. "Okay," he said. "Did you spend quality time with Glen?"

"We played poker."

"If you play out every hand, you'll lose money."

"Glen told me. We walked away from the table with a profit. It was fun."

216

"I spent several happy years in Vegas," Walter said wistfully. "How is your house coming along?"

"The progress is amazing."

"Paula shows me the bills. For what we're paying, it'd better be. When are you moving in?"

Moving in?

She had no conscious intention of moving in, but her subconscious had been busy. Walter's simple question crystallized her thoughts. The house exerted a pull like an irresistible tidal attraction. The idea flooded her mind and simply *felt* right. She *would* move in— as quickly as possible.

"The place is supposed to be ready on Friday, so I guess I'll move in on Saturday."

"Excellent. Take a day or two off if you need to. Movers can be booked far in advance, so you'd better get busy and line someone up. Needless to say, the company will cover that bill too. Invite me and Angela over for dinner—I'm curious about where the money is going."

When Gerusha looked up again, Walter was gone. It was eerie how he came and went so silently. She Googled 'Seattle' and 'movers' and paged through the search results. It occurred to her to wonder, again, what Glen's reaction to the place would be. Would he throw a fit over the expense of cleaning it up? Would he cast Rose out on the street? Would he order all the furnishings and decorations gutted? Would he think making a quick profit by flipping the house back on the market would be the best course?

She no longer wanted him to hate it. She wanted him to love it.

Ken Coffman

Glen and Raz

After the show, Raz requested a meeting. Glen tapped on the door of the suite. Jesus and Murphy were present. Murphy sipped a Diet Coke. Two of Raz's girls, sprawled on a couch with their legs intertwined, played a console video game displayed on a massive flat-screen TV.

"In view of your remarkable creativity, I have decided to let the promoters use bank transfers," Raz said. "Transferring your own money was a clever idea. I salute you." He gestured with a bottle of vitamin water.

"Does that mean I'm fired?" Glen asked.

Raz chuckled. "Murphy says she can use you on the security detail."

Jesus's expression was inscrutable while he nibbled macadamia nuts from a can.

"How'd you get half a million dollars?"

"The old fashioned way. I earned it." Glen stood. "Is that it?" he asked.

"You'll be a rover," Murphy said. "Walk around and watch for trouble."

A rover? Like I could, or would, do anything else... Did they think I'd wear a yellow security t-shirt and hold stoned idiots away from the stage?

"Murphy made a convincing case that it would be prudent to allow you to remain armed. She assures me you'll make every effort to avoid shooting your client."

"If you could, you guys would leach all the fun out of everything. What else?"

218

Raz shrugged. "Nothing, I guess."

"Okay. I'd better get busy roving."

Glen walked out and took the elevator to his floor. In his room, he selected a cold Heineken from the minibar and flopped on the bed to enjoy a siesta.

CHAPTER SEVENTEEN

Erik

Every few minutes, Erik lifted a strip of aluminum foil to make sure the SUV was still parked against the tree and not something conjured by his drug-addled imagination. The open wounds on his hands ached, but Buddha Bud took the sharp edges off the day. He had one concern. After the exertions of the prior day, he'd smoked the last of his stash. He was afraid to look. If there was no dope in the SUV, he'd be in trouble.

With the other Cambodians dead or scattered, how would he establish a new connection?

All the money in the world did no good without a source.

He collected energy and prepared to do an inventory of the SUV. He flipped up foil.

Yes, it was still there.

Waiting.

The sun was a pale smudge in the overcast sky when Erik came out. He walked around the vehicle, impressed once again at how large it was; it was like a prehistoric monster. He started his search with the drivers' side. Blood was crusted on the leather seat and dried in a pool on the carpet. He sighed. It was more work for the Simple Green.

Would the labor ever end?

In the door compartment, he found a small, chrome-plated automatic pistol. He stuffed it in his pocket. A rosary and air freshener hung from the rearview mirror. He pulled them free and tossed them out. Moving to the passenger side, he found a switchblade knife under the seat. The glove box was stuffed full of bundles of Buddha which spilled onto the floorboard when he released the latch. With extreme discipline, he smelled the packages, but did not light up a bowl. It was surely a year's supply or more. Erik's heart overflowed with joy.

In the passenger compartment, he found a few spliffs and paraphernalia, lighters and the like. From the gap between the seats, he plucked out a small pair of soiled panties. After a quick sniff, he tossed them in the yard.

The real score was in the cargo compartment. Under the pull-out privacy screen, he discovered bales of marijuana and, wrapped in plastic, black blobs of opium resin. Also, wrapped tightly in dense, plastic-covered bricks, he found cash—solid bundles of one-hundred dollar bills. He was rich. Under the cash, he found a one-gallon plastic zipper bag filled with little white pills. They looked like speed, so he decided to try one to find out. Almost instantly, after melting one under his tongue, he was filled with energy. After hauling the stash into his trailer and stacking everything on his table, he admired the impressive booty. The pile was a King's treasure.

Unable to sit still, he cleaned up Che's blood. That's when he found the AR-15. He wasn't sure how he missed it before; the bundle was in plain sight, wrapped in a piece of carpet and stuffed between the driver and passenger seats. The solid heft was impressive; it was clearly no toy. He had no idea how to work it. He'd seen movie heroes pull back the bar. He tried that, but it still wouldn't fire. Then he found the safety and flicked it. Aiming in the general direction of the Caprice, he pulled the trigger.

It was as if hell was unleashed.

The gun ripped the air like thunder and battered his shoulder. A string of bullet holes stitched across the Caprice and exploded through windows in a rising diagonal line ending in the trees.

With ears ringing, he tried to remember what was on the other side of the woods. There was a daycare sign on the highway. Which direction? He couldn't visualize it.

Never mind, what power!

He felt like God bringing down wrath on mankind. Jittery and elated, he practiced removing and replacing the clip. He'd never felt better in his life. The edges of the world shimmied and shimmered.

There were things that needed to be done. He stuffed the rifle back between the seats and started the engine. Carefully backing and forthing, he seesawed the huge truck until it was pointed down the long driveway toward the highway. He had to be careful; the accelerator was sensitive and the truck, like a caged animal, ached to be set loose.

After looking both ways with paranoid wariness, he eased onto highway. While driving toward civilization, through Index, Sultan, and toward Monroe, he punched buttons on the stereo. The MP3 player was loaded with metronomic hiphop beats, but the singing was some sort of nasty Asian gibberish. He found an FM rock station playing a TSS song. He took this as a positive omen. The song was *Cattle Call* and it had a slinky bass line, something overly-complicated that Raz dreamed up after Erik was unfairly fired.

> The siren summons Lucy to the mall
> She pays heed to the high-tech cattle call…

He pulled into the gas station across the street from Zack's to see if Trish was about. Her car was not there. It could have been his imagination, but it seemed that the cook watched him. There was a tap at the passenger's side window. With only a little fumbling, Erik found the control and lowered the deeply-tinted window. It was a nerdy kid with a round face covered in acne.

"Where's Che?"

"Don't worry about Che. What do you want?"

"Man, I'm hurting bad. Help me out."

"How much do you have?"

"Three-hundred, but I can get the rest tomorrow. Please."

"Let me see it."

The kid produced a wad of bills. Erik counted it.

"You're light, this is only two-fifty."

"Sorry. My dad doesn't keep much in his wallet anymore. I can get more, I swear."

Erik had so much dope that he almost felt guilty. He could spare some.

"Okay."

He flipped a bundle out the window and the kid lunged after it.

"Loser," Erik hissed as the window slid up.

Glancing back at Zack's, he re-imagined the scene with the cook, the spatula and the AR-15.

Taste death, you greasy, hamburger-flipping dickhead. Blam-blam. Can you laugh with holes ripped through your spine, asshole? Blam, finish him off with one last, merciful shot to the head.

Lights out, motherfucker.

There was a brisk rap on the window. It was the gas station attendant. Through the glass, Erik could not hear what he said. It didn't matter. He pulled back onto the highway and waited for the traffic light to change.

He was not sure why he'd never tried speed before. Amp working against the opiate was a perfect combination. He felt energized and focused. He'd not eaten for 24 hours, but he didn't

223

care. He wasn't hungry and he wasn't thirsty. He wasn't anything except happy.

He drove across the I-90 floating bridge and turned off on Rainier Avenue. Cruising the Central District, he found a discount autobody shop and negotiated a price with the paint-stained man behind the counter. The deluxe paint job would cost $129. Erik peeled a pair of hundreds off his roll and told the man to keep the change.

"You gonna come back for the car?"

"No," Erik said. "I'll be inside it. There's another hundred for you if you get it done quick."

The painter looked at him with curiosity, but did not comment. With Erik inside, watching and smoking a bowl, they did a quick wash, dry and mask. They sprayed ivory paint over streaks of remaining mud and dust. Soon, the black SUV was an eggshell white.

The rearview mirror reflected the scene on Martin Luther King Way. Old women waited for busses and homeless men searched through the garbage cans for aluminum cans. Lost in an opium dream, Erik lost track of time. The foreman rapped on the window several times before he could get Erik's attention.

"All done, my friend."

"Okay."

"There is the matter of an extra hundred?"

Erik was going to drive away, but noticed they'd raised a chain behind the vehicle. He popped a dose of amphetamine.

"Of course," he said. He peeled another hundred off the roll and they lowered the chain.

He loved the mixture of up and down. He felt good, mellow and at peace, but at the same time his mind was sharp. His mind explored many possibilities and he had the physical energy to implement his plans. He needed to get the SUV painted. It got done. He needed to fill the gas tank. It was expensive, over a hundred dollars, but it got done. He could afford it. In fact, he laughed. Over a hundred dollars to fill the gas tank, what a joke. If it was two or three hundred, he would not care. Money was no problem. He was a star and stars don't sweat small stuff like the cost of a tank of gas.

On a whim, he turned off 405 and drove to Bellevue Square. He was dressed like a bum. Stars don't dress like bums. There was a need to buy new clothes, so he got it done. He bought many things: a snazzy leather jacket, an expensive, distressed cowboy hat and a diamond-crusted pair of Oakley sunglasses.

Wearing his new clothes, he bought a round of drinks at the sports bar. Patrón Silver Tequila was eight bucks a shot and he did not care. Everything gleamed in golden light.

At closing time, he was escorted out by the bartender with special, gentle treatment. He handed over a hundred dollar tip. His car, gleaming like a white castle, stood alone in the parking lot. He started it and adjusted the heat against the cold. There was no heat in his trailer, so this was a magnificent luxury. All the warmth he wanted adjusted perfectly for the needs of his body. Then he found the switch for the heated seats and achieved nirvana. The deep warmth drove the chill from his bones.

Unfortunately, someone rapped on his window and would not leave him in peace. He straightened in his seat and found the window control.

"I'm resting my eyes a minute," he said.

"You can't sleep here."

Erik was surprised to find he was still in the parking garage. The security guard tapped the window with his MagLight.

"I can call a cab if you've had too much to drink."

"No, I'm fine," Erik said. "Give me half a second." He popped a pill. "Everything is fine, I'm cool. Moving along. Don't get your Wranglers in a wringer."

"Good night, sir. Drive carefully out there."

"Don't mother me."

Erik fought an impulse to pull the AR-15 and cut the guard in half. He was sick of people tap-tap-tapping on his window and nagging at him. People needed lessons on the proper respect and treatment of stars. With his hands gripping the steering wheel, he forced himself into calm. The rush of blood in his ears settled.

Through nearly-deserted Bellevue streets, he drove out of the parking garage and found the freeway and made the long drive home.

The next thing he knew, bright morning light, attenuated by the SUV's tinted glass, streamed in the windows. Sitting in the driveway near the Airstream, he was baking, and he could not throw off his clothes fast enough. His skin itched, not badly, but in places out of easy reach. He adjusted the air conditioning.

His neck was sore from the uncomfortable position he slept in. The gas tank was below half from running all night. With a deep throbbing in his head, he felt as if he'd been run over by a truck. Sometime during the night, he'd vomited on his new jacket and across the fine leather seats. The stench was disturbing and his stomach churned anew. What he needed was a bowl of Buddha and luckily, there was plenty. When the opium hit his system, he felt an immediate peace and fell asleep again.

When he woke again, the sun was directly overhead. He needed to smoke a bowl and take an upper, and then he'd be ready to face the day. He rinsed his mouth with warm Pepsi and spat out the window. With his head throbbing, he couldn't decide whether to smoke first or take the speed. Speed gave him the energy to get things done, but the opium helped his headache.

He smoked a bowl and drowsed with a warm sense of well-being. When he roused, he took a pill and washed it down with blood-warm Pepsi. There was no time to waste. He mixed up Simple Green and scrubbed the nasty vomit. Soon, except for a few stubborn stains, the interior was as good as new; clean and smelling good. He loved Simple Green. It worked great on vomit and blood and obdurate stains left behind by decomposing bodies. He vowed to buy it by the case and keep plenty of it around. Maybe he'd buy the company. He tasted it, but it was horrible, and he spat it out.

A part of his mind recognized the obsession. The varied colors of Simple Green soap bubbles were beautiful, but he needed to get a grip. There were chores, but what should he do first? How long had it been? He couldn't remember if it was time to smoke a bowl or take a pill, so he did both. His thoughts came together.

The long term goal was to punish Raz for firing him. However, the fake version of Toxic Shock Syndrome would not be in Seattle for another week. In the meantime, there was the cook at Zack's to deal with. Then he'd manage and promote Trish and her band. So, he'd deal with the cook and then work with the band to pull their songs together. First, he'd buy a bass, a good handmade one, not some Korean cheapy. Then an amplifier with vacuum tubes, not transistors. Speakers, big ones, massive 18-inch drivers. And cables and effects boxes and a tuner and picks and a cool guitar strap. It had been too long since he'd held a bass in his hands. The world tried to break him down, but he was a star and you can't hold a star away from destiny.

"Fuck yes," he shouted for the world to hear. "Let's rock."

He planned to wait until the burger stand was closed. The cook would be the last to leave and the back parking lot would be deserted. Erik put a loop of rope by the drivers' door of the cook's imported pickup. He planned to snare the cook's feet, pull the rope, topple him over, and before the stunned man could gather his wits, stab him with the switchblade. He imagined every step of the plan in vivid detail.

Unfortunately, the cook, yawning, looked at the loop incuriously and nonchalantly kicked it aside, so Erik jumped from behind a tree and stabbed him in the neck. The cook backed up to the car and held his hand against the wound with blood spurting from between his fingers.

"What the hell?" he whispered.

Darting in and out like a fencer, Erik stabbed him again and again until he fell.

"How do you like them apples, fucker?" he shouted.

He dragged the body deep into the woods, wrapped it securely in plastic garbage bags, and rolled duct tape all around and over. The completed package looked like a low-budget Egyptian mummy.

"Not so smart now, are you, fucker?" Erik said. He liked the sound of it, so he repeated it while kicking the body. Realizing he was acting compulsively again, he managed to get control after one last kick.

He drove the truck to a seedy tavern parking lot and left it with the engine running. Some drunk would steal it, or maybe drive it away by mistake. Elated, Erik found the possibilities endless and endlessly amusing.

While walking back to the burger stand, he jumped into the trees along the road when a car came by. He was sure no one saw him. He dragged the cook's body deeper into the woods and threw it down a ravine into a creek.

More than satisfied with the day's work, he traipsed back to the hidden Escalade. After smoking a bowl and dry-swallowing a pill, it began to rain. Massive drops pounded the moon roof. He watched raindrops pour from the sky and splatter against the darkened glass.

Perfect. All the evidence of my work will be washed away. The cops will have nothing.

Toxic Shock Syndrome

He turned up the music. On the FM radio station, Tears for Fears, like Erik, sowed the seeds of love. *Everything is possible.* The sound system in the Cadillac was beautiful with stereo imaging like nothing he'd heard in a car before.

Mark Levinson, whoever you are, I love you, man, he thought while tapping on the steering wheel in time with the beat.

In the dark, while rain poured from the sky like a cleansing shower of love, he eased onto the highway and pointed the car toward home.

His eyes were heavy and he almost missed the turnout. The car slewed like a supertanker as he overcorrected and thundered too fast down the driveway. The Airstream, illuminated in the headlights, looked like a giant, slimy slug. Its eyes, on stalks, turned toward him. As Erik pulled the SUV to a lurching stop, he realized he was hallucinating. The trailer was not a slug, it was a trailer. He wondered why he'd been so eager to get home. Without heat in the trailer, it would be more comfortable in the SUV. In fact, the cushy seats reclined to make a very comfortable bed.

It was cold when he woke. To-the-bone cold. He cranked the engine, but it would not catch. He noticed the yellow fuel gage warning light. Out of gas. With his pulse exploding in his head, he slammed his fists on the steering wheel. All the money in the world and he'd run out of gas. God wasn't punishing him, but issuing a warning. The Lord would provide, but Erik needed to pay attention and take care of business.

This was a setback, but not a fatal one. He could call for a tow truck to bring gas, but the phone did not work, so that was not an option. Slowly, a plan crystallized. He'd smoke a bowl, and then flag down some beaner driving by. For a hundred dollar bill, a kid would go to town and bring back a five gallon can of gas. Then, Erik would be back in play. With kindness overflowing in his heart, he decided not to kill the person who stopped to help unless it was absolutely necessary. There were already enough dead bodies on the property.

For security, Erik walked half a mile down the highway. He stood on a sweeping corner and waited for a prospect. He ignored fancy and expensive vehicles. Soon enough, a teenager in a red Toyota pickup with a crumpled fender putt-putted up. Erik waved him down.

"What's up man? You breakdown somewhere?"

The kid was dressed in flannel and wore an oily Seattle Mariners hat.

"Like a damn fool, I ran my car out of gas on one of the logging roads."

He showed off a crisp hundred dollar bill and ripped it carefully in half. "Bring me back five gallons of premium, and you get the other half. Get it?"

The kid's face split open with a wide grin.

"I'm on it. You want to ride along?"

"No," Erik said, "I'll wait here."

"Thanks, man, I can use the money. I'll be back in a flash."

Flash was not the word Erik would choose while watching the Toyota, rusted and held together with duct tape, lurch onto the highway with muffler blatting as it disappeared around a corner.

The Lord works in curious ways.

True to his word, the kid came back after an hour

"Do you want me to help? I can run you to your car and make sure it starts."

Erik handed over the remaining fragment of the money. He heaved the heavy can from the pickup bed.

"No, you've been a real help. I'm good from here."

230

"All right, thanks man. I can really use this money, I've been thinking of the best way to spend it all the way there and back." He pulled a few feet ahead and then stopped.

Maybe I will have to kill him, Erik thought.

"I just wanted to say, I love your hat, man, it's cool."

Erik had forgotten about it. He touched his head and adjusted the beret.

"Get your own," he said sternly.

The kid's grin faltered. "Whatever, man."

With tires crunching the gravel on the shoulder of the highway, the kid pulled truck onto the roadway and was soon out of sight.

Glen and Raz

Glen slept most of the next day, and then ordered an omelet from the room service menu. Leaning over the room's breakfast bar, he ate while reading through a selection of newspapers.

As usual, the world spiraled toward Armageddon; the news was a sordid compilation of elections, wars, gruesome accidents and actresses in rehab. He tossed the paper aside and looked through the drapes across the Las Vegas skyline. So far, his job as a rover was boring. He decided to find the rock stars and see what they were doing.

But first, a fortifying stop at the bar. The staging area of the Moon Nightclub held a line-up of wannabe patrons, but Glen bypassed them and showed his backstage pass to the doorman. A hundred-dollar-bill hidden behind the pass was smoothly liberated and Glen was immediately ushered through the doorway. The crowd in the Moon was fluid; by edging out a swooping Asian sporting a bleached fake-Mohawk, he commandeered a dirty table by a window

231

and looked outside while the busboy cleared away the clutter. The setting sun painted rosé tints onto wispy clouds. Another day shot.

Where did the day go and what did he have to show for it?

The nightclub décor was odd, like a Clockwork Orange dream gone bad. In the next booth, Glen thought he recognized the lanky man wearing a gaudy diamond stud in each ear. He was built like a basketball player; maybe that's what he was. He argued with his drinking companion, a fleshy woman who looked much older.

"We're young. I don't want no family tying me down, and you know that. You got knocked up on purpose to trap me."

"How can you say that?"

"I'll bet it ain't even mine."

"Then you'll want a paternity test. That's no problem."

"What does it cost for a coochy root canal?"

"I'm not killing our baby."

"Goddam it, Stephanie, it's not a baby, it's a blob of cells. It would be like spitting out a loogie, fer craps' sake. We're not having no baby."

"You're hurting me."

At this point the waitress stopped by.

"What can I get you, sir?" she asked.

Glen turned and was instantly distracted. The waitress had huge breasts exploding like popcorn from a silvery, over-stressed, halter top.

"Woah, what a question at a time like this. What's a bad girl like you doing in a nice place like this?" He took a deep breath and looked at her face. "I withdraw the question; I'm a married man. Christ on a sandwich, I hope you have a federal license for those things. Okay, I want three shots of Bacardi 151, neat, and a book of matches."

"There's no smoking here, sir. I can give you directions to the cigar bar..."

He fished a hundred-dollar bill from his shirt pocket and slid it across the table. She vacuumed it up efficiently.

"Right away, sir," she said.

The conversation at the next booth turned uglier.

"You bitches is always pulling shit like this. I'm on the edge of breaking through. Memphis and Oklahoma sent scouts. I need to concentrate on my conditioning for summer camp and you pull this shit."

"Dad says the job at the dealership is still open. You warmed the bench for two years. It's time to grow up. Man up and be a father to your baby."

An advantage to being a big tipper was excellent service. The waitress placed his drink on the table.

"Will there be anything else, sir?" she said with a sweet smile that reached all the way to her eyes.

"I'm going to cause a commotion," he said, flicking his eyes to the next booth. "Cover for me so I can slip out of here?"

He slipped another hundred under an art deco salt shaker.

She glanced at the neighboring couple with distaste.

"He's a crybaby flopper on the court too. The emergency exit says it's alarmed, but we got tired of the racket and flipped off the circuit breaker."

It must be hard to be a smart woman with large breasts. Were it not for my happy marriage, I'd plumb her depths.

"Thanks," Glen said.

After she was safely away, he prepared the matchbook and got up. Next door, the basketball player gathered a grip on his girlfriend's blouse; he appeared to be close to committing a blatant personal foul.

"Excuse me," Glen said. "I'd like to buy you a drink."

He placed the tall tumbler on their table.

"Get out of my face or I'll fuck you up, honk. We is havin' a private conversation. Piss off."

With his mutilated left hand, Glen slowly pushed the glass across the table and toppled it on the man's lap.

"Son of a bitch," the man complained, "I'll kill you dead."

"Big talk for a man on fire," Glen commented.

Smoothly, he struck the match, lighted the matchbook and flicked it. Immediately, pale blue flames erupted. Glen walked quickly to the emergency entrance partially hidden behind a curtain of gleaming black and white beads. After pushing through, he found himself in an austere stairway. Taking two stairs at a time, he descended.

Glen found Raz and the entourage in the big studio room. Murphy held up her hand to stop Jesus, mid-rant, and stomped up to Glen.

"What have you been doing?"

"My job. Roving." Glen said, "Researching the newspaper over a leisurely breakfast, lighting a basketball player on fire, odds and ends, nothing special."

Jesus stood and towered over Glen.

"I get sick of your bullshit. Lighting people on fire—"

"Back off, Jesus," Murphy said. "From bitter experience, I know the more outlandish his claim, the more likely it is to be true. It's not worth fretting over." To Glen she said, "Raz is looking for you."

"Cool," Glen said.

Raz, smoking his hookah, held court on a leather sofa on an elaborate Turkish carpet. Three of his girls attended and watched Glen approach.

"Ah, my best friend, Glen. I want you to meet a very special guest. This is Barry."

Barry, in his forties, wore a garish, neon Hawaiian shirt and gold neck chain. Absurdly, he wore a fluffy wig with wisps of lint trapped in the curls. Rising from his stool, he grabbed Glen's hand for a vigorous shake. His vintage watch was a platinum Patek Philippe. Glen did a quick appraisal. The watch was worth five grand on eBay.

"Nice watch," Glen said, "can I have it?"

Barry actually reached for the clasp before coming to his senses.

"No, it was my father's."

Raz looked on with mild disgust.

"Sorry," Glen said. "Sometimes that works."

"Barry won a VH-1 contest. He gets to spend six hours with the band."

"How delightful that it has nothing to do with me," Glen said.

Jesus pushed Glen aside. "I don't think it's a good idea. I said I'd play tour guide," Jesus interjected.

"And I told you Barry has ideas about the rock-n-roll lifestyle that are better served by *roving* with Glen," Raz said firmly.

"Side bet?" Glen suggested.

"What do you have in mind?" Raz asked.

"Five-hundred says by the end of the six hours *I'm* wearing the watch."

Raz's face erupted into a wide smile.

"Done."

Glen pulled out his wallet and handed Murphy a wad of bills.

Raz gestured to Charity. She did not approve, but got off her cushion and dug through a pile of coats to find her purse. She walked back with a motley assortment of bills. Murphy counted.

"I want to go on record that this is ill-advised," Murphy said.

"Duly noted," Raz replied.

"What just happened?" Barry asked.

"Don't give him your watch," Raz said.

Gerusha

The movers were gone and the condo was empty. Eloise, representing property management, walked though scribbling notes on a clipboard. Gerusha stood on the balcony and looked over the street one last time. Standing at exactly the right spot, she could see a horizontal slice of the Space Needle. It had not occurred to her she might miss the place.

Below, the Second Coming guy leaned his sign against the fender of a Mercedes SUV. Between bites of a greasy slice of pizza, he sipped from a large plastic water bottle. The center of his sign said 'The AND is near!!!' The margins were covered with scrawled Bible verses.

"Break time?"

He looked up and squinted into the bright sky.

"Hey, pretty lady," he said. "King Hezekiah had exceeding much riches and honor: and he made himself treasuries for silver, and for gold, and for precious stones, and for spices, and for shields, and for all manner of precious jewels. That's from Chronicles. Then, Hezekiah slept with his fathers. That means he died."

"The *AND* is near? What exactly does that mean?"

"It comes after the end times. The center of body, space, void and logos. All man's work scattered before winds of destruction. It's not too late to repent. Give me money?"

Gerusha considered the question.

"How about food instead?"

The man thought it over. "Okay," he said.

236

Inside, by the front door, rested the very last box. It was filled with cold stuff from her refrigerator. She selected a bottle of white wine and a salami.

After walking back to the balcony, she called down. "Are you ready?"

The man held out his arms and caught the salami. He stuffed it in his coat pocket. She dropped the bottle and he clutched it to his chest like a baby.

"You turned my water into wine," he said. "Do you have a corkscrew?"

"The Lord helps the man who helps himself."

"Thanks. I can handle it. The good book says God is just: He will pay back trouble to those who trouble you and give relief to you who are troubled."

"I'm relieved to hear that," Gerusha said.

She turned at a tap on her shoulder. Eloise looked tired. Deep, dark circles stained sagging skin under her eyes. Her gray hair bristled.

"There are marks on the wall in the bedroom. We'll hold back a hundred bucks for painting. It takes four to six weeks to cut a check. Sign and you're done."

Gerusha thought back. In prior years, she'd argue over damage deposits with teary-eyed, futile desperation. Her life was different now.

"Do you ever get tired of fighting over a few measly dollars?"

Eloise looked puzzled, as if she did not understand the question.

"No," she said. "It's my job."

"Good for you," Gerusha said while scribbling her signature on the form.

CHAPTER EIGHTEEN

Glen and Barry

"Where you from, man? Toledo?" Glen asked.

"No, Dublin. It's near—"

"I know where it is. Been to Vegas before?"

"A couple of times, but I was working trade shows, so all I saw was the airport, the hotel and the convention hall. I won twenty-seven dollars from a slot machine at the airport."

"That's nice. You have five hours and ten minutes left. What would you like to do?"

"I don't know. I saw TSS seventeen times last year. Can we check out the real Vegas so I can take home a few stories to brag about?"

"Ah," Glen said, "that's something I can help you with." He clapped Barry on the back. "Let's hit it."

They started with drinks at the Railroad Casino a few blocks off the strip.

"I think you need a woman," Glen said. "Pick one."

"What?"

"You're a prize winner and you need a woman. Pick one."

A pair of giggling Asian secretaries sipped umbrella drinks. Glen hoped Barry would not pick one of them. Well-dressed and classy, they would be difficult to win over. Otherwise, to Glen's eye the ladies in the bar were a motley mix of visiting LA hookers, drug addicts, slumming school teachers and rotund farm girls.

"Wow, any of them? You're kidding."

"This is Vegas, my man, there's no kidding. You got a girl back home?"

"Yeah, she's a day shift manager at Kohl's. She couldn't get a day off or she'd be here."

"Her loss. Got a Vegas girl in mind?"

"Are you serious? Any of them?"

"Your time's wasting."

Barry finished his drink and waved the glass in the air for a refill.

"You'd never get the girl at the bar. The one wearing red?"

It was invisible on the outside, but internally, Glen celebrated. To his trained eye, she was clearly a whore, and, over thirty, on the sad, one-way tail-end of her career. World-weary and rough around the edges, she was not a high-dollar piece though her blond hair flowed over her shoulders like an arctic wave and her nails were shiny. There was a lot of mileage on her chassis.

"Don't move a muscle," Glen said.

He walked to the bar and pressed himself between the flashy girl and a man sweating under a lurid black topper. Glen guessed he was an insurance salesman from Sacramento.

"Hey mister, the lady and I are having a conversation."

"Look, Mac. I'm an undercover cop. Unless you want your picture plastered on the front page of the Sacramento Bee, I suggest you take a walk."

"Cock-blocker."

"Beat it, Clem," Glen said sternly. "I don't have enough time to ruin your day."

The man drained his glass and shuffled toward the door.

"I like a man who takes command of the situation. What's your name, Sugar?"

"I have a business proposition for you."

He waved to the bartender for another drink and held up two fingers.

"What other kinds of propositions are there?"

"Take a look at the overheated dude in the corner. Ride with us and roll with the punches and there's a grand in it for you, plus tip."

"For a grand, baby, I'll bear his children."

"That's close to what I have in mind."

"The grand would be up-front, of course."

"Do I look like a man who is ignorant of tradecraft?" Glen, pretending to be offended, pressed a palm over his heart.

Shielding the transaction from Barry, he pushed a bundle of bills across the bar. Then, hand-in-hand, they walked back to the table. Barry, sloshing the drinks at the table, got up as they approached.

"Barry, I'd like you to meet my friend, Tiffany. Tiffany is an executive secretary from, where'd you say? Minneapolis?"

She looked at Glen with curiosity and unconsciously patted the pocketbook where the cash had been stuffed away.

"Madison."

"Yeah, same difference. Madison. She's been watching since you came in. She thinks you're a hottie. I told her you're a prize winner and she insisted on an introduction. Tiffany, meet Barry."

Flustered, Barry hesitantly offered his hand for a shake.

"Here in Vegas, it's more traditional to give a lady a kiss after being introduced."

Barry looked like he would prefer to bolt, but he craned his neck to kiss her cheek. She captured the kiss on her lips. Barry's eyes fluttered.

"You taste like a carnival."

"Thanks, I think," she said.

She made a wry face while exchanging a glance with Glen.

Is this guy for real?

Glen shrugged.

"The recipe for the evening calls for more alcohol," he said while gesturing for the waitress.

As professionals, Glen and Tiffany paced themselves with ginger ale while Barry, getting drunker and drunker, imbibed shot after shot of Jack Daniels. The evening passed in a kaleidoscope of images. Tiffany hanging over Barry's shoulders while, like a machine, he pulled the handle on a dollar slot machine. Tiffany, giggling and flashing her bosoms while Barry tossed the dice at a craps table. She screamed and planted sloppy kisses on Barry's neck after a fortuitous spin of the roulette wheel. Buying a cheap wedding set from a turban-clad Paki at an off-strip pawn shop. Standing in front of a new-age, black, amateur philosopher-preacher (with electric candles reflecting cheap sparkle from crystals strung around his neck) and exchanging wedding vows. Standing at the airport ticket counter and trying to find a JetBlue flight with the fewest connections to the newlywed's home to Ohio. Bleary-eyed, Barry stared at the flight schedules on flatscreen monitors. Tiffany tugged Glen's arm and pulled him aside.

"I don't want to go to Ohio," she said. "How far are you taking this?"

"Don't worry, we're in the final scene. Go to the restroom and wash off your makeup. Wet your hair and take off your heels. Get rid of the control-top panties and push-up bra. Let it all hang out."

"Damn it, Glen. I'll look like a shipwreck."

Glen shrugged. "Your call. They say the Ohio weather is great for ten days between the ice storms and soul-stealing humidity of summer. I'm sure Barry will let you drive his minivan to the White Castle on Friday nights."

"You're one-hundred-percent son-of-a-bitch, aren't you?"

"I'd be lying if I claimed to be anything else. Scoot."

A different woman came back. In the cold airport lighting, she looked ten years older and twenty pounds heavier. She grasped Barry's arm and looked into his eyes.

"We'll be so happy in Dublin."

It took a few minutes, but Barry sobered up. A look of panic spread across his face. He detached his arm and pulled on Glen's collar. They walked a few steps away.

"What have I done?"

"You married the woman of your dreams and you're headed home to live happily ever after. Congratulations, sport, she's a prize."

They looked back at Tiffany. Chewing a massive wad of gum, she turned her hand and admired the reflected sparkle of her wedding ring.

"This can't be happening. You gotta help me."

"What?"

"I can't take her home. Save me, please."

Frowning, Glen scratched his chin.

"She's not going to take this well. Didn't she say her father is a big-time attorney? This could be ugly. Wait. Maybe there is a way. Yes. Give me your watch and I'll make her go away."

"My father's watch? What does that have to do with anything?" Slowly, realization hit him. "That's what this is about?"

"She'll look fine with a few extra pounds of fat, don't worry about it. Women always gain a few pounds after they get married. Your mama will love her."

"You're an asshole."

"I've heard that one before. Am I getting the watch or not?"

"Oh," Barry groaned, "it was my daddy's watch."

"No sweat. Besides, I'll give you mine. It's only a Casio, but it keeps good time. I got it off a bell clerk in Orlando, but that's a long story and we don't have the time. To me, it has great sentimental value, but you can have it." He unclasped the band and dangled it. "Are we making a deal or are you taking Tiffany home and introducing her to your bowling league?"

Barry dropped his watch into Glen's palm.

"The best lessons are the tough ones," Glen commented.

"Screw you, jerk," Barry replied.

Pointedly not looking at Tiffany, he walked over and grabbed his carry-on bag. Glen, admiring the new watch on his wrist, followed and put his arm across Tiffany's shoulder. They watched Barry stomp toward the security line.

"Another happy customer," Glen said.

"You're a piece of work." She laughed. "Look, the night is young and the way I figure it, you still have time left on the meter. What say you we go to your room and watch the sun come up together?"

He pressed a roll of cash into her hand and wrapped her fingers around it.

"I'd love to. Go put your control top panties back on."

When she came out of the restroom, she knew he'd be gone. And he was.

At the Pearl, after waving his backstage passes at the security staff, Glen arrived in time to catch the last few minutes of Toxic Shock Syndrome's final encore. From sidestage, he watched Raz, backlit by globs of ruby-red lavalight flowing like blood, stalk the stage like a panther. Flurries of deafening, echo-laden riffs ionized the air like audio lightning. How it was done was not clear, but tendrils of electrical discharge snaked through Raz's body into the stage smoke. It was like an unhappy Christ was back in town.

Glen shook his head to clear the absurd thought. After the house lights were turned on, with ears ringing, he walked through the exiting crowd. Again, it struck him how well-behaved the kids were. An errant candy wrapper lasted only a few seconds on the floor before a teenager, grotesquely bearing lip studs and snaky braids, picked it up. Glen made eye-contact with the kid but could not interpret the calm confidence in his eyes.

"Good show?" Glen asked.

"Always," the kid replied.

Against the flow, clumps of girls streamed through the side stage entrances. Glen waved his pass and joined them. They formed a serpentine line weaving around backstage obstacles. Politely, the procession parted for the stage crew rolling heavy equipment cases. The girl before him was slim, about five-foot-six and wearing a TSS t-shirt tied over a slightly-protruding stomach. She seemed about 16, but must have been older. She wore a wedding band adorned with the TSS emblem on her ring finger. He tapped her on the shoulder.

"That's a cute ring. Can I have a look?"

Over her shoulder, she flicked a passive look at him, but did not respond. Charity walked up and kissed the girl on both cheeks before turning to address Glen.

"What are you doing?"

"My job. Roving. People keep asking, but it doesn't seem like that complicated a concept," Glen said. "Right now, I'm waiting in line to see Raz like the rest of the civilians. Is that okay by you?"

Her expression was sour. She bit off the words.

"If you need to see him, you don't need to wait in line."

"I'm fine, thanks," Glen said. "I'll wait with nearly infinite patience."

Charity turned back to the girl. Like old friends, they rested hands on each other's bulging bellies.

"We're operating on the theory that he's mostly harmless," Charity said.

"It's okay, I can handle it," the girl responded.

Glen watched Charity walk away.

"Who's the lucky daddy?" he asked.

It could have been imagined, but he sensed a transient shadow of smile flicking across her lips. She did not speak.

"Okay, be that way," Glen said.

The girls waited quietly.

Beyond a shared age and being physically similar, what did these girls have in common? They were small-framed and young, between 18 and 23 or so, but there was something else. They had dignity. They did not chomp wads of gum or giggle. They shared something... something grave, serious and solemn.

Generally, Glen was quick to spot undercurrents and underlying patterns. Now, he saw the vague outline of something, but the precise character escaped him. It tickled his subconscious.

Finally, they came to the end of the line. Leaning over to peer through a crack in the thick curtain, he watched the girl take her turn with Raz. On his throne, he was gentle. He took her hands and whispered in her ear. He placed his hands on her belly.

Was this a blessing? Ritual? Communion?

Raz got on his knees and pressed his face into her stomach. The girl ran her hands through his hair. After a minute, Raz climbed back on the throne. He took her hands and kissed the ends of her thumbs. Charity draped a chain and medallion around the girl's neck and her audience was complete. Without looking back, she walked to the exit and it was Glen's turn.

Raz puffed on his hookah.

"Char told me you got the watch. Does Barry still have his arm?"

"No fans were permanently damaged in the process."

"And I'm out five-hundred bucks. I'm impressed. I don't generally lose my wagers."

"Me either," Glen commented.

Raz laughed. "How goes the roving?"

"It's a job I was born to do." Glen gestured expansively. "This scene is interesting. I don't get it. What's your trip, dude?"

"Just another hard day at the office," Raz said. "After the show in Seattle, I'm taking some time off."

"Is that supposed to mean something to me, or is it just your smooth way of changing the subject?"

"Once the gig is over, I might actually miss you, Glen. Maybe. Shall we not keep the remaining ladies waiting?"

Glen smiled with his characteristic toothy grin.

"As you say, boss," he said.

CHAPTER NINETEEN

Erik

With an eerie sense of déjà vu, Erik pulled into Zack's parking lot and beeped the horn. Was this something he'd dreamed? The 'CLOSED' sign was prominent on the door, but he could see movement inside. He honked again. Trish came from behind the building.

"The cook is tardy, so we're closed."

"That's likely a long fuckin' wait. I'm not here for a grease burger. Hop in and we'll go for a ride."

She leaned her forearms on the door.

"I unrolled my Tox poster. You don't look much like the bass player. You're old, for one thing."

"That picture was taken a while ago and I'm not wearing makeup. Jump in. We'll party like rock stars."

"I'm gong to the library to meet my friends. I stopped by to get my paycheck."

"Fuck it. Let's smoke a bowl. If you still want to go to the library later, you'll be in the right mood for it."

Trish looked over the Escalade.

"This is a cool ride except for the shitty paint job. If you had wheels like this, why were you walking the other day?"

"For exercise. You getting in? The day is wasting."

She looked back at the restaurant. A pickup truck pulled in, then rolled away after the driver noticed the 'CLOSED' sign.

"I got time for a bowl, I guess," she said.

Internally celebrating, Erik pushed open the passenger door and she hopped in. Off the highway, he found a deserted church parking lot and parked the truck in a far corner.

"My dad was religious until my real mom died."

"That's nice," Erik said. He packed Buddha into his pipe and got it burning. "Go easy on this until you get used to it."

"I'm not twelve any more." She took a drag and held the smoke deep in her lungs. Erik was impressed. She only coughed a little. "What is this shit?"

"It's from the Garden of Eden. Shut up and find a cool radio station, will ya?"

She pressed buttons until she found a hiphop station. The throbbing bass pounded their ears.

"Old school shit, Young Jeezy and Jibbs," Trish said. "You know them?"

"I hate this jungle jive. I thought you liked doom metal?"

"I listened to it a lot when I was young. Not so much now."

"You said you're fifteen."

"Right. When I was little I dug the death-grunt stuff. But I still like TSS. We could pop in a CD if you have one."

"Find a metal station. They'll play some."

"Okay."

She scanned through stations until a Strapping Young Lad song blasted from the speakers.

"That's what I call music," Erik said.

They sat and smoked and listened.

"You have the best dope," she said languidly. "I'm warm and happy. Want to feel my titties? They're little, but they'll grow, I think."

"Maybe later," Erik replied. "Let's take an upper, then I'll buy you a bass guitar."

"Cool," Trish said.

The music store was busy. Shiny guitars in nearly infinite colors and shapes clung to the walls. Erik had been coming to the store for a year, but had never bought anything but a G-string for his last bass guitar before hocking it. The clerks looked him over quickly and averted their eyes. Ignoring the tag that said 'ask for assistance', Erik banged the headstock of an elaborately-tooled Alembic Buzzard bass against the Tobias Classic 5 bass next to it.

"What about this one?" he asked.

"Ugly," Trish said.

Pete, one of the younger clerks, approached.

"I'll put it away for you, sir," he said.

"It's about time I got some service. I'm buying my squeeze a bass. What's the most expensive thing you have?"

"Are you looking for something new or vintage? We have a beautiful 1964 P-bass that was owned by John Paul Jones. He lives nearby, you know. Comes with signed certificate. All original pots and never refinished; a collector's piece."

"I hate second-hand thrift-shop shit," Trish commented.

"Okay. We have a new one-of-a-kind Zachary bass but our consignment contract restricts who we can sell it to. The Alembic you're scratching up is nice, but the best piece in the store is a Ken Smith 5-string custom. It has a solid gold bridge." He feigned a look over his shoulder. "We're asking ten grand, but we'll take eight," he said with false secrecy.

249

He led them to a glass display case where the bass, displayed like a museum artifact, was illuminated by jewelry store lights.

"The quilted maple is stunning on this one."

"It looks like a woodpecker barfed," Trish commented. "I already have a Fender Squire bass; what I really want is a violin bass like the Guitar Hero game."

"We have several; do you want a classic Hofner Beatle bass or one of the Korean versions?"

"I don't care."

"Bring her the top-of-the-line one. I have the cash for it."

Pete perked up. "Are you finally scoring Tox royalties?"

"Don't worry about where the money comes from."

"This bass comes with a case. Shall we make up a package with strap, tuner, cables and extra strings?"

"Yeah, throw it all in," Erik said.

"Coolio," Trish said. She sorted through straps hanging from a display searching for one that matched her fingernail polish.

Erik peeled off five one-hundred dollar bills and tossed them on the counter.

"Keep the change," he said.

"Uh, sorry, with tax I need another fifty-seven bucks."

Erik, sighing with bored weariness, reached for his wallet. "Whatever," he said while adding another bill to the stack.

Carrying the bass and bags of accessories back to the car, Trish leaned over and gave him a kiss on the neck.

"Thanks," she said.

"You're welcome, baby," Erik replied.

Driving the Escalade through a residential neighborhood, they approached Trish's house.

"Drive slow. I need to see if my dad is home. I don't want him to see me bring this stuff in. He asks too flippin' many questions."

The house was a tan split-level in an older neighborhood. Behind a chain link fence, the grass was overgrown and dotted with vivid yellow dandelions.

"Okay, looks good. I'll jump out. You find a place to park and come back. I don't want the car sitting out front because the neighbors talk."

Erik found a spot around the block by a neighborhood park. He adjusted his sunglasses and rubbed a finger across his furry teeth. The street was nearly deserted. Erik wondered what day it was. Thursday? Apparently, most people were either at school or at work. When he got to the front door, Trish opened it. She looked around.

"Did anyone see you? Dad doesn't let me to have people over. He pops a gasket."

Erik pushed by her.

"No one saw me," he said.

"My room is down the hall."

They entered. Her twin bed was mussed. She had draped the guitar strap across her mirror. A TSS poster was spread across her desk in front of her computer's video monitor. On the walls, rappers with grotesque grill-decorated smiles leered down on them. She held the poster next to his face.

"Do you wear the black and white makeup anymore?"

"I will when I get back with the band. Put on some music."

"I have TSS on my Zune but we can't play it too loud or the neighbors will call the cops."

While peering nearsightedly at the tiny Zune screen, she thumbed through menus and found a collection. Softly, in the background, Raz sang about the Conquering Aardvarks of Armageddon.

"I never understood this song…"

251

Ken Coffman

"It's useless to try to understand Raz. He lives somewhere beyond crazy. Let's toke up."

They smoked a bowl and listened to the music. Trish twisted a strand of hair around her index finger.

"Thanks for all the shit," she said while gesturing at the bass hidden under her clothes in the closet.

Erik pushed the strap of her shirt down her arm and kissed her neck.

"Let's fuck," he said.

"I don't want you to get the wrong idea. I'll blow you if you wear a condom, but no vaginal. I'm a virgin and saving myself for my boyfriend. Give me a minute. Dad has a bunch of rubbers in his nightstand. I'll get one."

He heard the toilet flush, then she came back with a little packet.

"You're not ready," she said.

Erik said pointed at his crotch.

"Get busy."

She worked at his zipper and fished out his flaccid penis.

"You're not sportin' bone. I can't put a jimmy hat on that."

"Then rub me up," Erik said impatiently. "If you do it right, I'll get hard.

While she worked on his limp, useless penis, he reached over her head and snagged the music store bag. After unwrapping the bass strings, he looped the 'E' string around her neck and pulled tight. Her fingers, with nails painted pale pink, scrabbled at the string. After ninety seconds she was unconscious and after five minutes she was dead. Erik noticed he was now hard; his erection flopped like a deepsea fishing pole. He slapped her purple face.

"Great," he said. "Stupid bitch. Your virginity is safe now."

The metal string had dug into his flesh; dots of blood oozed from his sore palms. He coiled up the wire and stuffed it back in the bag. His mood was in turmoil and he felt disconnected. Did he need to smoke a bowl or take an upper? He couldn't tell.

"Why'd you off that bizzle?"

Erik looked around the small room.

"Huh?"

"I said, yo, bo-janglin' dopeshit, why'd you smoke that white ba-donka-donk shorty?"

Erik realized the rapper in the poster on the wall was talking to him. He stood up and studied the image. Bangin' Leroi Freekway had garish, diamond-studded teeth, a watch the size of a saucer and a hostile expression.

Wallpaper can't talk.

"You're a crumb-snatching poser goldfish. I liked to watch her get ready for bed. She wore panties with pink dots."

Now the rapper sounded like Raz.

"You'll take me back in the band or I'll…"

"You'll what, douchy?"

"I'll kill you too."

He picked up Trish; she was as light as a doll. So he wouldn't have to look at her mottled face, he turned her body so she faced the wall and arranged the covers. With tousled hair spread across her heart-shaped pillow, she appeared to be sleeping. His mind worked. Maybe they'd think the cook killed her and then ran away. He should leave as little evidence behind as possible. After making sure the receipt was still in the bag, he gathered all the purchases. Not wanting to carry it, he left the bass guitar in the closet. Standing at the front door, he scanned the neighborhood. All was quiet. Without encountering anyone, he walked to the Escalade and drove away.

Ken Coffman

Gerusha

Bubb's shiny new Lexus, bearing a custom plate reading *SOLDOUT*, was parked on the street. Sighing, Gerusha retrieved the box of cold food from the trunk of her little Mazda. The front door was cracked open; she pushed through and walked to the kitchen. After arranging the food on the racks in the refrigerator, she pressed a cool Diet Pepsi to her forehead, then popped the tab and took a sip.

"Ah Gerusha, my sweet," Bubb said with forced cheer. He grabbed her shoulders firmly and kissed her, European style, on both cheeks. He spoke quickly with a desperate, smarmy urgency. "I know you're going to be mad, but bear with me for a minute. We're talking about a lot of money. Hard cash money. They wrote me an earnest-money check for a half-million, off-the-books. They love, love, love the house. I found you a modern place more suitable for the princess you are. It's on Mercer Island, right on the water, with brand new slab-granite counters and a slate roof. It's ready to move in, with a Jacuzzi big enough for the Seahawks front line. It has the cutest, cozy sun room filled with ferns. You'll pocket a ton of cash. Did I mention the neighbors? Rock stars and movie people, big fun, dinner parties and cocktails with A-list big money folks. It's a dream come true."

"How did you get in?"

"Oh. Rosie let me in. Isn't she a sweetie? When you move to Mercer Island, will you take her?"

"I'm not moving."

She pushed past him and walked back to the entry. The floor, a checkerboard pattern of pink and tan marble tiles, gleamed under the massive chandelier. Like royalty, the prospective buyers floated down the curved stairway. The lady was dressed in a layered, peach-colored chiffon dress and gracefully maneuvered tall high heels like a Chinese

254

acrobat. He, a thin, older man, was dressed all in black and wore dark glasses.

The lady held out her hand and offered a limp handshake.

"You must be the mistress of the house. I can tell from the clever, simple elegance of your fashion sense." Gerusha, with a smudge of dust on her cheek, was dressed for moving furniture. She wore blue jeans with a hole ripped in the knee, a sweat-dampened cotton blouse and running shoes. "I love sophistication with modern touches. This house is like a cross between Tara and a Howard Roark modern classic. The wallpaper, paint scheme and decorative wainscoting in the master bedroom are pure genius, my dear. It will have to go, of course, because it will clash with our hand-made Italian furniture, but I very much admire your design choices considering your budget constraints."

A pellet of radioactive anger warmed Gerusha's midsection.

"I'm afraid you have been misled. This house is not for sale."

"Ah, Bobby was right, you're a pistol," the man said. "Please allow me to introduce myself. I'm Tom Kooper and I'd have to check, but I think I still hold the record for the most money ever made by a CEO in a single year." Conspiratorially, he mock-whispered: "You see, I was smart enough cash out early in 2000." He laughed and put his arm possessively around his wife's waist. "Our taste is particular. Rarely is what we want for sale. But, as you can imagine, we can readily afford indulgence. So, I am determined to buy this house and the only thing undetermined is how much of my cash you'll walk away with. As I understand it, you're clearing a net profit of three-million for a house you're not fully moved into. Only a lunatic or moron would say no to that deal and clearly you're neither. So, let's cancel the posturing part of our negotiation and move on to the bottom line and logistics, shall we?"

"I need to talk to my husband, Glen—" She noticed Bubb's self-satisfied smirk. She did not like the smug implication. "What?"

"I hope you don't mind. Paula gave me his contact information and we've been talking. Glen's ready, willing, even eager to sign right away and grab that easy money," Bubb said.

The anger in her belly expanded and filled her body with hot plasma. With super-human restraint, she stopped herself from grinding the Pepsi can in his face. The anger coalesced in scary, soulless cold. She looked around the kitchen, taking in the shiny new Sub-Zero appliances and copper pots and pans hanging over the granite-topped island. Overhead, recessed fixtures filled the room evenly with soft white light. With a steady hand, she plucked a coaster from a stack and arranged the soda can precisely in its center. She flipped open her cell phone and pressed the quick-dial number.

"Glen, I need you here," she said.

His response was quick. Somehow, she knew it would be. His hesitation might only have been the lag time between the cell phone signal bouncing from tower to base station to satellite and back to earth again.

"Okay, I'll call you when I land at Boeing Field," he said before breaking the connection.

She closed the phone and dropped it on the counter. "He's coming."

In the taxi hailed from the entry of the Palms, Glen called the airport and arranged for an Eclipse 500 pocket jet to be waiting on the tarmac. After paying the cabbie, a guard nodded and let Glen through a gate into the private terminal area. In bright sunlight, the air bore signs of the scorching afternoon coming later in the day; he walked briskly to the jet's stairway. The Captain, wearing a crisply-pressed uniform and peaked cap, shook his hand and gestured to the stairway.

In minutes, pressed back in the seat by aggressive g-forces, they were airborne. Glen glanced at his new watch. Gerusha's call had come 27 minutes earlier.

Over his shoulder, the pilot commented: "We'll press as much as we can. Flying time will be just over 90 minutes."

"Thanks," Glen replied.

"If you'll pass me your credit card, I'll get the billing taken care of."

"I'm paying cash if you don't mind."

The pilot glanced back. "That's no problem at all, sir."

They soared over the Nevada and Oregon desert. The horizon-to-horizon expanse of barren nothingness scared him. There was so damn much of it. It was a hostile, unforgiving and useless land.

How many bones had turned to dust under the unrelenting sun? How many lost souls wandered the arid folds of its landscape?

"If you choose to smoke a cigar, I'll have to close the door to protect the cockpit electronics."

Glen's thin lips stretched into a grin. Behind a cherry-stained cabinet door, he found a bottle of Chivas Regal and a small humidor of Romeo y Julieta Churchill Robusto cigars. With a crystal glass in one fist and a smoldering cigar in the other, the oppressive shroud of black depression lifted, dissipated into plumes of gray smoke. One day, death's miserable darkness would engulf and devour him, but this was not that day. By the time they crossed the white-capped Cascade mountains and saw the first sign of western Washington's verdant, misty, emerald-green rainforest, his wretched mood was a forgotten memory.

CHAPTER TWENTY

Erik

While driving home, Erik experienced a moment of clarity. The drugs balanced and aligned his thoughts… He needed to move out of the trailer. The cops would, by tracking the purchase of the bass guitar or finding DNA he left behind, find him. He'd seen the TV shows; the cops had mad skilz. The truck was filled with drugs, guns and money; he had everything he needed. Raz would be in Seattle soon. He'd never kill Raz or get back in the band if he was in jail.

The car behind him honked and he realized, while sitting at a stop sign, that he was drifting.

How long had he been sitting there?

There was a time for thinking and planning, but this was a time for movement. After popping an upper, his plan materialized. He pulled into a Safeway and piled supplies into an overflowing shopping cart. He was proud of himself for thinking of all the essentials: toilet paper, charcoal briquettes, matches, beer, hot dogs, buns, mustard, beer, doughnuts, tortilla chips, bean dip and beer. The bill, with tax, came to over two hundred and fifty dollars. He laughed at the cashier. The amount meant nothing. There was plenty of money. He peeled off hundred-dollar bills and dropped them in the cashier's outstretched palm.

"Would you like help loading your car, sir?" she asked.

"You're damned right," Erik said.

Toxic Shock Syndrome

After packing everything in the Escalade and pulling out of the parking lot, he needed to decide whether to go west toward the city or east toward the mountains. An image of an abandoned log cabin drifted in his mind. His former girlfriend, Moshi, had pinned a picture of one on the wall of their apartment. She dreamed of owning a cottage in the deep woods. Moshi was a stupid girl, but the image of the isolation was fixed in his mind. It would be a perfect place to hide. The cabin was east, on the dry side of the mountains, that much he knew. He turned on the left turn signal and pointed the massive vehicle toward the mountains.

The Escalade slewed on ice near the summit of Stevens Pass. A Subaru, partially blocking the highway, was lodged in a snow bank and the driver waved at him to stop and help. Erik gave him the finger and gunned the engine. The all-wheel-drive sprayed slush and Erik laughed. He wasn't stopping for a yuppie loser who did not know how to drive.

When he reached Leavenworth, it seemed he'd been driving his entire life; sweeping around corners and following the river through an endless scrubby forest. Leavenworth, decorated like a charming Bavarian village, made him nauseous. He stopped to fill the gas tank. After pissing, he bought a package of Doritos and a quart of beer.

"What do people do for fun around here?"

"There's a lot to do. I'm practicing for the International Accordion Festival in June. The best players from three countries come and we have a parade. If you're looking for something to do tonight, Rockin' Rick is playing the squeezebox at the München Haus. He polkas pretty good."

"I'll pass, thanks."

He continued east to Coulee City and then took Highway 155 north. He came to a sign that said 'Welcome to Elmer City'.

Elmer City.

259

He was tired of driving and was certain no one would ever think to look for him in a place called Elmer City. It was the last place on earth you'd find the world-traveling Toxic Shock Syndrome bass player. He pulled off the road and parked the car. An occasional car flying by interrupted the eerie hooting of an owl. Over the trees, a whisker of moon hovered on the horizon. The owl seemed to accuse him of murder, but the stereo drowned it out. After making sure the doors were locked, he crawled into the back seat and went to sleep.

Emma

Emma pushed her homework aside. She leaned back in her chair and adjusted the elastic bands that restrained her thick braid of hair. Feeling unsatisfied and on edge, she wondered what to do next. It was too early for dinner, but she was tired of studying. She sent Bennie a text message suggesting he drop his work and come play cribbage with her, but he did not reply. The phone buzzed.

"Emma, you have visitors in the lobby."

She pulled up her schedule on the computer screen. For the afternoon, there was one entry. Homework.

"I don't have any appointments. If it's a vendor, tell them to talk to Gerusha."

"It's two young women. They say they're with the AEF."

AEF. Advanced Evolutionary Force. What are they doing in the lobby?

"Okay, I'll come down."

Emma walked downstairs and entered the lobby, where the receptionist pointed toward the two girls. The pointing was unnecessary as the girls stood out compared to the three older,

260

formally-dressed sales people. One of the salesmen stood and offered a business card, but Emma waved it away.

The girls were older than they first appeared. Instead of teenagers, they were both in their mid-twenties. Both had dark hair; one wore her hair cut in a pageboy style, the other in a short, spiky, pixie style. They were slim and wore unmatched shades of pink jeans and petite t-shirts under leather jackets.

"Can I help you?"

Pixie pointed. "The receptionist says the vendor room is available so we can chat privately," she said.

Emma shrugged.

"Okay," she said.

The girls picked up silver flight cases. The vendor room was a small, undecorated room. The only furniture was a round, six-foot table holding a teleconference phone, and surrounded by four utilitarian chairs.

Emma sat. The girls stood beside her. One flipped latches on her case while the other began removing elastic bands from Emma's hair.

"Hold on. What are you doing?"

"We should introduce ourselves," Pixie said. "I'm Ali and this is my sister Wendy."

Wendy touched Emma's chin and tilted her head back.

"Your photographs do you no justice. You're very lovely. Above and beyond your ethnicity—I see why Raz has a personal interest in you."

Ali pulled a pink Mason Pearson boar-bristle brush from a satin drawstring bag and gently began brushing out Emma's hair.

"Excuse me," Emma protested.

"We're not genetic sisters, of course," Ali said.

"But *our* children will be," Wendy said.

Ali removed a badger blush brush and jar of blended face powder from her silver case while Wendy set up a miniature video camera and LCD monitor.

"I don't think she needs a superbalanced foundation, just a dusting of transparency powder."

"I'm not comfortable with you... handling me."

"You've been chosen for a direct inner-circle link with Raz. That's a singular honor. An honor I never got."

"Me either," Wendy said.

"You want to look your best, don't you?"

Emma calmed herself. Glen wanted her to join the AEF and report back.

I suppose I should see how this plays out.

"Okay," Emma said.

"We're almost ready," Wendy said. "Put in the earbuds and we'll start the video."

Ali arranged Emma's hair to frame her round face.

"You truly are extraordinarily pretty," she said.

Glen and Gerusha

Though the shiny floors had been trodden by royalty and presidents, the squat Boeing Field (King County Airport) brick building was microscopic and generic. After Glen's brief stroll through the terminal, the cool Seattle breeze was a shock to his system compared to the unrelenting heat of Las Vegas. Still puffing on the stub of his cigar, he stood under the front awning and waved to a taxi, but the turbaned cabbie was cut off by a swooping Lexus.

"Glen? It's Bobby Bobb with three B's in the first name and three more in the second. Welcome back to Seattle, sir." He waved a bundle of papers and flopped them on the roof of the car. "I have the faxed letter-of-intent, so this is just a formality, but could I get you to sign?"

After grinding the cigar butt into the pavement with the toe of his shoe, Glen took the proffered pen and scribbled on the paperwork.

With excess cheer, Bobby opened the passenger door and ushered Glen inside. As they navigated the surface streets toward downtown Seattle, Bobby babbled.

"I'm glad to finally meet you face to face, sir. To be frank—you know how women are—your lovely wife is acting all emotional, hormonal and irrational; she'll need your steadying hand if you follow my thinking. Sure, maybe she likes the house, but to think of walking away from a three-million-dollar windfall? Talk about flipping a house, this beats everything I've heard of. You could buy her one of those Kobe Bryant diamond blowjob rings if that's what it takes to smooth things over. Not that you'd have to. I'm sure you run a tight household and know how to keep a woman in line. Like the Bible says, spare the rod and spoil the wife, am I right? A man like you knows the score."

"Bobby?"

"Yes, sir?"

"Would you please shut the fuck up?"

Bobby clicked his teeth together audibly and nodded. With the steering wheel controls, he turned on the stereo and selected a track. The mellow sounds of Kenny Gorelick noodling on *What a Wonderful World* floated in the air of the quiet Lexus cabin. Glen reached over and turned the CD player off.

"You don't like Kenny G? I lost my virginity with my high school English teacher while *Songbird* played. Kenny's a cool guy. I almost sold him a cottage on Lake Washington before he got richer than God. A nicer chap, you can't imagine. I don't get the Kenny G bashing, but maybe you're more of a Kurt Cobain fan. I have Bleach on the flash drive. Let me find that for you."

He noticed Glen's forearm muscles rippling and knew, with undeniable certainty, that Glen would hit him if he kept talking. In silence, they drove through Seattle.

While stopped at a traffic light near Pioneer Square, Glen lowered the window and waved to a man holding a cardboard sign. After fishing bills from his pocket, Glen handed the man two dollars.

"God bless you, sir," the bum said.

"Yeah," Glen responded.

They followed the railroad tracks along Elliot Avenue and weaved until they got to the Magnolia neighborhood.

Unable to resist, Bobby spoke quietly. "This community is called Briarcliff. A lot of old Seattle money lives here." He parked the car on the street and turned to face Glen. "Contrary to my advice, she moved her stuff in. Cash deals close quickly. We have to get everything out in a couple of days."

"Thanks for the ride," Glen said.

Glen walked up the driveway. Craning his neck, he spoke to a swarthy man replacing a broken slate tile up on the roof.

"How's the roof holding up?"

The man grinned and tapped a slate shingle with a rough fingernail. A gold tooth gleamed from behind a bushy mustache. "It will outlive our sons," he said.

Gerusha, nibbling on a fingernail, walked onto the front porch and greeted him.

"Hey, Glen."

"Have you been crying?" Glen asked.

He hugged her and squeezed the cheeks of her ass.

"No," she said, "and don't molest my butt while there's an audience."

"What's the crisis?"

"No crisis. You're making a barrel of money flipping this place. I thought you should look over your windfall before it's gone, that's all."

"Right," Glen said. "Men don't bond to a place like women. We don't have the nesting instinct. A house is a house."

"I know," Gerusha said.

"We're clearing three-mil on a place we haven't lived in yet. It would be stupid to say no to a deal like that. Do I look stupid?"

"Not always. When you're done exploring my rear end, we'll take a quick look around and get out of here, okay?"

Tugging on his sleeve, she pulled him into the formal entry. Silently, Bobby followed at a discreet distance. In the grand foyer, Glen stared up at the chandelier.

"I'll bet that's a bitch to clean."

"They brought in a ladder."

She wore a wry smile that made Glen uncomfortable.

What am I missing? he thought.

"It's a grand old house, I get it. But, have you ever seen millions of dollars? Piles of cash are grand too."

"Of course," she said, "I'm not arguing. Five quick minutes to look around and we're out of here."

"Bobby is an idiot, but he makes sense in this case. We'll clear enough to pay cash for a fully-renovated place on the lake that comes with a boat. A five hundred horsepower boat. I'm not going to see anything around here I like better than three-million-bucks."

She walked part way up the curved stairway, then turned, paused dramatically and laughed.

"I'll grab my handbag and we'll go," she said.

Glen, tailed by Bobby, followed her up the stairs. Glen stopped to look at the old photographs on the hallway wall. They trooped through the bedroom. Glen poked his head into the master bathroom.

"Does that bathtub look big enough for two?" she asked.

"Barely," Glen said.

They marched across the bedroom. Gerusha pulled the curtains, opened the glass French doors and stepped onto the deck. Sunlight dappled the wrought iron table and chairs. The Puget Sound, glittering through the trees, blinded them with stabbing slivers of bright light.

"Where's my purse? I was sure I'd left it up here."

Glen ran his hand over the polished hardwood of the four-poster bed.

"This is nice woodwork. It reminds me of a long-ago love affair I had with South American doors."

"You get to take all the furniture when you move," Bobby said.

"Good," Glen said.

"Oh, I remember, I left my bag in the library."

Feigning carelessness, Gerusha flounced from the room.

"You're not fooling me for an instant," Glen called out after her.

The bookshelves were twenty feet tall. A large walnut desk gleamed under a colorful Tiffany lamp. At random, Glen pulled a book from the shelf. *The Mystery of a Hansom Cab* by Fergus Hume, 1931, bearing fountain-ink scribbles on the title page.

"Books bore me," he said while sliding the book back on the shelf.

"If we lived here, this'd be the only room where you could smoke your filthy, disgusting cigars, so maybe you'd learn to love books. I don't see my purse here either. Maybe I left it in my car. Why don't you grab a beer out of the kitchen while I say goodbye to Rose. Then we'll blow out of here."

Toxic Shock Syndrome

The stainless steel Sub-Zero industrial refrigerator was massive. Glen selected an Arrogant Bastard ale from the selection arrayed on the shelves and poured the murky beer into a tall German glass. While sipping the beer and looking over the acre of gleaming steel in the kitchen, it finally occurred to him to wonder...

Who the hell is Rose?

Carrying the beer, he walked back to the entry and followed the echoing trail of Gerusha's voice coming through a panel door partially hidden by a potted palm. The hallway was dark and took a sharp turn to the left before opening into a brightly-lit room. It was formerly a sunroom or greenhouse. Light streamed in through glass roof panels and the air was rank, dank and musty, like an old cellar. The walls were covered with lurid paintings. Dozens, overlapping in a mad array of color.

Glen stopped to examine a long strip of canvas hanging from a thumbtack. In this painting, a line of orange-robed penitents marched up a mountain trail. Near the top, the trail opened into a blood-splattered meadow where bears, wolves and eagles feasted on the raw flesh of screaming priests. The intricate, delicate brushstrokes created incredible detail; the closer he studied the scene, the more features emerged. Playfully, lion cubs batted at severed heads bearing eyes wide in horror. Hairy Yeti, with fur caked blood, tossed gnawed bodies into a precipice.

He did not turn when the strange lady spoke.

"That which was torn of beasts I brought not unto thee; I bear the loss of it; of my hand didst thou require it, whether stolen by day, or stolen by night," Rose said.

Glen turned and looked into her over-stuffed, blubbery face.

"Are you stupid?" she said. "That's from the Bible. Genesis. Jacob offers a sacrifice; it's allegory. Do you speak English? I don't like you. What's that? Beer? I don't like beer. Give me a sip. Yes. No.

It tastes like yak urine and I cannot abide the smell of it. You are forbidden to bring it into my studio. I like Tang and you will learn to stir it so the powder is mixed thoroughly as I can not tolerate hideous crystals on the bottom of my glass. Here's a paint strip. Notice the ochre tones? That's the right mixture of grenadine. It takes at least a minute of stirring to get the powder dissolved properly. Got it, stupid?" She turned to address Gerusha. "Does it talk?"

Glen pried open Gerusha's purse and extracted her camera-phone. He took a picture of the paintings stacked against the wall and pressed the keys to email them to Raz.

Bobby's voice echoed through the house.

"Where are you?"

Glen turned to leave.

"I would enjoy a hug."

Rose tugged at Glen's shirt and enveloped him in her doughy arms. She was damp with sweat and wet paint. She kissed his neck. "I'll let you diddle my goodies later, maybe. Ochre is a brownish orange. Colors, like an orgasm, are God's gift to mankind. They deserve respect. Now go."

Glen exchanged an inscrutable glance with Gerusha. She smiled and pointed at his white shirt. It was ruined with blotches and streaks of paint. He turned and walked out of the room.

In the foyer, Bobby stood with the buyers. While shaking hands with Tim Kooper, Glen's eyes scanned Tim's wife. His eyes caught the way her dress was vacuum-formed around her crotch. With distaste, she averted her eyes and smoothed the clingy fabric.

Kooper addressed Bobby.

"Did you know there's a Jaguar XK-120 in the garage?" Kooper said. "Personally, I think they're ugly, but it's a classic."

"Please allow me to introduce Mr. Glen Wilson," Bubb said.

Kooper studied Glen's face.

Toxic Shock Syndrome

"I remember you, Glen. We drank Cheoum Cheoreom soju and ate gaejangguk in Seoul in 1994. You cheat at cards. I see you've noticed my wife, Zia. Her father is the Korean Minister of Information and Communication; he'd remember that night too. Look, I don't mean to rush you guys, but can you get your stuff out tomorrow? We're eager to move in."

"I'm not selling."

"What do you mean? Bobby says the deal is done." Kooper looked between Bobby, Glen and Gerusha. "If it's the Jag, take it. It's worth a hundred grand, but that's fine."

"Bobby needs to take a closer look at the signature on the contract."

Glen walked toward the library while Bobby, with a look of panic on his face, tore open the contract folder. He studied the scrawled signature on the letter of intent, and then let the papers drift from limp fingers to the floor.

Two cheeks and the maw[14], it said.

"What does that mean? Shit. You lousy, conniving bastard."

Kooper looked confused. "Do we have a deal or not?"

Gerusha, with a smile dancing on her lips, leaned against the doorway and watched the scene.

Bobby followed Glen.

"A deal is a deal. What are you doing?"

Glen took a Lyman Plains black powder pistol from a walnut rack on the library wall. He poured powder from a horn and tamped the load.

---

[14] And this shall be the priest's due from the people, from them that offer a sacrifice, whether it be ox or sheep; and they shall give unto the priest the shoulder, and the two cheeks, and the maw.
Deuteronomy 18:3

"In about thirty seconds, I'm going to see if this old pistol still works by shooting at trespassers in my house."

"You're not serious."

"There are dead men who drew that same mistaken conclusion. I can't speak for the state of this powder, but I will pull the trigger."

Bobby scurried away. In the entry, he tugged at the Kooper's sleeves.

"There's a house, almost a mansion, on Lake Washington that I think you'll love. Waterfront, great neighborhood, it's two houses down from one of Craig McCaw's places. Very exclusive. Used to be owned by the ambassador to Australia. Paul Allen is flying in to look at it too, so we'd better hurry. It has a bathtub Queen Victoria once bathed in."

Bobby slammed the door as they left. Glen laughed, eased the hammer down on the pistol and placed it on an entryway table. On his way to the kitchen, he stopped by Gerusha.

"Okay?" he asked.

"Sure," she said.

"This is an interesting house."

"Yeah, I guess," she said. "Where are you going?"

"To thoroughly mix up a glass of Tang before I go back to Las Vegas. Want some?"

Gerusha could not stifle a giggle. "Sure, why not?" she said.

While stirring Tang in the kitchen, her cell phone bleeped.

"It's for you," she said while handing it to Glen. She took over the stirring.

"Yeah," Glen said.

"I need that painting for my CD cover," Raz said. "Do you know the artist's agent?"

"By odd coincidence, her agent is me," Glen said.

Raz breathed in the phone for a moment before responding.

"I suppose that means the purchase will be expensive."

"You suppose correctly, sir," Glen said.

"Very well," Raz said. "Give my very best, warmest regards to the artist. Pure genius."

"Sure."

Glen closed the phone and handed it back.

"Will you tell me the real, complete truth?" she asked.

"Maybe."

"When did you make the decision to keep this house?"

As if hypnotized, Glen watched Tang swirl in the pitcher.

"The instant you called, of course."

She brushed a lock of hair from her eyes.

"Is there any chance we'll be magnificently happy here?"

"Everything being possible," he said, "we can always try."

CHAPTER TWENTY-ONE

Glen

Reversing the trip back to Las Vegas was easily done. After calling the pilot on his cell phone, Glen agreed to meet him at Randy's Restaurant. On East Marginal Way, the sight of the French Concorde jet, poised as if for liftoff, dampened Glen's buoyant mood. At Randy's, the pilot sipped a cup of weak coffee and picked at a mountain of greasy hashbrowns. The waitress, Grace, topped off his cup, then pulled a stub of pencil from behind her ear.

"You want anything, Sugar?"

Glen glanced around.

"No thanks, I'm not hungry," he said. "How long have you worked here?"

"I started when this place was a Denny's and the 727 was the hottest bird in the sky."

Glen patted the pilot on the shoulder.

"If this guy would fly you anywhere your heart desired, where would it be?"

She tucked the pencil back behind her ear and waved a wisp of gray hair away from her face.

"Nowhere, I guess." She gestured back toward the kitchen. "I married Gomez a few years ago and he hates my cats. If I left town, he'd let them starve."

"Does Gomez treat you right?"

272

"On a good day, he has a couple of good qualities," Grace said. "I'm not exactly Eva Gabor. We get along fine. It's a life. I don't need rescuing."

Glen laughed. "That makes one of us," he said. He slipped a hundred dollar bill under the pilot's coffee cup. "Let's hit it."

On the flight back, Glen was quiet and pensive. Looking down on south-eastern Oregon's wastelands, he chewed a thumbnail and daydreamed.

"How are you doing back there?" the pilot asked.

"When I was poor, I didn't know how big the world was and what a man's life could be. I was too ignorant to make my dreams big enough."

"I meant, do you need a soda or a beer or something? There's a tin of cashews in the cupboard if you're hungry."

"Ah. Okay."

He popped open the can and munched while the landscape unrolled beneath the aircraft. At the airport, he jumped in a cab. It was dusk and glitzy casino lights reclaimed the evening. When he got back to the Palms, he picked up the house phone and dialed Murphy's room.

"I'll be down in a minute. I'm taking a crap."

Glen was surprised to hear a man's voice.

"Could I speak to Murphy, please?"

"Who is this?"

"Wilson."

"Well, you got a wrong number, pal. There ain't no Murphy here, so if you'll excuse me, I'm busy."

There was a rush of water. A toilet flushing. The connection was broken.

He went to the front desk and spoke to the clerk.

"What happened to Murphy in 4705?"

"That group checked out, sir. The final concert was last night. I didn't go, but I understand it was quite a spectacular."

With a frown, Glen flipped open his cell phone, turned it on and punched in Murphy's quick-dial number. When she answered, there was a lot of background noise.

"Where have you been?" she said. "I've been looking for you. The era of instant communication doesn't work if you keep your cell phone turned off."

"I've been around. Where are you?"

"You missed the plane. Raz held us on the runway for a while assuming you'd show up, but you didn't. Whoever the girl was, I hope she was worth it."

"She was."

"Get your ass to Seattle, jerk."

She disconnected.

With a self-depreciating smile, he looked around the lobby. With purpose, people in all sizes and shapes moved through. A covey of flight attendants, trim and attractive in pantsuits and sensible shoes, blew through the lobby dragging wheeled luggage.

Truly, I am an absurd person.

He thought about his money for an instant. Safe on Sylvie's truck? The thought amused him. Tired of airplanes, he thought of taking a bus or train, but decided to rent a car. He dropped his AMEX card on the Avis desk and the clerk promised a Corvette Z06 would be delivered to the hotel check-in circle in fifteen minutes. Thirty minutes later, the Vegas lights receded in his mirror and, at 100 MPH, the car ate miles on Highway 95.

Tired, he thought he might find a hotel in Indian Springs, but the village had nothing and he passed straight through. Under a sky full of stars, he pulled off the highway and leaned the seat back as far as it would go. Uncomfortable, he cursed his impulse to rent such an impractical car. While gazing at the stars through the moon roof, he fell asleep.

When he awoke, the car was still running and the gas gauge had drifted toward the half full mark. Rubbing his eyes, he looked around at the flat, desolate landscape and wondered where he was and why he was there. The tortured desert matched the barren, lonesome way he felt inside. Depression hovered on the edges of his mind like floating thunderclouds. Patches of scrub brush and scraggly mesquite marched to the ominous dark mountains. Clumsy and stiff, he got out of the car and pissed on a bush. In this dry climate, the bush seemed grateful. Overhead, a red-tailed hawk jeered. Glen raised his middle finger and waved it at the sky in response.

He folded his reluctant body back into the car. Without wanting to think about it, he kept the car pointed in the same direction and pulled back on the highway. The digital compass said west, so west it was. The temperature quickly increased. The terrain was baked and sand-blasted. It was God-forsaken, like Glen.

How did I end up here at the edge of death's valley?

He flew by the Highway 374 turn-off to Death Valley National Park. With a grumbling stomach and a burning thirst, he cursed himself for not laying in supplies. The endless highway, unveiled piecemeal after every sweeping turn, traveled over rocky terrain framed by dark mountain sawblades. Mileage signs counted to Tonopah. Finally, with a sigh of relief, he pulled into the Stage Stop Restaurant. The hotel-food-casino sign drew him with the irresistible magnetism of appetite.

The waitress, wearing a pale blue dress, filled his plastic cup with water.

"Just leave the pitcher," Glen said.

"Do you know what you want?"

"Bring me two specials."

"Our portions are mountainous. You sure?"

"Yeah," Glen said. "Bring it on."

His thirst was endless, unsated after drinking cup after cup of water. Soon, the waitress dropped two platters heaped with bacon, sausage, hash browns with gravy, scrambled eggs, and biscuits on the table.

"Think that will do ya?" she asked.

"It's a start."

"Which way you headed? Reno or Vegas?"

"How do you know I'm not headed to Pahrump?"

"Because no one goes to Pahrump."

"Reno. How do I get there?"

"Follow Highway 6 to Coaldale and turn north on 95. Follow the signs. Make sure you fill up your gas tank here; there ain't much out there. It's not scenic like the drive to Vegas."

Glen snorted.

"What?" she asked.

"Nothing," he replied.

He stuffed a forkful into his mouth.

"And you're stupid if you don't carry a couple of gallons of water with you. Just in case."

"Thanks, I'll do that."

She dropped the ticket on the table and Glen placed his hand on hers.

"You want to jump in my car and blow this town?"

She pulled her hand away.

"Everybody has to be someplace. I like it here. Thanks for the offer. I appreciate it. Eat your breakfast."

As she walked away, he watched her ass wriggle under the thin fabric before turning his undivided attention to the heaping platters.

When he was stuffed and could eat no more, he asked the waitress to box up the leftovers.

"They should hold you for a week or two," she said.

He slipped a hundred-dollar-bill under his water glass. Outside, the air was much hotter. He slipped on sunglasses and started the Corvette's engine with the remote to get the air conditioner running. Waves of heat radiated from the blacktop. After driving from the restaurant, he stopped at the Giggle Springs convenience store where he topped off the gas tank and bought two plastic gallon jugs of water. He gazed westward over the arid wasteland. The highway disappeared into black lava flows like a lonely highway to hell.

Driving too fast across the scorched-earth hell-fire moonscape with dark thoughts for company, he sighed and searched for a radio station.

How did it come to this after so many years of walking the earth? His hands ached with arthritis and he saw now-faint age splotches and wrinkles in his skin. Relentlessly, old age claimed his vitality. Most of his good years were behind him.

Why not run the speed to 140 and launch the car into space... Leave this worldly cesspool in a tangle of colorful shredded Fiberglas and blood?

At 110, the car slipped around corners as if glued to the pavement. It was the industrial magic of ground-effect surface tension.

Unconsciously, he decided to do it. Ahead, a sweeping corner and section of guardrail framed a wide expanse of alkali canyon. It would all be over in a glorious demonstration of mass times velocity squared. Then his cell phone buzzed.

"Where are you?" Bennie asked.

"I don't know. Nowhere. Thirty miles or so from Reno, I guess."

"What are you doing out there?"

"Nothing. Driving at high speed. Doing my best James Dean imitation. Committing suicide or something. I don't know."

"Well, knock it off, there's no time for nonsense. Grab a flight in Reno and get up here."

"What's up?"

"Emma is missing."

Emma? Sweet Emma? My favorite Inuit princess?

"I'm on my way."

He set the cruise control to 95, blew past semi trucks and RV rigs and only tapped the brakes on a few sharp corners. He thought of the first time he'd seen Emma in Anchorage. Some things simply belong together, like chocolate and peanut butter or pizza and beer. He could not imagine Bennie without slender Emma hanging on his arm and looking at him with love overflowing in her brown eyes.

How could she be missing?

He dropped the car off at the Avis rental return area.

"Leave the charges on the card, sir?" the turbaned Avis agent asked.

"Sure," Glen replied.

In no time, he was tightening his seatbelt in the First Class cabin of a SeaTac-bound Alaska Airlines 737.

The flight attendant handed him a pillow.

"Would you care for a cocktail, sir?"

"Only if I can't have two," Glen replied.

While the plane cruised at 35,000 feet, he worked things over in his mind. He'd asked Emma to join Raz's odd little fan club and now, the same day Raz plays his last concert in Seattle, she goes missing.

Correlations, compared to causes, are easy, but he knew with complete certainty. Raz was involved.

Erik

In the morning, he drank a beer for breakfast. An impulse struck him and he used the clasp knife to scrape off his hair and eyebrows. He removed earrings and studs from his eyebrows, lips and tongue. Pale, with dark circles under his eyes, his face in the rearview mirror looked ghostly. No one would recognize him now. Satisfied, he drove back toward Seattle.

After arriving in the city, he parked the Escalade in a parking lot by the railroad tracks and watched an Amtrak train cruise by. After smoking a bowl and popping a pill, he checked the magazine of the .45 and made sure his knife was in his coat pocket. He was ready. His mouth was dry, so he drained his large can of Budweiser and burped. It struck him as funny, so he burped again.

"Excuse me," he said to himself.

He pulled a stocking hat over his ears and jumped out of the vehicle. His boots crunched on the cinder gravel of the railway as he walked toward the concert hall. Near a shadow cast by an idling semi truck, he rattled the gate of a chain link fence. The security guard approached.

"This is a restricted area, sir," he said. "I need to ask you to move along."

"I need to ask you to die," Erik said.

He stabbed the guard in the throat and dragged the body into shadow. Hunched over, he worked the passes from around the guard's neck and draped them around his own.

The coat was big on Erik's wiry frame, but would do. The blood did not soak into the waterproof material; he blotted it with the guard's t-shirt. Ready, he walked toward the concert hall's loading doors.

Glen

After the cabbie dropped him off by a phone pole plastered with flyers, it took a few minutes for Glen to get his backstage pass from the will call window. He held his new watch up to the light. It was late and the concert must be nearly over. Through the walls, Glen could hear the roar of the amplifiers and the howling crowd. A man, wearing a flannel shirt over a huge belly, grabbed his arm. His breath was fetid with alcohol.

"You gotta help me, man."

Glen frowned. "I'm on a schedule." He fished in his pocket for currency. "Buy yourself a bowl of soup, brother."

"No," the man said. "My daughter was murdered by this guy. He used to be the bass player for this band and I think he's here somewhere. The cops won't listen to me."

Moving fast, Glen was twenty feet away before he stopped and turned around.

"What was that?"

The man leaned with his back against the wall clutching flyers to his chest. Glen tugged one free and looked at the picture. The headline said: Erik Olsen Killed my Daughter. The photograph was not helpful. Gaunt, with a thin mustache and a tangle of matted black-dyed hair, the kid looked like half of Raz's audience. Glen looked around and saw a dozen twins.

Toxic Shock Syndrome

"This creep wrapped a guitar string around my baby's neck and strangled her until she was dead. The cops won't do nothing. You gotta help me. I need to talk to the rock star."

"I don't think so, but I'll keep an eye open."

While navigating the eddies and currents of the milling crowd, he looked into the dead eyes of the pixelated photograph. Invisible forces of the cosmic vortex whipped his thoughts.

One day I will sit in a rocking chair with a bottle of rum and let the world swirl down the toilet. I will laugh and not lift a finger. Someday.

In the back of the cavernous concert hall, Glen watched. Raz stood in the center of a red spotlight and played a long, deafening, sinuous riff over and over, faster and faster as the arms of the crowd waved. The riff ended and infinite-echo feedback howled like a rabid wolf. Raz waved the guitar over the heads of the audience. A girl, wearing a maniacal grin, climbed on the shoulders of her boyfriend and grabbed it. The crowd milled like piranhas and the girl and guitar disappeared.

With a final wave, Raz walked off the stage and the house lights came up. Impatiently, Glen fought through the crowd and pushed through the line waiting for backstage access. A burly pair guarded the door and raised their hands to stop him, but parted when they saw the passes hanging from around his neck. Inside, he slipped between flight cases being wheeled off stage. Jesus spotted him and walked up quickly.

"As usual, your timing is perfect. Show's over, asshole."

"I don't have time to play with you, Jesus." He waved the flyer. "Watch for this fucker. Where's Murphy?"

"Playing tonsil hockey with some slit."

Shit. If Elke is here, Murphy will be distracted.

"We gotta move Raz out now," Glen said.

CHAPTER TWENTY-TWO

Glen

Glen pushed by Jesus and through the wall of hanging Turkish carpets. The air was filled with the thick haze of Raz's imported tobacco. Calmly, Raz puffed on his hookah. He tipped his head to his left and Glen saw Erik shifting a .45 pistol from hand to hand. The girls sat on the floor and watched Glen with wide eyes.

"I hope I'm not interrupting anything," Glen said.

"Erik and I were talking about his coming back to the band. He says he's learned new chops on the bass that I need to hear."

"Okay. I'll slip out and find a bass."

Erik, with mad intensity in his eyes, pointed the gun at Glen.

"You won't go anywhere until I tell you to."

It's been a while, but the feeling is familiar. Once again, I stare into the void. It's amazing how a half-inch gun bore can seem a mile wide when it's pointed at your head.

Glen's thoughts flashed to the Nevada desert highway.

Maybe I did it. Maybe I crashed through the guardrail and this is a dream.

Perhaps imagined, there were hints of brimstone in Raz's plumes of smoke. Futilely and self-consciously, Glen looked left and right for the devil's familiar obsidian shadow.

"Unless you want to impress Raz with your air guitar, I'd better go find you an axe. Anything special? Five string? Fretless?"

Erik pursed his lips.

"Just a regular one. Make sure it's a Fender. I don't want to play no crap bass."

"I'll see what I can do and be back in a flash."

He backed through the hanging carpets and found himself in the bustle of the backstage madness. He tapped Jesus on the shoulder.

"We have a security situation. Take me to Murphy."

"Look in the back-line control room," Jesus said, gesturing. "You'd better knock first if you get my meaning."

"Find me a bass guitar, preferably a Fender."

"Go find it yourself."

"Jesus, please. I'm not messing with you." He looked pointedly at Jesus' left leg. "Your best friend will be a wheelchair."

"Murphy says I need to humor you, so I'll do it. Otherwise, I'd kick your ass right here and now."

"Fine," Glen said.

He walked up a metal ramp and threw open the door of the control room. Murphy and Elke hurriedly rearranged their clothing.

"Damn it, Glen, we're having a conversation…"

"I see that. Murphy, you're still on the clock. While you're playing with your girlfriend, a psycho with a gun holds Raz hostage in his harem. Later, you girls can pick up where you left off. Right now, there's work to do. I want you by Raz's lair, stage right. Be ready to take the jerk down while I figure out the play."

"Should I call the cops?" Elke asked.

"Sure, after this is over, call whoever you want."

Glen walked back down the ramp. Jesus waited with an Ibanez bass.

"No Fenders?"

"Ibanez is a sponsor; it's all they have."

"Okay," Glen said. "Stay with Murphy and follow her lead."

He walked back to the lair. Outside, the girls patiently waited in line. The girl at the head of the line put out a hand to stop him.

"It's been a while. Will it be my turn soon?" she asked.

"I'm sure," Glen replied.

He slipped through the seams of the carpet wall. If it was possible, the smoke was thicker. Erik puffed on a hash pipe. The patterns on the Turkish carpets seemed to writhe.

Slowly, Glen walked over.

"I said Fender."

"For our purposes, this one will work the same," Glen said.

Moving slowly, Erik slipped the pistol into his waistband and eagerly reached for the guitar. With deft quickness, Glen flipped the bass around and hit him in the head. Erik fell off the stool like a bag of potatoes. Glen lifted his body and worked the pistol free. Raz, calmly watching, took a final toke from his hookah and stood up.

"Thanks, Glen," he said before slipping out through a gap in the rear carpet-wall.

"Hold on, I need to talk to you," Glen said to no one.

Raz was gone.

"It's safe, Murphy, come in," Glen said loudly.

Brandishing pistols, Murphy and Jesus came in.

"All you girls? Follow Raz; he's waiting for you out back."

The last girl stood for a moment by the back wall, then came back and gave Glen a kiss on the cheek.

"You're very brave," she said. "Thanks."

"Sometimes from the outside, stupidity looks like bravery," he said. "Now beat it." To Murphy he said "Who is this asshole?"

"I know him," Murphy said. "He played bass. Raz fired him a long time ago because he sucked."

Glen collapsed on a chair.

"I'm tired," he said.

"He's still breathing," Jesus said. "Let's duct tape him and hold him for the police."

"Fine. Whatever," Glen said while rubbing his eyes.

"He was Moshi's old boyfriend," Murphy said.

Glen raised his head.

"What did you say?"

"Haven't you put this together? This is the original Toxic Shock bass player. He was Moshi's boyfriend."

Glen's body was stiff and robotic as he walked over to look down on Erik. Jesus, looking at Glen's face, took a step back.

"Uh, hey? What's going on?"

Glen's voice was quiet. Nearly inaudible. He pulled the flyer from his pocket and smoothed it on his thigh. "Call this guy on his cell phone. Find him and bring him back here."

Jesus shot a look at Murphy. She jerked her head and raised her eyebrows in silent command.

Go.

Glen's taut muscles twitched. While looking down at Erik, Glen picked up the bass guitar and slowly unwound the 'E' string.

"I'm sorry, Glen. I didn't mean to upset you."

"It's okay, Murphy. I'm not upset."

It took twenty minutes for Jesus to return with the troubled father in tow. The small crowd looked down on Erik for a few moments.

"Everyone else out," Glen commanded.

Murphy tugged at Jesus' arm.

"You heard the man," she said.

Jesus was reluctant, but allowed himself to be pulled away.

Glen handed the distraught father the guitar string.

"I'll give you two a little privacy," he said.

285

Five minutes later, the ashen-faced man came through the carpet wall. The guitar string dripped blood. He dropped it on the floor. In shock, he moved slowly.

Glen touched Jesus' arm.

"Make sure this man gets home. Don't leave him alone until you know he's alright. I'll take care of the fucking trash."

Jesus put his hands on Glen's shoulders and looked into his eyes.

"I can't decide if we're friend or foe."

"If we meet again, you can let me know your verdict," Glen said.

Jesus grinned and turned away. He gently took the stunned man's arm and pulled him away.

Glen found a big-enough equipment case and stuffed Erik's body into it. He retrieved the guitar string and tossed it in.

"See you in hell," he said.

He spit on the body before closing up the latches.

Murphy glanced at the transit case.

"Let's call the tour officially over, okay?" Murphy said.

"Yeah," he said. "We're done."

The next day, after topping off the equipment case with concrete blocks, he rented a fishing boat and pushed Erik's roll-around coffin into the deepest water he could find on a Puget Sound nautical chart.

Next came the search for Emma. He could not face Bennie. Murphy and Walter would search for Emma in their way. Murphy would work with the cops and Walter?

Who knew what bizarre rites or convoluted pathways he would pursue.

Glen knew at some point, Raz would visit Moshi's grave.

Staked out at the Evergreen Cemetery, Glen read magazine after magazine, ate convenience-store sandwiches and pissed into a 2-liter soda bottle. Three days later, on a cool autumn day with the wind scattering leaves and bearing a hint of the winter's approaching cold, his patience paid off.

Raz, nearly unrecognizable in a furry fleece coat and cowboy hat, visited Moshi's grave and left a bundle of pink roses next to the fresh red rose that was dropped off every day. After resting his hand on Jimi Hendrix's nearby monument, he walked back to his SUV.

Hanging far behind, Glen followed as Raz drove his black Tahoe north on I-5 through Seattle, Everett and Marysville.

To Canada? Glen wondered.

But they turned off and headed toward Arlington, and then north on Highway 9. The landscape, fervently green, grew more and more desolate. Once Raz turned on a road the GPS said had only one destination, Glen pulled off on a wide spot on the gravel road and waited.

The road ended at Lake Cavanaugh.

The lake was a shiny jewel nestled in evergreens. The banks were crowded with expensive weekend homes. Driven by an easterly wind, the surface was choppy. Slowly, he drove completely around the perimeter and did not see Raz's car. He stopped to talk to a teenaged boy carrying a fishing pole and walking a bicycle with a large black dog at his side.

"Any fish in the lake?"

"Sure, of course. Bass and trout."

He opened his wicker creel to show off his catch.

"Nice," Glen said. "Someone told me the rock star has a place up here…"

Silently, the kid pointed at a giant cedar house built on a ridge over the water.

"Thanks."

Glen drove around the lake and did not find the entrance until noticing a well-worn dirt road that snaked under a thick stand of trees. He followed the road. He stopped at a huge black gate decorated with the TSS symbol. On a post, there was an intercom. He pressed the button, but there was no response.

"Tell Raz I'm happy to sit here all day until he lets me in."

He held his thumb on the button while the speaker grated with harsh buzzing. Eventually, the gate retracted and Glen drove up the steep driveway to the house. The compound was massive, essentially a lodge with several large outbuildings. A brick wall, topped with wrought iron spear tips, ran down the property line toward the lake. Two young women, wearing long cotton dresses, looked up from stacking firewood. Raz appeared on the porch under an elaborately-carved archway.

Glen got out of his car and stretched his back. The air, crisp and fresh, bore the smell of spruce.

"You followed me from Moshi's grave. I didn't see you."

"I stayed quite a ways back."

Raz stared at Glen, then sighed.

"You might as well come in, I guess."

They walked down a hallway lined with doors. Hearing voices, Glen opened a door and looked inside. It was a classroom. Twenty young kids, about three-years-old, swiveled their heads and silently turned their dark eyes on him. They were nearly identical, with swatches of black hair and piercing eyes. Raz reached around Glen and eased the door closed.

They continued down the hallway into a great room. A bank of windows looked out over a deck. Far below, the wind-swept lake glittered. Rain, driven by a gust of wind, splattered on the deck.

288

Toxic Shock Syndrome

The room was filled with young women and children. Some of the girls were in varying stages of pregnancy. They stared at Glen with calm, passive eyes. Raz settled into an overstuffed leather chair. A girl handed Raz an infant. Raz kissed the baby's cheek and handed it back. Another girl handed him a steaming mug, and then sat down on the floor, resting her head on the arm of his chair.

"We don't drink coffee here, but I could offer you a cup of herbal tea. It's my personal blend; you'll like it." He gestured with an index finger and soon Glen held an aromatic mug. He took a sip, and then placed the mug on the floor. A girl lifted his mug and placed a coaster under it. They sat in uncomfortable silence for a few moments.

"This is quite a scene," Glen commented.

"Did you know the average, healthy man's ejaculation has between 40 million and a billion sperm cells? No matter what, a large number of them will be wasted. I decided to waste fewer of them, that's all."

"How many babies are we talking about?"

Unconsciously, Raz patted the belly of the girl sitting beside him.

"Worldwide, including the ones in the pipeline?"

Glen nodded.

"Not so many yet. Maybe twenty thousand. If we stick to schedule, we'll have a hundred-thousand in two years."

"Why are you doing this?"

Raz tilted his head back and laughed.

"I like you Glen, so I'm going to honor you with an honest answer. The bottom-line truth is, I'm not sure. I'm building a big machine, a social army if you want to call it that, but the reason has not been fully revealed to me. Yet."

"You couldn't possibly service twenty thousand girls."

"Of course not." He reached over and lifted the pendant from the girl's necklace. "Only certain special girls actually, uh, directly interact with the master. For the rest? Well, I get milked by a machine. Believe me, it's very unpleasant. A computerized system sorts the sperm and we use clinics around the world for insemination. There's nothing magic about it—anyone could do the same."

"Given enough money and a supply of willing girls."

Raz laughed. "Yes, it's an expensive operation. You can't blame me for trying to save a buck or two where I can."

"By stealing from yourself to avoid taxes..."

Raz shrugged. "Seemed like a reasonable idea at the time. Plus, I enjoyed challenging you." He leaned forward. With his nearly-black eyes, he pierced Glen. "Now you know what I'm doing. Where do we go from here?"

"There's one I will not allow you to keep."

"Yes. I know. Beautiful Emma. She's very special. With the right seed stock, the result would be—phenomenal. Anyway, you know these girls are here voluntarily? They can leave any time they please."

"Yeah, I get that. But, this one you'll cut loose."

"Or else?"

"I'm not making any threats."

Raz sighed. "I held off on seeding her, though the temptation was—extraordinary. Her genetics... Well, never mind. I'll let her go." He gestured. "Bring her up."

After a minute, Emma walked into the room. Braided hair framed her round, perfect face.

"I was teaching the kids Tai Chi..." Her voice trailed off when she saw Glen. "Oh."

With eyes pointed at the floor, she kneeled before Raz. He raised her chin and kissed her forehead.

"It's time for you to go home," he said gently.

Glen stood. He took Emma's hand and, under the watchful, calculating eyes of the other girls, they walked out. He worked the car around in the driveway and pulled through the already-opened gate. On Lake Cavanaugh Road, they crossed the outlet creek.

"How do you feel?" Glen asked.

"I'm fine. Can we listen to one of Raz's albums? I've developed a taste for his music." She turned to Glen. "He truly is a genius, you know."

"I know."

"I suppose Bennie is freaking out."

"Yeah."

"I missed him too, but the kids... So sweet and beautiful. And Raz... Maybe I wasn't thinking clearly."

She slipped a disc in the player and filled the cabin with a TSS song that started with a contrapuntal chant before launching into an intense, syncopated beat. With her eyes closed, Emma tapped her finger on the armrest.

They traversed the long road back to Seattle without speaking. Glen parked in a handicap parking space in front of the company. He studied the Immortality, LLC infinity logo for a moment before unlatching his seatbelt and entering the lobby. He waved at the receptionist and took a seat. Nearby, several salespeople patiently waited. At the elevator, Emma turned.

"Are you coming up?"

"You go ahead. Tell Bennie I'll see him later."

Glen felt empty. Drained. Used up. The receptionist, with a curious look on her face, dialed her telephone and spoke a few words.

"You work here, don't you?" A salesman wearing a garish, splotchy necktie spoke hopefully. "I represent a world-class manufacturer of—"

"Please. Just let me be," Glen said.

Why am I sitting here? Why don't I go in?

He felt too tired to move an inch. Gerusha, wearing a short skirt and flowery blouse, came out.

"Hello, Gerusha," the salesman said.

She waved him back. She took Glen's hand and led him to a private corner of the lobby.

"I saw Emma. You found her and brought her back."

"I did."

"Bennie is going to overflow." Sitting with her warm hip touching his, she stared at a painting on the wall. "Is this what our marriage will be like? You'll disappear and I won't know if you're alive or dead, coming home or gone forever?"

"Probably."

"You are maddening. This would be easier if I hated you."

Glen shrugged.

Bennie, dragging Emma by the hand, rushed down the stairs like a whirlwind. Glen stood. Bennie picked him up and spun him around. He kissed Glen on the mouth. Glen turned his head and wiped his mouth.

"Let's not go overboard, my friend. Put me down."

"Glen."

"Yes, Bennie?"

"I owe you a really, really big one."

"It's okay."

"No, it isn't," Bennie said.

He puckered up. Glen rotated his head so Bennie kissed his cheek.

"Let go, Bennie."

"Sorry," Bennie said. "I just wanted to thank you personally before you disappear again." He glanced at Gerusha. "I suppose you two are talking. We'll go back upstairs. Thank you, Glen, from the bottom of my heart, thank you."

Emma and Gerusha hugged and cried. Bennie tugged at Emma's arm. They walked back toward the stairs.

"Mr. Jackson, could I get a moment, please?" asked a salesman offering a brochure.

Bennie ignored the plea and, climbing two stairs at a time, pulled Emma along. Glen sat back down.

"I have to get some sleep," he said. "I'm wiped out."

"Are you coming to the house?"

He buried his face in his hands and rubbed eyes.

"If it's okay with you," he mumbled.

She looked at him for a long moment.

"Yeah, Glen. It's where you belong. I want you there." She stood and smoothed wrinkles in her skirt. "I'll see you tonight," she said, before walking away.

EPILOGUE

Glen

It was a game he had not played for a while.

Where the hell am I?

Blinding planar light slipped through a gap in heavy curtains. The diesel engine of a garbage truck rumbled outside. It was a cosmic puzzle.

Where am I?

A firm breast floated six inches from his face. It was an unfamiliar breast, perfectly round and decorated with a precise circle of brown aureole. The woman attached to this breast lay on her side; she had tousled blond hair. In dream or memory, he'd emptied into her during an endless orgasm. Gerusha. Lightly, he flicked with his tongue; she took a deep breath and arched her back.

Where the hell am I?

Home, he thought before thinking stopped again.

THE END